"What are you d[...]
between clenche[...]

Lenore moved swiftly [...] question as he followed behind [...] door. She moved to the oversize desk at the front of the room and began to search through the drawers.

"Are you serious right now?" he asked. "This is a violation of—"

"You are welcome to leave at any time," Lenore said, cutting him off. She continued to rummage through the desk. "I don't recall asking for your help or your permission."

King huffed. Although he was curious to know what she was trying to achieve, there were protocols, and rules, and she was breaking every one of them. That didn't sit well with him, but he made no earnest effort to stop her. "What are you looking for?" he whispered loudly.

"I don't know. But I'm sure when I see it, it will make sense."

Finding nothing, she reached for the bottom drawer and suddenly paused as she peered inside. Her expression changed, the color draining from her cheeks.

Dear Reader,

Are you ready to join me on this newest adventure? We are going to have such a great time getting to know the daughters of Claudia and Josiah Martin, starting with eldest daughter Lenore's story. A private investigator, Lenore Martin is not to be played with. She will break hearts and heads to catch a criminal. She's also been known to push the boundaries of the law a time or two.

Lenore going toe-to-toe with NOLA police detective King Tobias Randolph makes this a read you won't soon forget. They are fire together and King's stately moniker epitomizes his stern demeanor and love for the rules of law. He will challenge Lenore as much as she will challenge him, and a man who will keep a woman on her toes is a man to keep your eye on.

I loved writing King and Lenore's story as they join forces to find a serial killer trolling the local high schools. Getting to know the Martin family and the bonds they share has been the sweetest icing on some really good cake! I'm excited to share a slice with each of you!

Thank you so much for your support. I am always humbled by all the love you keep showing me, my characters and our stories. I know that none of this would be possible without you.

Until next time, please take care and may God's blessings be with you always.

With much love,

Deborah Fletcher Mello

www.DeborahMello.BlogSpot.com

PLAYING WITH DANGER

Deborah Fletcher Mello

HARLEQUIN
ROMANTIC
SUSPENSE

HARLEQUIN®

ROMANTIC SUSPENSE™

Recycling programs
for this product may
not exist in your area.

ISBN-13: 978-1-335-73843-1

Playing with Danger

Copyright © 2023 by Deborah Fletcher Mello

For questions and comments about the quality of this book, please contact us at CustomerService@Harlequin.com.

Harlequin Enterprises ULC
22 Adelaide St. West, 41st Floor
Toronto, Ontario M5H 4E3, Canada
www.Harlequin.com

Printed in U.S.A.

A true Renaissance woman, **Deborah Fletcher Mello** finds joy in crafting unique story lines and memorable characters. She's received accolades from several publications, including *Publishers Weekly*, *Library Journal* and *RT Book Reviews*. Born and raised in Connecticut, Deborah now considers home to be wherever the moment moves her.

Books by Deborah Fletcher Mello

Harlequin Romantic Suspense

The Sorority Detectives
Playing with Danger

To Serve and Seduce
Seduced by the Badge
Tempted by the Badge
Reunited by the Badge
Stalked by Secrets
In the Arms of the Law

The Coltons of Colorado
Colton's Secret Sabotage

The Coltons of Grave Gulch
Rescued by the Colton Cowboy

Colton 911: Grand Rapids
Colton 911: Agent By Her Side

Visit the Author Profile page at Harlequin.com for more titles.

To Walter and Corrine Fletcher

I do this because you gave me the guidance

and the strength to pursue my dreams.

I am grateful for all you have done for me.

I will love you always!

Chapter 1

The body of a young woman dressed in denim shorts and a T-shirt with the Tulane University emblem had begun to decompose. The corpse was propped awkwardly against an oversized cypress tree that rose majestically out of the dark, murky waters of the marshy wetlands. A thick rope was wrapped around her waist, her torso folded in a distorted backbend. Her arms and legs were splayed haphazardly, tangled in the wire and mesh of a bait trap, and a chunk of flesh was missing from one calf. A Nike sneaker was tied snugly around her left foot. The other floated on the water a few yards away, and a pink-striped sock hung from her big toe.

The brutal sunrays and intense midday heat beating down on the landscape were wreaking havoc on everything they touched. The police officers milling around all looked haggard, drenched in perspiration that fell like rain. Sweat stained their blue uniforms. There was some shelter from the bright sunshine under a wooden pavilion, but nothing could deflect the high heat and humidity.

The property was owned by a man named Claude Beaumont who ran a local tour business in Orleans Parish. Beaumont had been prepping one of his flat-bottomed boats for the day's business when he'd found the body. Despite his best efforts to contain his emotions, there was no denying his annoyance at having to cancel on the group of tourists who'd paid him well for the opportunity to explore the ecosystem. He was past ready to toss the lot of police officers off his land. Tired of answering the same questions over and over again. Wanting instead to get back to the business of making money. New Orleans police detective King Randolph found the man's annoyance palpable.

King stood on the edge of the dock, staring out at the water. Across the way, a large gator sat sunning himself on the shoreline. Another had just slipped beneath the wet blanket, disappearing from his view. Behind him, his team of officers was taking statements from the tour company's staff. The heat was stifling, but King found the intrusive noise of Claude Beaumont's whining even more throttling. He'd had to walk away from the man, every ounce of effort needed to keep him from punching the fool in his face. He turned his attention back to the body hanging above the water.

The call had come hours earlier, dispatch pulling him from his bed. News of a body being found had prepared him for the worst, but he still hadn't known what to expect. It also hadn't taken him long to realize that another body added to an already full caseload would soon have his superiors breathing down his neck.

A forensics team stood in a police airboat beneath the oversized tree. One had taken a wealth of photographs before they slowly lifted and dragged the body into the vessel. Watching until the corpse was tagged, King knew his window to find the killer was closing quickly as the outside elements waged war against them. Evidence was deteriorating right before his eyes, Mother Nature playing a cruel game of hide-and-seek with every gust of wind and each crest of the slow-moving stream. He imagined that identifying the body might prove to be an even bigger challenge, rotting flesh leaving them little to work with. He found it all infuriating.

"Detective Randolph?"

King turned, the interruption pulling him from his thoughts. A female officer was eyeing him nervously. She was small in stature with an unflattering pixie cut and mousy features that gave her a waiflike appearance. She was not a member of his team, and he didn't know her name.

"Yes? Patrolman…?"

"Flagg. Janette Flagg."

"How can I help you, Patrolman Flagg?"

She held out a cell phone sealed in a clear plastic bag. "This was in the victim's pocket. It was ringing a few minutes ago."

"Did anyone answer it?"

"No, sir. And the battery just died."

"Did they dust it for prints?"

She nodded. "Yes, sir."

King took the bag from her. "Let evidence know I have possession. I'll sign it into the evidence locker when I get to the station."

"Yes, sir."

Patrolman Flagg hesitated for a split second before turning from him. King watched her walk away, sensing there was something more she wanted to say. Under different circumstances he would have called her back, but for now, whatever was on her mind would have to wait. He had too much on his own mind to be concerned with anything that didn't have to do with the case. And then she turned back around, returning to stand in front of him.

"Excuse me, sir," she said, her voice a loud whisper.

King took a deep breath. "Yes, Patrolman Flagg?"

"I think I know her."

King blinked, his brow lifting at her statement. "Excuse me?"

"The victim. I believe I know who she is. I recognized that heart tattoo on her ankle."

King's eyes narrowed till they were nothing but thin slits. "Go on," he said, prodding her to continue.

"I think it's Michael-Lynn Jeffries. She's a junior at the high school where my brother graduated."

"You think? You're not sure?"

The young officer shook her head vigorously. "No, sir, I'm sure. It's Michael-Lynn. She and my brother used to date."

"What's your brother's name?"

"Patrick. Patrick Flagg. He deployed to Afghanistan about six months ago. He enlisted in the army right after his graduation. But he and Michael-Lynn were good friends. They went to his senior prom together. She lived down in Pine Village with her grandma, Hattie. Hattie Jeffries." A single tear rolled down the woman's face, and she brushed it away with the back of her hand. "She was a good girl, sir. This ain't right. It's going to break Mama Hattie's heart."

King gave her another quick nod of his head. "Thank you, Patrolman. And I'll need you to keep this information to yourself, please. Once we confirm it is Ms. Jeffries, I'll need to notify her family before we release any information to the public."

"Yes, sir." Patrolman Flagg did a one-eighty and headed back toward the end of the dock.

The forensics team had finally pulled the body away from the tree, lowering it into the boat beneath. A sad pall settled through the air, no one speaking as a final show of respect for the victim, and then Claude Beaumont's voice broke through the silence, his Cajun accent thick and heavy.

"Does this mean I can start my tour now?"

Disdain painted King's expression, irritation dancing in his frown. He turned and headed back to his car. Settling in the driver's seat of the state-issued sedan, he allowed himself time to think through his next steps. For a quick minute, he studied the cell phone. It was an older model Apple device with a cracked screen. The back cover was adorned in stickers, hearts and smiley faces suggesting a grade-school mindset. King inhaled swiftly, unable to fathom why anyone's child would be hanging dead in a Louisiana swamp. But this was not the first body, nor the first child, left to the elements. This was yet another case on his watch that he was suddenly anxious to resolve. He always felt personally responsible to bring closure to their friends and families. But once again, he had more questions than he had answers, and he was quickly running out of time.

Lenore Martin cursed her baby sister as she blew her car's horn for the umpteenth time. It was too early on a Monday morning, and with a full workweek ahead of her, she couldn't afford to be late. In that moment, she was past the point of being annoyed. Her sister Sophie Martin was dragging her feet, and Lenore wasn't taking her stalling kindly. Lenore and her sisters often joked that Sophie would be late to her own funeral, needing to arrive in full regalia to make her entrance the talk of New Orleans. But this particular morning, Lenore was neither amused nor patient.

She dialed the young woman's number, and when Sophie didn't answer, the call going directly to her voice mail, she left an expletive-filled message that left no doubt about her feelings.

The front door to Sophie's Metairie home suddenly flew open, and her sister flipped her middle finger at Lenore. The abrasive gesture contrasted starkly with the young woman's innocent expression. Lenore laughed, not at all moved by her sister's sophomoric efforts to be shocking. She gave her an eye roll as Sophie finally slid into the passenger seat of her Mercedes coupe.

"Really, Sophie?"

"I had to finish my makeup!" the young woman exclaimed, tossing her hands up for emphasis. "You should have thought about using some. Maybe a little foundation and some mascara," she said snidely.

Lenore cut her eyes in her sister's direction. Sophie knew full well that Lenore had dusted her face with a bronzing powder and had dashed her cheeks with a hint of blush. A touch of eyeliner and her favorite rose-tinted lip gloss completed her look. It was her go-to look and took her less than ten minutes to accomplish. "You've got jokes now," she said with a soft chuckle.

Sophie laughed with her. "I'm just saying you might want to think about stepping it up a notch." She lowered the passenger-side visor to stare at her reflection in the mirror. Her own makeup was perfection, her contour and shading at a master's level.

Lenore was only slightly envious, and then, with the blink of an eye, she wasn't. "What I think is that you're going to get us both fired. We're going to be late, and you know how your mother is about punctuality!"

Sophie laughed. "You say that like she isn't your mother, too!"

"She isn't. Not when she's mad. When she's mad, she won't claim any of us."

"We're her best agents. She won't fire us. Besides, she likes me. I'm her favorite daughter."

The two women exchanged a look and then both burst out laughing heartily. Both women and their sisters, Celeste and Alexis, worked for the family business, a local detective agency owned by their mother, Claudia Martin. Working for Claudia came with a unique set of challenges, and they had been working for her since the inception of the business, learning on the job, case by case. Claudia Martin was not a woman to be played with. Lenore knew, favorite or not, her mother would not be happy with either one of them.

The drive to the New Orleans office took them just over thirty minutes, with traffic on the I-10 backed up for two miles after a three-car accident. Despite her annoyance, Lenore enjoyed the time with her sister, the two of them having much in common. Since they'd been babies, Lenore had been protective of all her sisters, but she was overly protective of Sophie, the youngest child in the Martin brood.

"He exposed himself at the table," Sophie was saying as she was sharing details about her recent date with a local attorney. "We'd just finished the appetizer and were starting on the entrée when he suddenly unzipped his pants and shook his wacky at me, talking about what he wanted to do for dessert! He did that crap at the table!"

Lenore laughed, a gut-deep chortle that had her eyes tearing. "Wacky? Really? Is that what you're calling it now?"

Sophie giggled. "Trust me when I tell you, it was not a pretty penis. Had it been a pretty penis, I might have given it some consideration. But it was not pretty at all." She shuddered, her expression exaggerated as she squinted her eyes and wriggled her nose in disgust.

"So, what did you do?"

"Smiled my prettiest smile, gave him an eye wink, then excused myself to go to the ladies' room. I walked right past the bathrooms and out the front door. Then I called Daddy."

Lenore's eyes widened, the smile across her face spreading from ear to ear. "Please tell me you did not call and tattle to Daddy! Were you trying to get that man killed?"

Sophie laughed again. "Not killed," she said with a shake of her head. "Just hurt!"

Lenore pulled her car into her assigned parking space and shut down the engine. It wasn't quite ten o'clock in the morning, and already the temperature was well in the nineties. The sky was clear, a stark canvas of royal blue with the barest wisp of a cloud in the distance. The humidity was thick, blanketing the atmosphere heavily. There was something in the air Lenore couldn't quite put her finger on, but she sensed things were amiss, and it knotted her stomach with nervous energy. She took a deep breath and then a second.

Stepping into the Dorgenois Street property, they heard their mother screaming at the top of her lungs. Her high-pitched tone seemed to vibrate from wall to wall through the renovated warehouse space. Both women threw each other a look. A man was screaming back, or trying to, the couple in the midst of a heated argument. Neither woman seemed at all concerned. Lenore grinned as Sophie shrugged her narrow shoulders. The two women laughed again, amusement dancing across their faces.

"Good morning," Lenore chimed as she stepped through the door.

"I don't know how good it is," Piper Long responded. The office manager stood with two piping hot cups of coffee in hand. She passed one to Lenore and the other to Sophie, then rounded the reception desk to retake her seat. "They've been at it for a good hour now."

"What did my mother do?" Lenore questioned as Piper reached for the telephone ringing on her desk.

"Your mother didn't do anything," a deep alto voice answered, moving them to turn and stare.

Claudia Martin stood in the entrance to her office, an index finger pointed toward the exit. A young man half her age stormed past her in a huff. He was tall and lean and easy on the eyes with a head of dark curls that complemented a pale complexion. He shot them all a look but said nothing as he stomped across the hardwood floors and out the door.

"Well," Lenore said, "he didn't look happy."

"His happiness is not my problem," Claudia quipped.

"What's he all emotional about?" Sophie questioned.

"His feelings are hurt. Someone else escorted me to that black-tie banquet last night. For some reason he was under the impression we were exclusive."

"Clearly he doesn't know you," Lenore said with a soft chuckle.

Her mother's gaze narrowed ever so slightly. She stole a quick glance down to the diamond-encrusted watch on her wrist. "And why are you two just now getting to the office? Did I miss something?"

Sophie pointed at her sister. "Lenore took forever to get ready this morning!" she said, her expression smug.

Claudia looked them both up and down, then shook her head. "Staff meeting in ten minutes. Be on time for that or find yourselves someplace else to work." She turned on her high heels and moved back into her office, slamming the door behind her.

"I'm going to kill you," Lenore said as her sister laughed warmly.

"You need to be quicker on the draw. It's why I never got in trouble," Sophie quipped.

"That and you lie," another voice countered.

Both women turned toward their sister Celeste, their other sister Alexis following close on her heels. The two women had been seated in the conference room, poring over a stack of file folders.

"I don't lie," Sophie said. "I'm creative with my explanations."

"She lies," Alexis responded. "She lies like a pro."

"She got that from our father," Lenore added. She grabbed the stack of mail Piper was holding out for her.

The young woman also gestured toward the telephone. "You have a call, Lenore. I'll transfer it to your desk when you're ready."

"Who is it?"

"Hattie Jeffries? She said it's urgent she speak with one of you."

"Mama Hattie?" Lenore said, calling the neighborhood matriarch by her nickname. "How'd I get lucky?"

"Sophie took the last case. You're next on the list."

"How would you define *urgent*? Was it hysterical urgent or I just need to speak with someone very soon urgent?"

"She wasn't hysterical, if that's what you're asking. But she did seem frustrated. She wouldn't tell me what it's about. Just that she needed to speak with one of you. That, and she called your name two or three times during the conversation. I figured that was her way of saying she wanted you specifically."

Lenore nodded. "Get a number, please. Tell her I'm in a meeting and will call her back as soon as I'm finished. Tell her it should only be about an hour or two." She turned and followed her sisters into the conference room, Sophie updating the others on her date with the attorney. Laughter rang warmly through the space.

As Lenore and her sisters made themselves comfortable, their mother strode into the room, her cell phone pressed tight to her ear. Her expression was tense with annoyance. The matriarch suddenly cussed, profanity rolling effortlessly past her thin lips. The Martin women exchanged looks, grateful that they were not on the receiving end of their mother's wrath. They pitied the man who was getting it with both barrels. When the conversation ended, Claudia slammed her phone down against the table and threw her petite frame down in the upholstered chair.

"What is it with these men? I don't need a father or a warden! Why is that so hard to understand?" Claudia exclaimed.

"Boy toy still having issues?" Celeste questioned.

"That child is acting like I took his pacifier when it wasn't his to have."

"You're always telling us to date mature men, but you never take your own advice," Alexis interjected.

Their mother's eyebrow lifted slightly. "I'm not looking for Mr. Right. At my age, I'm very happy with Mr. Right Now as long as he can handle my needs."

Lenore winced. "Too much information."

Her sisters laughed.

"You'll appreciate these lessons when you get to be my age," Claudia concluded. "Now, where are we? I need to meet a client in an hour."

The mood in the room shifted abruptly, the girls taking their mother's cue to focus on business. Celeste started them off.

"I'm finalizing the Michael Hinton case today. We found nothing to support Dr. Hinton's concerns that his wife is cheating on him."

Claudia nodded. "What did you find?"

"Mrs. Hinton has been taking design classes at the community college. But clearly, she doesn't want her husband to know."

"And what do you plan to tell him?"

"Only that there is no secret lover. She hasn't lied. She just skips over the fact that she's in school. If she says she was at the coffee shop, she always makes a stop at the coffee shop."

"What's your impression of the husband?"

"Overbearing. Controlling. Slightly obnoxious. I have some concerns that he might be abusive, but nothing concrete."

Claudia nodded. "Be discreet without tipping our client's hand, but let her know her husband is suspicious. See if you can get a feel for why she doesn't want him to know, and let her also know that her secret is safe with us. If she's wanting to get out of her situation and she's afraid, let her know she'll find a friend here if she needs one."

Celeste nodded.

After updates from Sophie and Alexis, Claudia turned to Lenore. "Where are we with the John Simon estate?"

"I found his son and connected him with the attorney. We've officially closed that file."

"What else are you working on now?"

"I received a call this morning from Hattie Jeffries. She said she needed to speak with us."

"Did she say why?"

"No, ma'am. Just that it was urgent."

"Call Mama Hattie back. If she's calling, something's wrong."

"Who is she?" Sophie asked, her eyes skating back and forth across their faces. "Do I know her?"

Claudia answered. "Her late husband was pastor of Church of Christ down in the Twelfth Ward. You probably don't remember her. You were a baby when we were all acquainted."

"Her husband and Daddy had history," Lenore stated.

"What kind of history?" Sophie questioned.

Their mother raised an eyebrow but said nothing, the question needing no answer that she was willing to give. Her silence was almost deafening, the moment suddenly feeling awkward. The sisters exchanged a look between them, neither daring to push the issue further.

Sorority Row Detective Agency had been born out of necessity. Their mother, Claudia, a former cotillion debutante and fashion model turned wife and mother, had constantly navigated unknown territory to help family and friends resolve their problems. Problems that always seemed to drop in her lap by way of her ex-husband, Josiah Martin.

Having been married to a known drug kingpin in the streets of New Orleans had put the matriarch in a unique position to seek out answers where others feared to tread. It had also afforded her the opportunity to keep eyes on her husband, his philandering ways eventually leading to their separation and divorce. Many of their clients had history with the family that didn't need to be explained when they came calling. Hattie Jeffries was one of those clients.

Lenore gave a nod of understanding, knowing her mother only told them what she wanted them to know. Understanding that no answer to her sister's question was forthcoming. "I'll call Mama Hattie as soon as we're done here."

"Unless there's something else I need to know, we're finished. Call her now," Claudia said, rising from her seat. She paused to eye each of her daughters directly, then dismissed them with a wave of her hand. "Let's get it done, ladies. Someone out there needs saving."

Chapter 2

Hattie Jeffries was pissed. Lenore had heard the irritation in the woman's voice when she returned the call. When she entered the modest two-bedroom home, she could feel the wealth of the old woman's anger painting the walls a dark shade of discontent. Anger wrapped around fear and hopelessness, hoping to conceal emotion she was unwilling to show. She was ranting as Lenore stepped through the door.

"Something ain't right! My baby girl would not stay out all night long and not let me know where she is. Michael-Lynn ain't like that!" she was saying.

"When's the last time you saw your granddaughter?" Lenore asked. She drew a warm hand against Mama Hattie's back.

"Yesterday morning, right before I had to go to my

shift down at the dry cleaners. Said she was going to meet her friend Tralisa. They volunteer at the library together. But Tralisa said she didn't show up."

Lenore nodded. "Did you believe her?"

Exasperation wafted through the look Mama Hattie gave her. "They're both good girls! If Michael-Lynn said she was meeting Tralisa, she was. Tralisa said she never showed up, and I believe her. Them girls wouldn't lie to me."

Lenore wanted to say that all teens lie at some time or another, but instinctively knew the matriarch wouldn't take her comment kindly. She made a mental note to go visit Tralisa when she was done at Mama Hattie's. "Does Michael-Lynn have a boyfriend?" she asked.

Mama Hattie shook her head. "Last little boy she liked went into the military a few months back. They write letters to each other talking about they in love. His name's Patrick. Michael-Lynn has it bad for Patrick, so I know she didn't go off with no other boy all night long unless he forced her. Michael-Lynn ain't like that. She's a good Catholic girl."

Lenore gave her a slight smile. She too had been a good Catholic girl. Even when she hadn't been. "When I spoke to you on the phone, you said that you had called the police to report her missing?"

Mama Hattie grunted as venom wrapped around her words. "A lotta good that did me!" she spat. "They said she had to be missing for forty-eight hours. Even suggested she might have run away. They wouldn't even send over a patrol car to take a report. Told me to call back tomorrow." She grunted a second time, her irritation furrowing her brow.

Lenore nodded. "May I see Michael-Lynn's room, please?"

The old woman pointed her toward the back of the house. "Her door is on the right. I need to go take my medication."

Lenore was dismissed as Mama Hattie headed for the kitchen. She wore her age like a shroud, her thick frame moving unsteadily on legs that looked like tree trunks. Without saying so, she had given Lenore free rein, knowing the young woman wouldn't do anything to tarnish her trust or have her calling Lenore's mother to complain. There was a level of behavior she expected, Lenore knew it, and neither needed it to be a discussion between them.

The exterior rooms were a shrine to everything Mama Hattie loved. The walls were lined with photos of family and friends in dollar store frames. Stacks of magazines lined polished wood tables. The furniture was old and well-worn, and there was little that Mama Hattie ever discarded. It was cluttered, but meticulously organized, the old woman able to put her hands on anything she wanted without giving it a second thought.

Lenore maneuvered her way down the narrow hallway, past the bathroom, to the bedroom on the right. Michael-Lynn's name decorated the door in a personalized license plate with pink flowers around the border. Pushing the door open, Lenore stepped inside. The space made her smile. Michael-Lynn had taken a more pragmatic approach to her home decorating. Everything was pristine. Bright white curtains dressed the one window. The room had been painted a pale shade of lavender, and a floral print, purple-and-white spread was draped across the full-size bed. An oversized poster of the K-pop group BTS covered the wall behind the bed like a headboard. The seven-member boy band were a pretty lot, sporting similar bowl cuts in varying shades of the rainbow.

There was a white makeup table and chair under the window. A dozen tubes of lip gloss, all neutral tones, rested in a crystal bowl, and two eyebrow pencils were neatly positioned beside it. A Dell laptop rested on the nightstand beside the bed. Her clothes were hung neatly in the closet, and one chest of drawers sat in the far corner. Beside the computer there was a framed prom photo of Michael-Lynn and a handsome young man hugged up against each other, both smiling as if there was nothing at all wrong in the world.

Lenore stood for a moment studying the photo. Michael-Lynn had her grandmother's eyes. Her makeup looked like it had been professionally done, and she wore her hair in a cascade of curls that danced around her face. She was a very pretty girl, her expression angelic. The boy in the photo was beaming with adoration, joy brimming out of his eyes as he stared at his friend. Their affection for each other pulled you into the photo and held you hostage. If young love was corporeal, Lenore thought, they could be the poster couple for it.

Lenore moved to the bedside and took a seat, pulling Michael-Lynn's computer into her lap. She powered it on, not at all surprised that it was not password protected. Intuition told her that much like her own mother, Mama Hattie didn't allow locks of any kind in her home. If Michael-Lynn had something to hide, it wouldn't be in the space her grandmother ruled. Whether the old woman was interested in checking her grandchild's internet history didn't matter. It just mattered that she could.

Michael-Lynn had been working on a paper, researching the 1936 Olympians Tidye Pickett and Louise Stokes. The two had been the first Black women allowed to participate in the Berlin games, but racism and sexism had stolen their thunder. Lenore skimmed the first draft, impressed by the young girl's observations. She was astute and thorough in her research and had given much thought to what she wanted to convey.

The day before she disappeared, she'd browsed a popular clothing site, the product and prices cheap. Two summer dresses and a pair of sweats had been saved to a favorites folder. Michael-Lynn had also looked up movie schedules and hours for a local pharmacy, and had spent a fair amount of time surfing YouTube videos.

On her initial search, Lenore found nothing unusual. But she knew that didn't necessarily mean anything. She'd get their assistant, Cash Davies, to do a more intensive search, seeking out files and folders that might be secreted away in hidden drives. Cash was a vital part of the agency. She was a convicted computer hacker turned professional technical guru to legitimize her sometimes illegal operations. Lenore couldn't imagine them ever doing without her.

Lenore shut down the laptop and slid it into the leather tote that she carried with her. She stood and moved to the closet. Michael-Lynn favored denim jeans and bright white shirts. There were a few dresses, all conservative styles with high collars and knee-length skirts, and Lenore reasoned the girl probably only wore them to Saturday Mass or for special events at school.

Lenore stood in the center of the room. Her initial impression was that Michael-Lynn was everything her grandmother believed her to be. She did well in school, was respectful, obedient and not at all problematic. Lenore had closed her eyes, taking it all in, when she heard the doorbell ring. A man's deep baritone voice suddenly echoed from the entrance. Mama Hattie's tone was terse, the visitor neither expected nor welcomed. And then Mama Hattie screamed, the blood-curdling shriek piercing through the afternoon air.

As Lenore rushed back to the living room, she found Mama Hattie on her knees. The old woman sobbed as she rocked back and forth. The man standing above her looked perplexed, his expression a mesh of sympathy and confusion. He was bent at the waist, his hand clutching Mama Hattie's elbow. Lenore sensed that he had tried to keep her from falling, helping instead to lower her to the floor. Now he looked like he wasn't quite sure what he should do.

Lenore didn't need to ask who he was or what business he had with the matriarch. He wore his badge on a chain around his thick neck. He was local police, and Lenore knew he was there in an official capacity.

He was dressed in tan slacks and a white dress shirt that showcased his brown-and-blue paisley necktie. He was a good-looking man. His Hershey's dark chocolate complexion was butter-slick, and he was handsomely rugged with his full beard and mustache. His hair had been freshly cut, the short edge up with a high-low fade having just enough length to see some kinky curly texture on the top. Another time and place and Lenore might have been moved by his good looks. At the moment, though, he was the bearer of bad news, and she sensed that her search for a missing teen had become something else altogether. The case was technically over before it had even begun.

"He said my baby's dead! My baby's dead!" Mama Hattie cried. "Lord, help me! My baby's dead!"

"I'm Detective Randolph," the man said, directing his attention toward Lenore. He still held on to Mama Hattie's elbow.

Lenore shook her head. She moved to the old woman's side to help lift her back onto her feet and into one of the cushioned wingback chairs that decorated the room. As the officer watched her, Lenore moved into the kitchen. She could be heard rummaging through the cabinets and minutes later returned with a glass of ice water, a shot of dark whiskey and a box of tissues. Mama Hattie clutched the booze between both her hands and tossed the shot back before taking a sip of the cool beverage. She swiped at her eyes with a clean tissue and blew her nose clear. As she sat back in her seat, her tears still flowing, Lenore sent a quick text message to her mother. She knew that passing the bad news on to Claudia would bring a cavalry to help the old woman get through the heartache.

Lenore slid her phone into the back pocket of her slacks and then extended her hand. "Lenore Martin, I'm a friend of the family," she said, the statement more truth than lie. "What happened to Michael-Lynn?"

King took a deep breath. His voice dropped to a loud

whisper, not wanting to burden Mama Hattie a second time as he glossed over the details. "We found Michael-Lynn's body earlier this morning over in Tangipahoa Parish. It's officially a murder investigation."

"What happened to her?" Lenore questioned a second time. "What was she doing over there?"

King's brow lifted slightly. For a family friend, the woman wasn't showing emotion he would have expected. There was no shocked expression, no tears, no palpitations or hand wringing. Reaction had barely registered on her radar, and he couldn't help but wonder why, especially with the queries she was throwing at him. He didn't bother to answer. "I really just need to ask Ms. Jeffries a few questions," he said. "We're in the initial stages of the investigation, and I can't share much information."

"Now's not a good time," Lenore said, suddenly feeling very protective of the old woman who was still rocking back and forth, her tears saturating the front of her plaid housecoat.

King nodded. "I understand." He reached into the pocket of his dress shirt and pulled out a business card, passing it to her. "I'll reach out again in a day or two. Again, it's really important that I speak with her. If there's anything she'd like to tell me before then, please have her call."

Lenore eyed the card briefly before palming it in her hand. "Thank you," she said as she moved to the front door and opened it. "We appreciate you stopping by."

King gave her a nod. "I'm very sorry for your loss," he said. "Please know that we're going to do everything that we can to find her killer."

The timing couldn't have been more perfect. As King stepped back across the threshold, the first of many women began to arrive. The cavalry of church mothers eyed the duo with reservation before pushing past them to hurry to Mama Hattie's side.

As the detective moved back to his car, Lenore watched him walk away. His stride was confident, with the barest hint of arrogance. He had presence and drew a wealth of attention from those hurrying past him. She watched until he was out of sight, taking the briefest moment to enjoy the rear view. When he had rounded the corner, she pushed Dial on her cell phone and pulled the device to her ear. Her sister answered on the third ring.

"Celeste, hey, I need a favor."

"What's up?" Celeste responded.

"Ask your friend down at the police station to get me everything he can on a body that was discovered this morning. The victim is Michael-Lynn Jeffries. A detective named Randolph caught the case."

"Is that your missing person?" Celeste questioned.

"Yeah." Lenore sighed. "It's now a murder investigation," she answered. "Someone killed our client's granddaughter, and we need to figure out who."

"If the police are on it, Lenore, then there's not much we can really do."

"She's a young Black girl from the poor side of town, Celeste. Her grandmother called us because she couldn't get the police to help. She called them first, when her grandchild went missing, and they ignored her. Stereotyping her and claiming Michael-Lynn was probably a runaway. Mama Hattie doesn't trust them to do right by the little girl, and if I'm honest, I don't have much faith in them either."

A quiet pause rose like a morning mist between the sisters as both considered Lenore's comment.

"I hear you," Celeste said finally. "I'll call you as soon I find out something."

King sat in his car and watched as Hattie Jeffries's neighbors and friends began to occupy her home. It was a ritual of sorts that he knew all too well. They would take over her kitchen to feed the mourners who would come to console her. She would want for nothing, all her needs cared for until her granddaughter was buried, and everyone went back to their daily lives. Prayers would ring randomly through the air, someone or everyone needing the litanies to promise strength and courage as they struggled through the tragedy. There would be a protective wall around Hattie Jeffries that he would have to push past to ask questions she had no interest in answering.

He was just about to pull off when he saw Lenore Martin again. The family friend was hurrying toward her own car, tossing a quick glance left and then right before sliding into the driver's side of her vehicle. She was a stunning woman, King thought as he shifted forward in his seat.

He hadn't missed the spattering of freckles that dotted her nose and cheeks. Little chocolate chips that peppered her warm complexion. She was a natural redhead, lengthy waves cascading past her shoulders. And there was no missing the wealth of curves, a full bustline and wide hips complementing the tiniest waist. Her hourglass figure could easily bring a strong man to his knees, King thought.

Who was she, he wondered? And how was she connected to the Jeffries family? How had she known his victim? She had politely pushed him out the door, and he had let her. He knew he'd get further giving the family that moment to themselves. They'd be more willing to lend him help if he allowed them their pain without being intrusive. But he had questions that he needed answered. He was determined to find Michael-Lynn's killer. He owed that to the young girl.

Hours later, Lenore sat in her car, watching the front door of a shotgun-style home. The long and narrow, single-story residence had been freshly painted, its wood exterior a vibrant shade of tangerine with a neon-green door. The original Victorian embellishments beneath the large front eave were a classic white and added to the home's charming character. Someone had invested a fair amount of time on the landscaping, and the whole property reminded her of a gingerbread house with candy decorations. From the outside, it looked like a happy place.

The man who had answered the door, however, had not been happy to see her. He worked third shift and was leveraging a few more hours of sleep before he would have to ready himself for work. Her leaning on his doorbell had disturbed his dreams, and that had been all he was interested in. His name was Shaun Morgan, and he was Tralisa Taylor's stepfather. Tralisa hadn't gotten home from school, and Shaun claimed not to know where she was or how to contact her. But Mama

Hattie had given Lenore Tralisa's cell phone number, and after an exchange of text messages, the young girl had promised to show as soon as she was finished with cheerleading practice. Until then, all Lenore could do was wait. She glanced at her wristwatch, noting the time. Either she was early, or Tralisa was running late.

It was excessively warm, and she sat with the windows lowered. Her mind kept wandering back to the detective and how he had disregarded her questions. Lenore wasn't accustomed to being ignored by any man, and it rubbed her the wrong way. Detective Randolph had been purposeful with his silence, and now she planned to be a thorn in the man's side until the case was solved. He couldn't begin to know what was going to come at him, and she would do it for no other reason than that she could. Lenore could be a raging storm in high heels if the moment moved her, and this case had her moved.

She blew out a soft sigh as she reflected on what little she knew about the young girl who had disappeared and turned up dead. There were few clues for her to go on, and she found her rising frustration disconcerting.

Michael-Lynn had an active social media presence. Lenore scrolled through her Instagram, Twitter and Tik-Tok pages. There were hundreds of photos of her, her with her friends and random things that caught her eye. She'd been quite adept at taking selfies, was opinionated, socially conscious and had a keen sense of humor that many gravitated toward. She was well-liked and was considered one of the more popular students. She participated at school, church and in the community, and she'd been a shining light who led with conviction.

Like many young people of her generation, her entire life played out on social media. At face value she was every parent's dream come true. She made her grandmother proud and would have been a force to be reckoned with in the world. Lenore was suddenly filled with sorrow, the devastating loss hitting her hard.

"Hey, are you Miss Martin?"

Lenore was suddenly startled from the reverie she'd fallen into. She looked up to find a young woman who reminded her of a Bratz doll, peering into her passenger side window. Her pursed lips were a deep shade of burgundy, and her eye makeup with the blue shadow and black liner gave her a wide-eyed, deer-in-the-headlights gaze.

Lenore swiped at a tear that had fallen against her cheek. She nodded her head. "Are you Tralisa?"

"Yes, ma'am."

Across the way, Tralisa's stepfather was standing in the doorway, staring at the two of them. The gesture was meant to be protective, him noting that he had his eye on her and his child whether he said anything or not. He folded his arms across his broad chest and leaned into the doorjamb. He would not be moved until Tralisa crossed back over the home's threshold and was safely inside.

Lenore turned her attention back to the teenager. "I need to talk to you about Michael-Lynn."

"Mama Hattie called to tell me," she said, her voice dropping an octave as she suddenly fought back tears.

Lenore nodded again, understanding that Mama Hattie had cleared the way for the girl to cooperate. She opened the driver's side door and stepped out. Tralisa moved around the front of the car to the sidewalk to stand with her. She held on to a bright red Schwinn bike, pausing to lower the kickstand before turning to stand toe-to-toe with Lenore.

"What do you need to know?" Tralisa asked, her bottom lip quivering.

"Anything you can tell me that Michael-Lynn didn't want anyone to know about. Was there a boyfriend, a girlfriend, or someone she liked to hang out with that her grandmother would have had a fit about if she found out? Something she was into that would have gotten her into trouble. I need to know if she had any secrets that she shared with you but kept from everyone else."

There was a moment of pause, and Lenore couldn't tell if the girl was deciding whether to share something or if she was trying to remember if there was something that should be shared.

"Nah," she said finally. "Michael-Lynn was straight as an arrow. If she had secrets, she didn't even tell me what they were, and I was her best friend."

"Do you know where she might have gone off to yesterday?"

"No, ma'am. We were supposed to meet up and go volunteer at the library. They were doing an afternoon program for the little kids, and we was supposed to help out with the art project. I waited for her as long as I could, but she never came. She never showed up to help either. I called her like a million times, and she didn't answer. Then her grandma called looking for her. We called everyone we knew, and no one had seen or spoken with her. Mama Hattie called the police, and they wouldn't help, and that's when she said she was gonna call you."

"Thank you, Tralisa. Just one more question. Was there anyone Michael-Lynn was afraid of? Someone who might have scared her?"

The girl pondered the question for a quick minute. She shook her head. "Just her granny. Mama Hattie can spit fire if you look at her sideways. But it was all love. She just wanted Michael-Lynn to do right and be happy. It was the best kind of scared, and Michael-Lynn appreciated that her granny loved her enough to care." Tralisa swiped at the tears that rained down her cheeks.

Before Lenore could respond, the car pulling into an empty parking space in front of the gingerbread home drew their attention. Lenore recognized the driver, Detective Randolph, catching her eye as he passed.

"Who's that?" Tralisa asked, noting the look that passed between the two.

"Police. He's come to ask you questions about Michael-Lynn," Lenore answered.

"Should I talk to him?"

Lenore smiled. "I don't know him well enough to answer that, baby girl. I'll let you decide."

Tralisa nodded. "If my stepdad says I have to, I will."

"That sounds like a good idea to me," Lenore answered.

"I have to go," the girl said, giving Lenore a slight wave. "Shaun is going to be mad. He has to go to work, and I need to watch the other kids."

"Thank you, Tralisa, and I'm really sorry about your friend."

The young woman gave her the faintest smile. "Please find who did this, Miss Martin."

"I'm going to try my best. If I have any more questions, I'll text you."

Lenore watched as the girl crossed back over to the other side of the street. Her stepfather had stepped out of the doorway and stood on the front stoop, his arms still folded. His expression was grim, annoyance pulling his thick lips in a frown. As Randolph moved toward them, Mr. Morgan gestured for Tralisa to go inside. The girl went obediently, disappearing behind the brightly painted door.

As Randolph moved in front of Mr. Morgan and extended his hand, introducing himself, Lenore chuckled softly. She instinctively knew the conversation would be short and sweet, any access to Tralisa denied. He would be hard-pressed to find someone in the neighborhood willing to talk to him. He was a stranger with a badge, and that made him suspect in many of their eyes. They would shut him out until someone they trusted gave him a pass. But no such license was coming anytime soon.

The two men stood talking briefly, and then the father dismissed him with a wave of his hand. He too disappeared into the home, closing and locking the door behind himself. Frustration painted Randolph's expression as he turned his gaze toward Lenore. He called her name and he gestured for her attention.

"Ms. Martin! A moment of your time, please!" He moved toward her, sturdy legs carrying him swiftly in her direction.

"Detective Randolph. How can I help you?"

"Perhaps you can explain what you're doing here?"

Lenore bristled ever so slightly. Her eyes narrowed. "I could ask you the same thing, Detective."

"I'm trying to conduct an investigation, and it feels like you're trying to get in my way."

She gave him the slightest smile. "I'm visiting a family friend. That's all."

"Another family friend who also happens to be connected to my victim. That makes two today for you."

"I didn't know we were keeping score."

"I like to know who all the players are."

Lenore stared at him, her eyes doing a slow two-step over his features. His brow was furrowed, frustration seeping like water from his eyes. She sensed there was something he wanted to say, but he was holding back his words, assessing her as intently as she was studying him. She turned, reaching for her car door. She didn't bother to respond as she slid into the driver's seat.

Detective Randolph grabbed the top of the driver's window before she could close the door. He stood majestically, leaning into the car to meet her eye to eye. "If you get in the way of my investigation, Ms. Martin, I will arrest you," the handsome man stated, his expression stern.

Lenore laughed, the warmth of it like a summer breeze dancing with the heat. Light shimmered in her eyes, and the faintest hint of color tinted her cheeks. "Good luck with that, Detective," she said, still chuckling.

King took a step back as she pulled the door shut and started the car's engine. She tossed him one last look before she pulled into traffic, disappearing down the road and around the corner.

Chapter 3

"Get me everything you can on a woman named Lenore Martin," King snapped as he entered the South Broad Street police station.

Detective Christian Forel jumped from his seat, following him as he headed to his desk. He was a bear of a man with a head of dark curls and the beginnings of a serious beer gut. At King's comment he came to an abrupt stop, many in the room seeming to fall quiet. Then someone in the back laughed, other officers looking at King like he'd just made a joke.

King turned, eyeing everyone around him. "What's funny about that?" he questioned.

"Most of us around here know the Martin family," Christian said. "It's not often anyone asks about them."

"What do you need to know?" Captain Juan Romero interjected, moving toward the two men.

King shrugged. "What everyone else knows, apparently," he said.

"She's mean as spit and has been known to bite," Juan said.

A round of laughter rang through the room.

Had his boss not looked so serious, King would have thought he was being pranked, an initiation of sorts to welcome him to the department and see what he was made of. The captain gestured with his head toward the conference room, and King followed, Christian still on his heels. The three men dropped into the pleather chairs around the table.

"What am I missing?" King said, his eyes skating between the two men.

"Lenore Martin is most likely working the case you caught this morning," Captain Romero stated.

"Working? How?"

"She's a private investigator. One of the best. She works for her mother's business, Sorority Row Detective Agency. Let me guess. She's running interference, and no one will talk to you."

"Yeah," King answered. "Something like that."

The captain nodded. "The Martin family history goes way back. Her parents are legendary. Her father, Josiah Martin, controlled every illegal operation in this city, from drugs to prostitution. While he did that, her mother had them hobnobbing with the city's elite, running in all the right circles. It's told that Josiah has three former presidents on speed dial. But he's also as cutthroat as they come, and in these streets, he is still the law. And don't get me started on her mother. She makes her ex-husband look angelic. That woman is highly regarded in the community, but she can be vicious. People bend over backwards for her. The New Orleans police department included."

Christian nodded. "They ran this city. Still do. People trust them. Their philanthropic endeavors are legendary. There is a generation in this community that will call on them before they call on us, and that's because many of them worked for Josiah. Some kept his secrets, and he is still protecting them and taking care of their families."

"The loyalty to them can't be denied," Captain Romero added, "and it's been extended down to their daughters. Because they can sometimes get answers that we can't, we've used the agency to open doors for us."

"So, you've worked with them before?"

Captain Romero nodded. "We have. In an unofficial capacity, of course. So why is Lenore interested in this case?"

"I'm not sure."

"You may want to ask. She may know something that can help." He stood. "I have an appointment with the mayor in an hour. He's going to want to know where we are with these murders. Are they connected? Do we have a serial offender on our hands? Questions I can't answer. Do you two have any answers for him?"

King shook his head. "I'm headed to the state examiner's office when we're done here. I'll know more after I speak with the coroner."

Captain Romero nodded. "Keep me updated."

"Yes, sir."

"And reach out to Ms. Martin. Find out what she knows. And watch what you share. It's need-to-know only. You don't want the prosecutor's office hanging you up by your balls and bringing you up on criminal charges. If you're unsure, check with me just to be safe. That's an order."

King and Christian exchanged a look. "Yes, sir," they chimed in unison.

When the senior officer was out of earshot, Christian blew out a sigh, then spoke. "What the captain didn't say was that he and Lenore dated for a quick minute. He never talks about it, but I heard it wasn't pretty. They say she chews men up and spits them out for entertainment."

"I can believe that," King said, thinking about his brief encounters with the beautiful woman. "I can definitely believe that!" Curiosity suddenly pulled at King. "How long was a quick minute?"

"Maybe a month or two, if that. But it was a crash and burn to the nth degree. He's still licking his wounds although he won't say it. He's a little sensitive about the subject."

"I'm surprised he's still willing to work with her."

"He might be butt-hurt, but he's not stupid. She's good, and if I'm honest, her father could shut this city down with one phone call. He's got that kind of juice."

King eyed his associate warily. "I find that hard to believe."

"I did, too, until I saw it for myself."

"So, me threatening to arrest her probably didn't have any weight."

"I'm sure it gave her a good laugh," Christian said with a hearty chuckle.

King shook his head. He was not amused.

* * *

King used a pushpin to add Michael-Lynn's high school picture to the photo gallery that hung on the oversized bulletin board. Since his official first day with the New Orleans police department, it was the eighth murder assigned to his desk, and he'd barely been there three months. Of those eight, five remained unsolved. The first two had been acts of domestic violence. The third had been a robbery gone wrong. Those offenders had all been caught in record time. The last five were proving to be elusive, testing King's skills on a whole other level.

Maximillion Broussard had been the first of the five cases yet to be solved. He'd been eighteen years old, recently graduated, headed to Job Corps to figure out his future. He'd been tangled in a gator trap, little left of him when he'd been found. The body of fifteen-year-old Jessica Guidry had been found just two days later. Jessica should have started her freshman year in high school. Barely three weeks into that investigation, fishermen had discovered Kyle Tanner, then Lissette Broman. Now Michael-Lynn Jeffries. All had been in their teens. Each had been left in the swamps, discarded like trash.

King knew the problem was bigger than any of them wanted to admit. Whether it was said out loud or not, there was a serial predator at large, and he was nowhere near identifying a suspect. He was no closer to solving the case, but he was determined. He refused to be beaten. He folded his arms over his chest as he leaned back against the desk, staring at the smiling faces of each child. They had family and friends, and their lives had been important. They had deserved better. He owed them justice no matter what it took, and it might take him working with a woman folks claimed made mincemeat of the male species.

The more he thought about Lenore Martin and the stories fellow detectives had come by to share, the more he wondered if the Pandora's box he was about to open would be worth the effort. Many of the men he worked with had made it clear that she could be a vicious adversary when challenged, and what he needed right then was an ally.

Moving to the leather executive's chair, he flipped through a stack of folders left on his desk. After a quick review, he slid them into the attaché that was resting on the floor. Minutes later, with the twist of a key, he locked his desk for the night and headed out.

Celeste dropped a file folder onto Lenore's desk. "You owe me," she said, her expression smug.

Lenore grinned. "I won't ask what you had to do to get this. How is Officer Douglas?" she asked, referring to the man her sister sometimes allowed in her life.

"Still hopeful."

"You shouldn't string that poor man along. He loves you."

"Your mother says love is overrated. I tend to believe her."

"Maybe so, but it does come in handy," Lenore muttered. Her attention was focused on the autopsy report inside the folder and the note clipped to the inside. "The coroner has tied Michael-Lynn's case to four others." She sat back in her seat, her mind racing.

Celeste nodded. "Four of the five victims had identical burn marks on their lower backs. He branded them postmortem. One had been eviscerated by the local wildlife, but the assumption is that he also fit the MO."

"So, we have a serial killer?"

"Starting to look that way. Of course, there's no official statement saying such from the police department."

Lenore cussed, an expletive slipping past her lips as she continued to read through the autopsy report. The details were gruesome, and it broke her heart to know that Mama Hattie's beloved granddaughter had suffered. She blew a sigh and slammed the folder closed. "So now we need to figure out if the victims were random or if they had something in common that linked them to each other." She reached for the phone on her desk and pushed the intercom button.

Cash Davies answered instantly. "Yes, Lenore?"

"Cash, I need to know…" Lenore started, and then she was interrupted.

"Your sister already asked. All five victims were students at the Thomy Lafon Academy. One had graduated. One was a rising freshman. Two were juniors and the other a senior. Two cheerleaders, one math whiz and three were in the chess club. They were acquainted, but nothing across their social media says they were besties with each other. I already emailed you a report. You have family histories, contacts, health records and anything else I thought might be relevant."

"You're too good to me!" Lenore exclaimed.

"Love you, too!" Cash chimed back as she disconnected the call.

Celeste gave her sister a smile. "We're on it. You can

go beat the pavement, and we'll make sure you're covered here. If I can't anticipate it before you ask, Claudia will."

The intercom on the desk suddenly chimed.

Lenore stole a quick glance at the ID screen and pushed the response button. "Yes, Piper?"

"You have a visitor."

Confusion washed over her expression. "A visitor? I'm not expecting anyone."

"He said he doesn't have an appointment, but he's certain you'll want to speak with him." Amusement danced in the receptionist's tone, a hint of laughter ringing over the line. Neither Lenore nor her sister missed it.

Celeste crossed her arms over her chest, her brow raised as she eavesdropped on the exchange.

"And who might *he* be?" Lenore questioned, rising from her seat.

"Police detective King Randolph!"

King had entered the Dorgenois Street office with a hint of trepidation that he hoped did not show. Pulling his shoulders back and standing as tall as he could, he introduced himself, asking to speak with Lenore Martin. As he waited, he inhaled deeply to calm his nerves. His discomfort was coming from the blatant stares he was getting from the women in the room. He was feeling slightly out of sorts, their gazes stripping him naked. Or maybe he was just imagining it, he thought. It might have more to do with seeing Lenore Martin again. Because if he were honest with himself, he was excited to see the woman despite the circumstances.

There was something about Lenore Martin that he found exhilarating. She made him pause, and that was a rarity with him and any woman. She clearly had an agenda that excluded him, and that made him curious to know more. His captain had ordered him to reach out, but it was that curiosity that had him there hoping to meet with her.

He took a seat in the reception area. The space was minimalistic: a contemporary love seat, two cushioned chairs, a coffee table with issues of *Architectural Digest* laid neatly atop and an original Jon Moody hanging on the wall. The room colors were muted, soft shades of gray interspersed with pink and ivory. The painting added a juxtaposition of vibrant greens and purples that danced off the wall. The setting was tasteful and refined.

King crossed one leg over the other and folded his hands casually in his lap. The women were still watching him closely, and he had no doubt that he would be the topic of at least two conversations to come.

The receptionist who'd greeted him when he arrived and had asked his name suddenly stood before him, her gaze sweeping as she gave him a bright smile. "If you'll follow me, Detective," she said. "Ms. Martin will see you now."

"Thank you," King said, his deep baritone voice echoing through the space. He stood, brushed his damp palms down the front of his suit jacket before he buttoned it closed, and followed the woman.

"Why is he here?" Lenore quipped as she moved to stand in front of her desk.

Her sister laughed. "Clearly he wants to talk to you. Why are you acting so squirrely?"

"I'm not being squirrely! I'm just surprised."

Celeste peered through the closed blinds that shielded the room from the reception area. "My, my, my! He's gorgeous!"

"Shut up, Celeste!"

Her sister's laughter rang warmly through the air. "I'll let you two have some privacy," she said as she opened the door, coming face-to-face with Piper and the handsome detective. Celeste gave the other woman a wink of her eye and smiled brightly at King. "Good evening," she said politely.

King nodded. "Good evening."

Celeste stepped to the side to let him enter, and as he passed, her eyes widened. As Piper pulled the office door closed, the two women giggled like teenagers.

Inside, Lenore rolled her eyes skyward, a wave of embarrassment washing over her. She shook her head. "My apologies," she said. "They don't get out much."

King chuckled softly. "Not a problem. I appreciate you taking time to see me, Ms. Martin."

Lenore folded her arms over her chest. She sat back against the desktop, her legs crossed at the ankles. "To what do I owe the honor?"

King smiled. "May I sit down?"

Lenore gestured toward the empty chair with her open palm. She moved back behind the desk and took her own seat as he settled himself in the cushioned chair. Their gazes met and held, both inhaling swiftly as they stared at each other. Something heated rose swiftly between them, the intensity of it giving them both pause.

King blinked first, shaking the sensation away. He

pulled a closed fist to his lips and cleared his throat. "Excuse me."

"Why are you here?" Lenore asked after taking her own deep breath to stall the sensations sweeping down her spine.

"I believe you're working the Jeffries murder. I wanted to ask you some questions."

"Asking me questions should be the least of your concerns," Lenore responded. "You have a bigger problem you need to be focused on."

"Excuse me?"

"You should be trying to find your serial killer," she said matter-of-factly. "Not interrogating me."

King's brow lifted as he tried to mask his surprise. "You're right," he said finally. He added, "But I could use your help."

"Where are you from?" Lenore questioned, seeming to change the subject. She shifted forward in her seat.

King looked confused.

"You're not from N'Orleans," Lenore stated.

He nodded. "I was born and raised in Chicago. I moved here about six months ago to take care of my grandfather. He's almost ninety, and his health is beginning to fail him. I've been with the police department for three months."

"Who's your grandfather?"

"Tobias Randolph."

Lenore leaned forward a tad more, folding her hands atop the desk. "So, what do you need from me, Detective?"

"A partnership of sorts. People will talk to you. You

know the pulse of this city. They're wary of me, and I need to find this killer before he strikes again."

"I prefer to work alone."

"As do I. But if we can work together and can give Mrs. Jeffries closure, I'm willing to do that. Are you?"

There was another pregnant pause that swelled thick and full between them as Lenore pondered his comment. He'd struck a nerve mentioning Mama Hattie, and she wasn't sure she wanted him to know it.

She took a breath and held it deep in her lungs. "Fine," she said, blowing the air past her full lips. "Where would you like to start?"

King smiled, a brilliant row of pearl-white teeth gleaming at her. "The coroner's office. I'm headed there now. And I know it's late, but I thought you might want to go with me. You won't be able to go in, but we can talk after."

Lenore's expression was smug. "You'll really need to catch up, Detective! I already have the coroner's report."

Chapter 4

As King followed Lenore to the Orleans Parish coroner's office, he found himself angry about her having access to the autopsy reports. There was clearly a flaw in the system that he fully intended to question. Lenore Martin was a civilian and should never have been able to access records for an ongoing case. He was still learning how they did things here in Louisiana, but he couldn't begin to fathom that it was that much different from what they did in Illinois.

Who was this family? This woman? And more importantly, who were the people in the judicial system supporting their endeavors and giving them free rein? Foret had said they ran the city of New Orleans, and he still couldn't fathom how such a thing was possible without law enforcement being equally culpable in their illicit activities. He had known dirty cops, but he also knew that most police officers believed in the tenets of the law, and they worked hard to carry out their duties responsibly. But it was always the few bad apples in the barrel that spoiled the whole damn lot of them.

His list of questions was rising with no reasonable answers in sight. He suddenly regretted that Lenore had decided to drive herself to the coroner's office. He would have welcomed the opportunity to have a conversation and learn more about her. But she'd insisted she needed her own car for personal reasons, leaving him standing outside his police-issued vehicle as she'd hurried off to a Mercedes-AMG GT four-door coupe.

As they pulled into the lot of the Earhart Boulevard building, Lenore pulled her car into one parking space, and he pulled his beside it. As he stepped out of the vehicle, he could see she was on her phone. She held up an index finger, waving it at him. He hesitated, feeling slightly out of sorts as he waited for her to join him. As he stood there, the sun in the distance beginning to disappear over the horizon, he found himself second-guessing the decision to partner with the woman. Wondering if he should have ignored the captain and just struck out on his own to solve the case. Doubt was waving a red flag for his attention, and he had no choice but to ignore it.

"Sorry about that," Lenore muttered minutes later when she finally exited the vehicle and joined him.

"Everything okay?" he questioned. She seemed flustered, purposely avoiding eye contact.

"I'm fine," she said, spinning around on high heels as she headed toward the entrance.

He hesitated, watching her as she walked away. He found her rear view distracting, a distinct side-to-side shimmy in her hips that caused a ripple of heat to blow through his lower quadrant. He closed his eyes and took a deep breath, stalling the wave of sensation that had risen unexpectedly.

Lenore suddenly called his name.

He opened his eyes and stared toward her, his brow raised inquisitively.

"Are you coming?" she snapped brusquely, as if he hadn't just stood waiting for her to get off the phone.

With a nod of his head, King took another deep breath and followed after her.

Lenore couldn't begin to explain why she was entertaining the idea of having a partner. Or why she found herself bothered by King Randolph. She liked working alone, getting the job done on her time, her way. The prospect of working side by side with the man went against the grain of everything she trusted. Besides, Detective Randolph was proving to be a distraction and she wasn't happy about that fact.

That call had been from her sisters, the trio phoning to tease her about her situation with the handsome man. They had given her a hard time about taking her own car and not riding along with him to discover what she could. With them knowing her reluctance about him, the conversation had been annoying at best. Then there he'd been, standing so close that she could feel the heat simmering against his skin, emboldening the scent of the cologne he wore. He smelled like a man should, reminding her of wood and leather rich with notes of cedar, cinnamon and sandalwood. She'd made the mistake of taking a swift breath, inhaling him deep into her lungs, and just like that her knees had begun to shake, leaving her dizzy. She knew she could become easily addicted to the aroma, his fragrance completely mesmerizing. Snapping at the man had given her a quick moment to regain a semblance of balance as he followed her through the glass doors and into the building.

Once inside, she focused on the case and why they were there. King hadn't read the coroner's report, wanting to talk face-to-face with the medical examiner. She would have done the same if she hadn't already been privy to the details of Michael-Lynn's death. She was there because she needed to see the body, to confirm for herself that the young girl was actually gone.

The building's exterior had an industrial feel to it, looking more like a prison than a medical facility. Its barred windows and gated perimeter gave Lenore a moment's pause. The inside of the property was bland with cream-colored walls and industrial carpet. The coroner's logo was painted on one wall in the lobby, a fusion of medical caduceus symbols as scales, representing the concept of medicine and justice.

For obvious reasons, under Louisiana law, Michael-Lynn's death had been deemed a coroner's case, requiring a thorough investigation. Death investigations at the Orleans Parish Coroner's Office were conducted by highly trained professionals: a team that included forensic pathologists, medicolegal death investigators and morgue technicians. Their sole responsibility was to determine the cause and manner of death of the bodies that passed before them. They found the scientific answers that explained the *how* of what had happened, but rarely *why* that something had happened.

As the elevator descended to the lower level, Lenore cut her eyes in King's direction. The two hadn't spoken a word to each other since arriving, and she found the moment awkward. She wanted to ask him a host of questions, curious about his professional and his personal life, but it was neither the time nor the place. Nor did he look particularly interested in a conversation with her.

As the conveyor came to a standstill and the doors opened, King shot her a look and gestured for her to exit ahead of him. On the other side, Dr. Benjamin Mayhew stood waiting. He was a man of average height with a bad comb-over and the bluest eyes. He greeted them politely, a hint of surprise washing over his expression.

"Good evening," he said.

King extended his hand. "Dr. Mayhew, thank you for meeting with us."

"I'm glad to be of assistance, Detective Randolph." The doctor nodded, his eyes darting nervously toward Lenore. He was visibly taken aback, not expecting to have seen her. "Lenore, how are you?"

She smiled politely. "I'm well, sir. Thank you for asking."

The doctor nodded his head a second time. He took a deep inhale of air before asking his next question. "How's your mother?"

Lenore's brow lifted ever so slightly as she stared at the man. Dr. Mayhew was a forensic pathologist who'd been employed by the city for longer than Lenore could remember. He had also briefly dated her mother. She smiled. "She's good. How's your wife, and family?" she asked, the smugness in her tone cutting.

The doctor cleared his throat, giving her the slightest nod. Color flushed his cheeks, his face turning a brilliant shade of embarrassed. He didn't offer a response. He turned his attention back toward the detective, gesturing for them to follow. He moved slowly down the length of corridor, the conversation shifting from pleasantries to the business at hand.

"The body is in better condition than the others, but there are marked similarities to the traumas the earlier victims suffered."

"What traumas?" Lenore questioned.

Dr. Mayhew tossed her a look over his shoulder. "Ligature marks from where they'd been restrained. They'd all been tied with barbed wire that tore at the flesh. The bodies show evidence of sexual assault and sodomy with a foreign object. And then there's the postmortem brandings. But I've detailed all that in my reports."

"I need to get copies of the previous reports," Lenore said, her eyes shifting toward King.

Knowing her connections, he was surprised she didn't already have the documents. There was a snarky quip on the tip of his tongue, but he bit it back. Instead, he nodded. "I'll get them to you," he said, then added, "if the captain approves me sharing the information."

Dr. Mayhew looked from one to the other, then continued down the hall to an autopsy room. He pushed open the door to enter, and they followed him inside.

Mama Hattie's baby girl lay prone on the stainless steel table, a cotton sheet covering her naked body. Her eyes were shut, and the dark strands of her hair were matted badly against her head. Her once crystal-clear complexion was blotched black and blue from bruises that darkened her skin, and remnants of a brilliant red lipstick still speckled her lips.

Lenore came to an abrupt standstill, staring toward the young girl's body. Dr. Mayhew was talking, but it was nothing but noise in her ears. The words weren't registering in her head as she closed her eyes and drew in a deep breath. The smell of death filled her lungs and clung to the little hairs in her nostrils. The stench seemed to permeate the blood vessels and nerves through her body, leaving her desperate for an ounce of fresh air. For just a brief moment she thought she might vomit, but that Cobb salad she'd had for lunch stayed put.

King suddenly stood at her side, noting her distress. He cupped a hand beneath her elbow, concern washing over his expression. "If this is too much for you…," he started.

Lenore glared in his direction. "I'm fine," she snapped, her voice a loud whisper. "I just…" She paused, and a single tear suddenly ran down her cheek. She tugged lightly at the arm he was holding on to, wanting to free herself from his grasp.

He nodded, releasing the grip he had on her arm. "I'm sorry," he whispered back.

Dr. Mayhew seemed to miss the exchange, still chattering away. "We've sent tissue samples to the lab, but it's going to be a few days before we get them back. There appeared to be human tissue under her fingernails, indicating she might have scratched her attacker.

We hope to get a DNA hit when the test results come back. But that's all in my report."

"Have you analyzed her lipstick?" Lenore suddenly asked. She'd moved closer to the table and was staring down at the body. Her eyes were dancing all over the young girl's face, trying to connect what she saw there with the images of Michael-Lynn in her grandmother's home.

"We're trying to identify it now. Is that important?" the doctor questioned.

Lenore thought back to those things that had rested on the girl's makeup table in her room. She said, "Michael-Lynn wore gloss, not lipstick, and she would never have been allowed to wear such a bright color."

"You think the killer put it on her?" King asked.

She nodded, the length of her hair waving against her shoulder and face. "Maybe. I just know it's out of character for the girl," she said matter-of-factly. Although truth be told, Lenore was only guessing, not able to fathom Mama Hattie approving. But what if there were things about Michael-Lynn her grandmother had no idea about? Was she that girl who changed her appearance the minute she was out of parental view, trading her schoolgirl uniform for something tight and bright to draw attention to herself?

"I'll follow up and get the results of all the lab work back to you as quickly as I can." Dr. Mayhew said, interrupting Lenore's thoughts.

She could feel King staring at her, seeming to read her mind, and she found the attention disconcerting.

King extended his arm to shake hands with the other

man. "Thank you, Dr. Mayhew. We appreciate your time."

The walk back to their respective cars seemed to take forever. When Lenore reached the outdoors, she took a deep breath, bending forward to stall the panic threatening to consume her. With her palms pressed tightly to her upper thighs, she gulped air, struggling to catch her breath. King moved to her side, concern sweeping through his own body. He pressed a gentle hand to Lenore's back, his touch sending a wave of heat down her spine. She stood upright, moving herself from his touch. Then she screamed at the top of her lungs, a deep guttural roar sounding like a wounded animal. Her hands were clenched in tight fists, and her face had turned a deep shade of burgundy red.

King eyed her warily. "Are you okay?" he questioned.

"No," she snapped. "I'm pissed! We need to catch whoever did that to her, and then I want to see them suffer! She was a baby! She had her whole life ahead of her. Why would someone want to do this?"

"It's pure evil, plain and simple. It's evil rearing its ugly head. And we will catch them. They will have their day in court."

Lenore rolled her eyes skyward, because in that moment, the justice she wanted to see could only be delivered in the streets, not a courtroom. "What's your game plan?" she asked, her tone sharp. She folded her arms across her chest, shifting her weight from one hip to the other. "What's next?"

"I'm headed to the school tomorrow morning to speak with her friends and teachers. You're welcome to join me," he said, knowing she'd probably beat him there if he didn't extend an invitation.

Lenore passed him her cell phone. "Give me your phone number. I'll pick you up at nine o'clock," she said brusquely.

King took the device from her hands. He entered his telephone number, then passed the unit back to her. He gave her a slight smile and then said, "I'll pick *you* up at nine o'clock, Ms. Martin. In case you've forgotten, I'm in charge of this investigation. And I don't want to have to keep reminding you of that. You're only being allowed to tag along as a courtesy."

Lenore's brow rose, her gaze narrowing. Before she could think to reply, he continued.

"Have a good night, Ms. Martin," he said softly. "I'll see you in the morning." Then he moved back to his own car, slid into the driver's seat and exited the parking lot.

Before getting back into her own car, Lenore texted her sisters to let them know that she was leaving the coroner's office alone. She didn't bother to share how things had gone between her and Detective Randolph. She had no doubt they already knew she'd gone full mean girl toward the man, and she wasn't interested in the lecture that would come about her bad behavior. She hadn't wanted to give him a hard time, but that hard time had helped her ignore the interest he had generated. When her body had threatened to betray her, being mean had shifted her feelings in the other direction.

She had debated whether or not to call at least one of her sisters to vent. Maybe elicit a little sibling sympathy. She changed her mind knowing that none of them would say what she wanted to hear, so she decided not to waste her time. Instead, she called her father.

Josiah Martin answered on the second ring. "Are you okay?" Josiah said in greeting.

"Hi, Daddy," Lenore responded. "I'm fine. I was calling to see how you're doing."

She could feel her father nodding into the receiver of his phone. "I have no complaints," he said. "Where are you?"

"Leaving the coroner's office. I was here about Mama Hattie's granddaughter."

"The funeral home says they haven't released the body to the family yet. You know anything about that?"

"You talked to the funeral home?" Lenore questioned.

"Yeah," her father said. "Your mother and I are picking up the expenses for the funeral. What do you know?"

Lenore turned onto Notre Dame Street, heading toward her fourth-floor apartment. Her eyes darted back and forth as she eyed the traffic.

"Whoever did this is brutal, Daddy," she said, her voice dropping an octave. "Whoever it is needs to be stopped."

"I understand the detective investigating the case is new to the department. Have you vetted him? What do you know about him?"

"His name is King. King Randolph. He moved here from Chicago to take care of his grandfather. Cash pulled a background check on him, and he checks out."

"Who is his grandfather?"

"Tobias Randolph. Do you know him?"

There was a lengthy pause, and Lenore knew her father was rifling through the Rolodex in his head. He finally said, "Yes, I do. Nice old guy. If I remember correctly, he and I played chess a time or two."

"Well, I'm not sure about how nice his grandson is," Lenore said.

"Why do you say that?"

"I'm just not feeling him." She shrugged her shoulders.

There was a moment of silence between them. And then her father chuckled softly. "He can't be too bad," Josiah said. "He's not on my payroll."

She laughed. "He's definitely not on your payroll."

"Should he be?" her father questioned.

"I hope not," Lenore said, amusement tinting her tone.

Lenore and her sisters were acutely aware of what their father did and how he did it. Their parents had never hidden the truth from them. Or more specifically, their mother had ensured they weren't in the dark. It had been important to her that her daughters understood why, if friends and family shunned them. That they knew why the hired bodyguards never let them out of their sight. That they were prepared if it all came crashing down around them and Josiah suddenly disappeared from their lives.

Lenore always said they inherited the lifestyle. During Prohibition, her father's family had been bootleggers. They smuggled rum into the city via Lake Pontchartrain and then through St. Bernard Parish. They had made a fortune, and their criminal enterprise had grown substantially. If it was dirty—drugs, prostitution, extortion—the Martins had their hands in it. Her grandfather had been one of the first to run drugs through New Orleans, and he'd never been caught. Josiah had inherited that cunning, taking it a step further by *legitimizing* a lengthy list of illegal endeavors. Laundering dirty money through legal businesses the family owned and operated had become an art form.

The police knew Josiah Martin was neck-deep in the game. He was still at the top of their watch list, but they had never been able to pin anything on him. Not anything they could get to stick, and they had tried multiple times. As for his daughters, Claudia had kept them as far from their father's choices as was physically possible. Claudia Martin had refused to let them fall into the trappings of easy money and dangerous connections. College had been a requirement, an education deemed necessary and nonnegotiable. Their mother had opened doors to high society. Their father had taught them how to handle themselves in the streets of New Orleans.

"Have you spoken with Mommy?" Lenore asked.

Thinking about her parents, Lenore found herself smiling. Josiah often said that he had married up. Claudia Edouard had been born into one of New Orleans's more prominent families. She'd been the belle of every ball. Beautiful, intelligent and quite the challenge for every man in the city. But Josiah had won her heart. Even though they were now divorced, there was still a connection between them that could not be denied.

"Talked to her earlier today. We plan to meet for a late dinner tonight. Why do you ask?"

"She and one of her boy toys were going at it earlier

today. She said she wasn't worried, but I didn't like how he kept calling and hammering at her."

"I'll see what she says," Josiah said. "Either way, I'll take care of it. But back to you and the detective. You still haven't told me what about him bothers you. Has he done something?"

Lenore sighed, trying to find the words to explain how she was feeling. She told her father about her day and meeting King. She recounted every conversation and the moments where there should have been some discussion, but she had shut him down. She was a daddy's girl, and there was little about her that her father didn't know. Since she'd been little, she'd never thought twice about telling him everything, trusting that he would never judge and would always love her.

"It sounds to me like you might have met your match. You couldn't run over this detective like you run over everyone else."

"I don't think I was trying to run over him."

"Daughter, you know damn well that's exactly what you were trying to do. It bothers you that he challenged you and put you in your place. And don't roll your eyes!" Josiah said as if he could see her through the phone line. The patriarch knew his daughter well.

Lenore closed her eyes instead and took another deep breath. Maybe calling her father hadn't been a good idea, she suddenly thought. Because he wasn't telling her anything she wanted to hear either.

Josiah continued. "Your mother made dinner reservations, so I need to go. Bring this detective by my office tomorrow. I want to meet him."

"You sure about that, Daddy?" The request surprised

Lenore. Her father rarely invited anyone new into his world, and Lenore had never before taken any man, friend or foe, to visit her father on his turf.

"It's what I said," Josiah concluded. "We can talk more tomorrow."

"Yes, sir," Lenore responded.

"Be careful, daughter. I don't want you getting yourself into anything that could get you hurt. I love you!"

"I love you, too," Lenore said just as the phone line went dead in her ear.

She'd waved a hand at the uniformed security guard who stood in position at the entrance to her apartment building. His name was Patrick. He was a bear of a man in a starched blue uniform and a military haircut that gave him an air of authority. He waved back, greeting her warmly before turning back to a phone call, someone complaining about a delivery that hadn't made it upstairs. She stepped into the elevator and pushed the button for the fourth floor.

Stepping into her luxury condo, Lenore closed and secured the door behind her. The aroma of lavender and vanilla greeted her in the entranceway. The space was everything she could have wanted. Her father had gifted her the home when she'd graduated from Tulane University, where she'd double majored in political science and legal studies in business and minored in art history. Her mother had taken her to Europe for a two-week tour of the continent.

Lenore was the first to admit that she and her sisters had been spoiled rotten, raised with the proverbial silver spoon between their lips. Except their spoon had been gold, the handle embellished with diamonds and gemstones. They had wanted for nothing and had been given everything.

The spectacular corner condo boasted three en suite bedrooms, four bathrooms, a large gourmet kitchen with top-of-the-line appliances, hardwood floors, high ceilings and an open floor plan with two balconies. For all practical purposes, it was more space than she needed living by her lonesome, but she loved every square inch of the three-thousand-square-foot property. Located in the heart of the Warehouse District, its proximity to fabulous restaurants, shopping, art galleries, museums and the French Quarter was icing on some very sweet cake.

Lenore dropped a trail of clothes from the front door into her bedroom. After she'd stripped down to her black lace bra and matching panties, she flung herself across the padded mattress, sinking into the comfort of the down comforter. She was exhausted, and she knew the following day would be equally as tiring.

She suddenly thought of King Randolph. Curious to know if there was someone he went home to every night. Whether or not there was a woman in his life who made the end of bad days bearable. Who held his head in her lap and stroked his brow as he recapped his hard day of work. Because of her own schedule, she didn't even have a cat, let alone a man, and it had been some time since there'd been a DOC in her life who provided dick-on-command. She sighed, a loud gust of stale air blowing past her lips.

Why she'd let her mind go there made no damn sense. She didn't need any man, and she surely didn't want one whose regal moniker promised riches and rewards he surely didn't have to give. She didn't need to be thinking about King Randolph when there was a murderer still out there who needed to be found.

King sat on the front porch of the family home. His long legs were extended atop an ottoman in front of him, and his feet were crossed at the ankles. He held a vintage cut-crystal rocks glass half-filled with bourbon. For the first time that day, he was feeling relaxed, his entire body no longer feeling like he was wound around a wringer.

Lost in thought, he didn't hear his grandfather when the patriarch joined him outside. His mind was on Lenore Martin, revisiting the time he'd spent with her. She was an anomaly in the world of women he was usually surrounded by. She played by rules others didn't have the luxury of following. From everything he gathered, she controlled and manipulated the games she played to her advantage. Her confidence was unsettling. In a man, it would have been pure arrogance. He wasn't sure *arrogant* was the right word to use for a woman without it being insulting or the thought misogynistic. His initial impression made him think she wasn't overly sensitive, but he had no doubts that if offended, she would go for the jugular to get even.

She was an enigma of sorts, leaving him bewildered. He wanted to know more, but he was also scared that whatever he learned would have him desperately yearning for her, petrified for himself, or both. He lifted his glass to his lips and took a large swig of the drink inside, the bourbon sliding smoothly down his throat.

"Rough day?" Tobias Randolph asked.

There was no denying the familial connection between the patriarch and King. Their resemblance was striking, both standing tall and imposing. They came from a noble bloodline, their chiseled features distinguished and handsome. His grandfather's hair was silver, cut short and edged up pristinely. The older women in the church called him dashing, treating him like a class pet that needed to be cared for. They brought by trays of food and platters of sweet treats for him to binge on. Younger women found his maturity enticing, deeming him sugar daddy material. The sweet treats they brought by were less binge-worthy.

The old man found the wealth of female attention flattering. King found it annoying, the revolving door into their home, determined by his grandfather's foolish whims and the audacity of women hoping for a payday. He sighed, cutting an eye in the old man's direction.

"It was," he said, taking another sip of his drink.

"I saw on the news they found that little girl's body. Damn shame!" His grandfather rocked back and forth in the metal glider that decorated the porch. "Lots of evil people in this world," the old man concluded, his head bobbing up and down.

"Is Josiah Martin one of those evil people?" King questioned with a serious side-eye.

His grandfather suddenly stopped rocking. He shifted his body to turn and stare, and his grandson stared back.

"What's this case got to do with Josiah Martin?"

King sighed. "I'm working the case with his daughter Lenore. And not by choice. She's a private detective the grandmother hired when the little girl went missing. Now she's determined to find the killer, and my captain says I need to work with her."

Tobias sat back and resumed the back-and-forth sway of his chair. He seemed to drift off into thought, not saying anything for a good few minutes. Finally he responded, "Martin's a good man. He's lost his way a time or two, but he cares about the folks here in N'Orleans."

"You know him?"

"I've had some business dealings with him back in the day. Every now and again we would play some chess to pass the time." He chuckled softly. "He'll give you a run for your money on that chessboard!"

King nodded, a slight smile bending his full lips upward. "Well, his daughter Lenore plans to give me a run for my money with everything. I have never before met such a beautiful woman so intent on being disagreeable for no reason whatsoever." He suddenly went on a rant about his day with Lenore.

Tobias listened, the slightest smirk pulling across his face. He listened as King sighed and huffed and professed his annoyance with a woman he called beautiful six times in the expanse of ten minutes. If he hadn't known anything about her before, he surely knew now that his grandson thought her the most exquisite female he'd ever had the pleasure of laying eyes on. The old man laughed as he stood. He stretched his body upward to ease the stiffness that had settled in his limbs.

"Where are you going?" King questioned.

Tobias nodded his head toward the home across the street. Soft jazz billowed out an opened window, and a single light glowed softly past sheer white curtains. He could see the outline of a female frame passing back and forth, putting on quite the show.

"Miss Williams is expecting me," the patriarch said, a soft giggle wrapped around his words.

King shook his head from side to side. Elora Williams had lived in that house since King had been a little boy. She and his late grandmother would sit in each other's kitchens, drinking hot tea and gossiping about the other women in the neighborhood. After his grandmother had passed, she'd slid into his grandfather's life like warm molasses, professing her intent to help him get over his grief.

Miss Williams was a robust woman, reminding King of bread dough, warm and malleable. She had the bluest eyes, and although they'd dulled slightly in her old age, there was still a shimmer of mischief that some men, like his grandfather, found bewitching. Their jaunts through her silk sheets had slowed substantially over the years, but at least twice per month, Josiah would saunter over to savor the treats she readily offered.

"You plan on spending the night?" King asked.

"I don't know. Depends on how comfortable I am."

"Well, I'm locking this door at midnight, old man. If you ain't inside when I do, you'll have to sleep on the porch tonight."

Tobias laughed. "I hear you, Daddy!" he said sarcastically. He had often told King the same thing when he'd been a boy.

King laughed with him, still shaking his head as his grandfather eased his way across the street, knocked on the front door and then let himself inside the home. Minutes later he watched as the duo danced in the shadows of that light, the jazz billowing with the late-night breeze.

King finished the last of his bourbon. He stood, took a deep breath, then headed inside to ready himself for a new day. He tossed one last glance over his shoulder, the light inside the Williams home flickering off. Stepping over the threshold, he couldn't stop himself from thinking of Lenore, pondering what a late-night rendezvous might be like if he ever showed up at her door.

Chapter 5

Lenore was sleeping soundly when her cell phone rang. So soundly that she barely heard the obnoxious chime as it pushed its way into the sweetest dream she was having. With her eyes still shut, she fumbled on the nightstand for the device. By the time she pulled the phone into her hand, the call had disconnected. She opened her eyes to stare at the screen, not recognizing the number.

Wondering why it even existed, she cursed the government's Do Not Call Registry. When bill collectors and scammers could still reach you at all hours of the day and night, it clearly didn't work. And not that a bill collector would be calling, because her bills were paid. But it was seven o'clock in the morning, and she still had thirty good minutes before the alarm would sound. She rolled back over to the other side of the bed, dropping the phone to the mattress beside her. Just as she adjusted the pillow beneath her head and started to doze back to sleep, the phone rang again. Lenore grabbed it before the third ring.

"Hello," she said, her voice still groggy with sleep.

"Miss Martin?"

The breathy voice on the other end pulled Lenore upright in her bed.

"Tralisa?"

"I need your help…" the young girl started, tears muffling her voice.

"Tralisa, what's going on?" Lenore intoned. "Where are you?"

"School," she said, her voice a low whisper. "Please, can you come get me?"

Lenore could hear another muffled voice in the background calling Tralisa's name.

Tralisa began to sob. "I know who killed Michael-Lynn…" she started, and then there was a loud commotion on the other end. The girl screamed, a blood-curdling screech that left Lenore shaking with dread.

"Tralisa! What's going on? Tralisa!" Lenore screamed into her own device. And just like that, the phone line went silent.

Jumping from the bed, Lenore rushed toward the bathroom, dialing her phone at the same time. King answered, sounding too chipper for the early morning hour.

"Ms. Martin, good morning," he said.

"Tralisa Taylor's in trouble," Lenore said. "I need you to meet me at the high school."

"What kind of trouble?" King questioned.

"The kind that has her screaming in fear," Lenore snapped.

The panic in Lenore's voice moved King toward his front door. "I can be there in twenty minutes," he said. "And I'll send a patrol car right now."

On the other end, Lenore closed her eyes and took a deep breath. "Thank you," she said, her voice softening with gratitude. "I'll meet you there."

Despite their respective distances from the Thomy Lafon Academy, one of the magnet schools in Orleans Parish, the duo arrived within mere minutes of each other. Lenore knew she'd broken all kinds of records getting dressed, and a law or two, to get there as quickly as she had. King credited the light traffic and his siren for moving him swiftly toward the downtown area. The school was within walking distance of Tralisa's home, but Lenore imagined the girl had probably ridden her bike to get there.

A city patrol car was parked in the circular drive in front of the school, and two uniformed police officers were exiting the front door. The duo paused to give King an update, shrugging their shoulders dismissively. There was no sign of the young woman, and as they stood outside the brick building, there was nothing out of sorts that gave them reason to pause. King waved the two officers back to their vehicle.

Lenore hit the redial button on her cell phone, calling Tralisa for the umpteenth time. It went directly to voice mail.

"She hasn't called you back?" King questioned.

"No, and I spoke with her stepfather. He said she left early for cheerleading practice."

"It's a little early for extracurricular activities, isn't it?"

"That's what I thought, but he said she frequently had morning practice on game days." Everyone following the high school football circuit knew Thomy Lafon was facing off against Chalmette in a midseason playoff game.

King gestured for Lenore to follow as he led the way to the rear of the school and the sports fields. Sure enough, the cheerleading squad were going through their paces down on the football field. Twelve young women were dancing in sync, the choreography including hip gyrations, shoulder shimmies and some quality tumbling that was better than expected.

Lenore followed as King moved toward the older woman who appeared to be directing the lot of them.

They all came to an abrupt halt as the coach spun toward them, clearly irritated by the interruption.

"Can I help you?" she asked, eyeing the duo suspiciously. She was tall and lean, her athletic frame indicative of a long-distance runner. She wore navy track pants with a matching jacket and an off-white T-shirt with the school's logo beneath. Her eyes darted back and forth, watching the girls closely, and then back to them, her stare even more intense.

King flashed his badge and introduced the two of them. "We're trying to locate Tralisa Taylor. We were told we might find her here."

"Did she do something?" the woman questioned.

Lenore's gaze narrowed. "I'm sorry. We didn't get your name."

The woman tossed her a look, her gaze gliding from Lenore's head to her toes and back. She blinked, then shifted her gaze back toward her team. "Maxine Carmichael. I coach the cheerleading and track teams and teach advanced placement science courses the rest of the time."

Lenore gave her the slightest smile. "Well, Ms. Carmichael, we just need to ask Tralisa a few questions about her best friend's death. She's done nothing wrong." She didn't bother to add that the woman's question, immediately presuming guilt of some kind, had irritated her.

The woman named Maxine tossed Lenore another quick look. "It's sad what happened to Michael-Lynn. She was one of our brightest. The girls are dedicating their performance tonight to her memory. As for Tralisa, she was supposed to be here an hour ago. She knew we needed to restage the lifts since we lost Michael-Lynn, and now we've had to redo them without her."

"You're not concerned about her not showing up?" Lenore asked.

"Should I be?"

Lenore tossed King a look. He read the annoyance on her face and knew she was biting her tongue. He appreciated her restraint but sensed it wouldn't last long. He took two steps, putting his large body between the two.

"If I can bother you with a few more questions," King said as Lenore turned, moving toward a group of girls who were staring in their direction curiously.

The coach mumbled something incoherent, her eyes

boring into the back of Lenore's head. Lenore kept walking, knowing that if the woman dared say one thing to her, she might snap. She took a deep breath.

"Hey," she said, greeting the girls warmly.

A chorus of morning greetings sounded in the early morning air.

"My name's Lenore. I'm looking for Tralisa. Have any of you seen her this morning?"

Eyes darted back and forth as heads waved from side to side.

"She didn't show up for practice," one young lady said.

"Coach is pissed, too," another added, her voice a loud whisper.

"Does Coach always have attitude?" Lenore asked, tossing a quick glance over her shoulder.

The girls giggled. "That's putting it nicely," the first girl responded. "When she gets mad, Coach is a royal…!" She cut herself off.

"Run it again!" Coach Carmichael suddenly bellowed. "I didn't say you could take a break!"

The girls standing with her ran back to the field and moved into position. The first kid hesitated, meeting Lenore's stare. "I thought I saw her bike when I got here. Tralisa locks it in the bike rack by the gym door. But it wasn't there when I came out after changing into my gym clothes for practice."

"What's your name?" Lenore asked.

"Amber. Amber Gaines."

She nodded. "Thank you, Amber!"

Lenore watched as Amber scurried off to join her friends. She stood staring as they lined up in a single row and began to go through the routine they would perform later that day for a crowd of fans and family. They were good, performing in near perfect sync.

The morning temperature was already pushing toward the midseventies. Storms were predicted for later in the day. The humidity made the air sticky and uncomfortable, feeling more like eighty-plus degrees. Lenore applauded the girls putting forth their best effort so early in the day. Especially with the unkind conditions. They were perspiring and panting, stopping now and again to chug ice water for breakfast.

When King finally moved to her side, she was staring off into the distance, something on the other side of the football field catching her eye.

"Did you get anything?" he asked. He stared where she stared.

"A bad feeling," she muttered, beginning to walk across the field toward the tree line that bordered the property.

King followed after her, studying what had grabbed her attention. The tree line was sparse, bordering a fence that divided the property line. There was a parking lot on the other side and the back side of a row of brick buildings. In the sky overhead, a large flock of black buzzards soared against the backdrop of a darkening sky. Buzzards that were rising in number with each rotation above their heads.

As they approached the fence, he saw a hole had been cut through the wire, a path between the two properties beaten down by the students who cut through to get to a sandwich shop on the other side. Behind the brick buildings was a row of military green dumpsters. Trash littered the ground around them, and the vultures were hopping from the blacktop to the inside of one dumpster and back. They pulled at the trash and debris tossed out by the restaurant. At least that was what the two hoped as they drew closer.

Lenore came to an abrupt stop and shot him a look. She pointed her index finger toward the back of the dumpster. A shiny red bicycle rested against the side of the metal container. She took a deep breath and held it, the color draining from her face.

King suddenly moved past her. "I'll look," he said. "In case we have a crime scene, I can't have you contaminating it." His demeanor was stoic and commanding.

Lenore nodded her head, watching as the gregarious birds pushed each other about, their display intensely territorial. They stared at her with beady, evil eyes, also annoyed by the intrusion. She knew the black vultures were feeding on something dead inside the dumpster Dining like they'd been proffered a meal at a Michelin-starred restaurant.

She detested the sight of them, most especially when they congregated together like a scene from an old Hitch-cock movie. Their feathers were jet-black. They had scaly heads—featherless, grayish-black and wrinkled like their necks—short tails, and hooked beaks. Those that flew above their heads had silvery or whitish wing tips with respectable five-foot wingspans. They circled in a mixed flock of larger turkey vultures and hawks, all looking for a taste of whatever had been found.

King leaned forward into the opening of the over-sized container. He leaned back quickly as one of the vultures suddenly flew at him and out. Later he would swear it hissed at him. He leaned forward a second time to peer down inside. He folded his arm across his face, tucking his nose into his elbow to ward off the stench of garbage and filth. When he stepped back, turning away quickly, his face confirmed what Lenore had feared most. They hadn't gotten there in time to save Tralisa Taylor.

Thirty minutes after finding Tralisa Taylor's body, a forensics team had cordoned off the area and were gathering evidence. The birds had been shooed away, some still flying overhead, and the young girl now lay in a black body bag, waiting to be carried to the morgue to be autopsied.

On initial inspection, King observed bruising around her neck, suggesting she'd been strangled, but the sheer volume of blood she'd lost and the gashes to her garments indicated she'd been stabbed multiple times. If it had been the same serial killer, he'd not had time to toy with her, to watch her cry and scream. Her death had been quick, and although violent, she had not endured the torture of his previous victims. Nor had she been branded. Others in the department were already declaring the murder was not connected to his other cases, but he instinctively knew differently. Now he just needed to prove it.

Lenore stood with her back pressed against the brick wall of the sandwich shop. The popular lunch spot was owned by a man called Dutch. Dutch was a hulking six-foot-tall brute with a teddy bear spirit. He was broken by the events playing out behind his store and even more torn up about the security cameras being down. He had no explanation for why they were off or why they hadn't been turned back on, other than to complain about the fees the security company charged for their services. Once again, they had nothing that could help solve this case other than speculation, conjecture and a host of gut feelings.

Lenore hadn't said much since he'd called for backup. Despite his objections, she too had looked where he'd looked, taking in every fathomable detail of Tralisa's dead body. Tralisa's lips had been blue, her makeup smeared across her delicate face. Tears had smudged her mascara over her cheeks. Her clothes were shredded and saturated with her blood. One sleeve was missing from the white blouse that had been pristine when she'd left her home that morning. Her navy blue skirt was shoved up around her waist, showing off her cotton panties. They were a pale shade of Carolina blue, also spattered with blood. Her legs were angled awkwardly looking like one might be broken. One athletic shoe lay by her side. And those damn vultures had begun to shred her flesh like she'd been dinner.

When Lenore finally stepped away, her jaw had locked tight, her eyes had narrowed and her expression had become unreadable. If there had been tears, King never saw them. When backup had arrived, she'd eased out of the way, standing alone as she studied every person who'd come within twenty feet of the crime scene.

As if she read his mind, her gaze lifted, meeting his eyes with a stare so intense that he suddenly felt naked and vulnerable. His entire body shivered as if cold. He inhaled a deep breath and moved from where he stood with other NOPD officers. He sauntered slowly to her side. Her hands were pushed deep into the pockets of the silk blue blazer she wore.

"No, I am not okay," she remarked before he could ask the question that sat on the tip of his tongue. "I am far from okay."

"Is there anything I can do to help?" His voice was soft and warm, like a sweet caress. It hugged her, wrapping around her shoulders.

Lenore sighed softly. Her own voice came out as a loud whisper, barely audible if one hadn't been listening for it. "We need to head back to the school. Someone had to have seen something."

"We actually have a meeting with the principal in twenty minutes," King said as he stole a quick glance at his wristwatch. "We should probably head in that direction."

Lenore gave him the slightest nod. She cast one final glance toward Tralisa's body, then turned, heading in the opposite direction.

Chapter 6

Dr. Morris Brandt met them in the high school's office lobby. He was a small man with a slight frame and a bulbous head of blond curls. He wore an expensive silk suit, his attire meticulous, and he was not happy about having them in the building. The school's secretary shifted her eyes from the couple to her superior nervously.

He stuck out his hand. "Detective Randolph, how can I help you?" he asked brusquely.

King gave him a slight nod. "Dr. Brandt, I appreciate your time. Is there someplace more private where we can speak?"

There was a moment of pause as the principal eyed him anxiously. He took a deep breath and gestured for them to follow as he led the way to his office. He closed the door, then moved to the leather chair behind the desk. He pointed the duo toward the two upholstered seats that decorated the space.

"We were devastated by the loss of Michael-Lynn," Dr. Brandt started. "She was a bright star here at the school. Her friends are dedicating tonight's game to her."

"How have the students reacted to the news?" Lenore questioned.

"As expected. Those closest to Michael-Lynn are devastated. The others are saddened, and some have been very nonchalant about the whole thing. But we've brought in counselors for them to speak with, and that has helped students and staff."

"Is there anyone Michael-Lynn didn't get along with that you're aware of? Or maybe a teacher she butted heads with?" King asked.

Dr. Brandt shook his head. "No one I'm aware of. Everyone liked her. She was a very popular student. And all of her teachers always spoke quite highly of her."

"We're going to need to see her locker," Lenore said, her voice commanding. "And we'll need to speak to everyone who was close to her."

The principal nodded. "Everyone's been made aware that you'll be in the school today. We haven't been able to contact her best friend, Tralisa. She didn't show up to school today. But then, you know that. I understand you two were looking for her this morning at cheerleading practice?"

King took a deep inhale of air before speaking. "Tralisa Taylor's body was found a few hours ago in a trash dumpster next door. We believe the two murders are connected."

Dr. Brandt gasped. Loudly. His face reddened, color creeping into his alabaster cheeks with a vengeance. He began to shake, gripping the arms of his chair tightly. Both King and Lenore were staring at him intently, studying his reaction for anything that seemed out of place. He pulled a starched white handkerchief from the inside pocket of his plaid blazer and swiped away the sweat that had beaded across his brow.

"Have her parents been told? I'll need to reach out to them."

King nodded. "They have. We didn't want them to find out on the news. I've also posted a patrol car out front. The local news stations are going to want a story, and they'll be trying to talk to the students. We will do everything we can to keep them from being an intrusion."

"I'll need to cancel tonight's game," Dr. Brandt mumbled. He seemed to be talking to himself, trying to ascertain what he needed to do or how best to do it.

"Don't cancel the game," Lenore said.

The comment surprised King as both men shifted their gazes toward her.

"Why not?" Dr. Brandt questioned. "Under the circumstances, it's the respectful thing to do for both girls."

"Let the kids honor their friends. Give them a moment of silence. That would be respectful." She shot King a quick glance. "Detective Randolph and I will both be here to observe. Sometimes killers like to witness firsthand how their handiwork has impacted their victim's family and friends."

The man frowned, the muscles in his face pulling toward the floor. "Are my other students in any kind of danger? I'm not willing to put any of them at risk!" His voice rose an octave.

King shook his head. "No, sir. There will be a strong police presence. You need not worry."

Dr. Brandt seemed to consider the request. He finally nodded his head. "Fine, but I want it on record that I'm not totally comfortable with the idea."

"Noted," King responded.

Dr. Brandt left them in front of Michael-Lynn's and Tralisa's open lockers, the girls having maneuvered to get two side by side. The hallway was empty, students in their respective classes.

King narrowed his gaze. "Do you always just volunteer other people's time? How did you know I didn't have plans for tonight?"

"I really didn't care," she quipped. "I'm sure it's nothing you can't cancel. Besides, I would think finding our killer would be a priority over some bad date you had planned." She snatched her gaze from the look he was giving her. A wave of heat had bubbled in her tummy, feeling like an army of butterflies firing all weapons.

The hint of a smile lifted his lips, amusement dancing in his expression. "I never said I had a date," he quipped back.

His tone was smug, and that disarmed Lenore completely. She bit down against her bottom lip, eyeing him for a quick moment before responding. "Then what are we arguing for?" she said tersely.

Lenore reached into Tralisa's locker, noting the book bag resting inside. Photographs of her and Michael-Lynn and other friends had been plastered on the door's interior. A sticky note was attached to the back wall, *Harvard Bound* printed in big, bold, black ink. Her cheerleading uniform hung from a hook, and there were a change of clothes and two pairs of running shoes tossed on the floor. Michael-Lynn's locker was practically identical.

"Anything?" King asked as he flipped through the pages of a science journal.

Lenore was unfolding a note she'd found tucked in the side pocket of Tralisa's book bag. She read it once and then a second time. She passed the pink slip of paper to her companion.

They exchanged a look as King read, refolded the note and tucked it into his pocket.

"Did Tralisa mention this boy to you when you spoke with her?" King asked.

Lenore shook her head. "No. She said there wasn't anyone Michael-Lynn kept hidden from her grandmother. I never asked her who she was hiding."

"But clearly the two had a disagreement about this Kevin person."

"Clearly," Lenore said, the words on that note spinning through her head. Michael-Lynn had criticized her bestie's choice of a boyfriend. Whoever Kevin was, she'd spelled out in no uncertain terms that he was too old for Tralisa and there was something "weird" about him. Tralisa had taken offense, calling her friend out for being jealous because she didn't have a man.

That note had gone back and forth between them, one writing in dark blue ink, the other in a neon green. Lenore wondered why pen and paper and not a text thread on their phones. But she knew that answer. Knew that forgetting to delete that one message on their cell phone that either's guardian could find would cause hell neither girl wanted. That a conversation in a classroom was easier with pen and paper than risking a zealous teacher snatching the devices from their hands. But Tralisa had held on to the page torn from a notepad. Maybe it had been her turn to respond. Or maybe she needed it for leverage if things went any further left between her and Michael-Lynn. Then Michael-Lynn had gone missing, and that note lay forgotten in a book bag.

"Now we need to figure out who Kevin is and how he plays into this," King said.

"That shouldn't be too hard."

"You don't think so?"

Lenore shrugged her narrow shoulders. "You can bet that two teenage girls fighting over some man-boy is good gossip in high school. Someone knows something."

They slammed the two lockers closed at the same time, the harsh clang of metal echoing through the hallway.

The two teenage girls had only shared one class together. Lenore and King had spoken with their respective teachers and were heading down to the science lab for a final conversation with Coach Carmichael. Her classroom was nearest the gym, and when they found her, she was on a break, no students or other faculty in her room. She didn't seem surprised to see them, almost as if she'd anticipated their visit.

"Detective. Ms. Martin. How can I help you?"

"You've heard that we found Tralisa?" Lenore said. "Someone murdered her."

Coach Carmichael cut her eyes in Lenore's direction. The two women seemed to be sizing each other up. She finally nodded. "The whispering started hours ago. My girls are devastated."

"We had a few questions about Tralisa and Michael-Lynn," King said. "We understand the two girls were in one of your classes together?"

The woman nodded. "My fifth period AP Science class. Both were doing exceptionally well academically."

"Did either girl have any problems with any of their peers that you may have been aware of?" King asked.

She shook her head. "They were both well-liked and ran with the popular students. Besides being on the cheerleading squad, they were also on the debate team, and if I'm not mistaken, I believe Tralisa was also on the math team. Michael-Lynn was more interested in the arts versus the sciences. She was quite the writer."

"Who's Kevin?" Lenore suddenly asked, the two women locking eyes.

The coach seemed startled, the question unexpected. Her eyes suddenly darted from side to side as she contemplated a response. She finally replied. "Kevin?" she asked.

"Apparently, he's a young man Tralisa was dating. I

was wondering if he might have been one of your students as well."

The coach paused again, seeming to fall into thought, and then she shook her head. "I don't think that I'm familiar with anyone named Kevin that either girl would have been involved with. I could ask my other students if you'd like. One of them might know."

Lenore shrugged nonchalantly. "That's not necessary. We appreciate the offer, though."

"I'd like to do anything I can to help. Those girls didn't deserve what happened to them. They had so much promise!"

Before Lenore or King could respond, a tall young man dressed in designer jeans and an expensive silk jacket stood in the doorway. He leaned against the door frame as he stared inside, his gaze skating from person to person. He smiled, his grin canyon-wide as he and Lenore locked eyes. His gaze widened, and then he turned his full attention to the other woman.

"Is this a bad time, Mother?" he asked, giving Coach Carmichael the slightest nod.

"No," she answered, tossing a glance toward the clock on the wall. "You're right on time." There was a moment's hesitation before she made an introduction. "This is my son," she said. "Everyone calls him Junior."

The young man shook his head, responding sarcastically. "No, Mother, you're the only one who calls me Junior." He extended his hand. "Charles Carmichael," he said, shaking both of their hands firmly. He held on to Lenore's slightly longer than necessary.

"It's nice to meet you, Charles," King said.

"Are you a student here, Charles?" Lenore questioned as she pulled her fingers from his.

He smiled. "I graduated three years ago. Now I only pop in to see my mother and support the team. I study mechanical engineering at the University of New Orleans." The timbre of his voice carried an air of confidence wrapped around a wealth of arrogance.

"Do you by chance know any of the students in your mother's classes?" Lenore persisted.

The young man shrugged. "Not well. I know a few of the cheerleaders by name, but that's usually with some prompting. I don't spend enough time here to want to know any of them better. Besides, I wouldn't want to risk any of these young girls getting me hemmed up with their drama. I can't have people giving me the side-eye, and I'd never risk embarrassing my mother."

Coach Carmichael lifted her thin lips, her efforts to smile feeling forced. She was past ready to be rid of them. She shifted the conversation. "If you don't have any more questions, I promised my son lunch."

"Do you have any other children?" Lenore asked, still fishing for information.

The other woman's gaze narrowed ever so slightly. Charles answered for his mother. "I'm an only child," he said. "Which makes me spoiled rotten, and right now I need to eat!" He chuckled heartily.

King shook his head. "Don't let us keep you. We appreciate your time."

"It was nice to meet you," Lenore said as she and Charles stared at each other.

He grinned again. "The pleasure is all mine."

They all exited the room, and Lenore turned to watch

as the coach locked her classroom door. She bid them one last goodbye before scurrying down the hallway with her son sauntering easily by her side. Charles tossed Lenore one last look over his shoulder and winked his eye. She was not amused, but she feigned a coy smile as if she were.

As they turned the corner out of sight, King blew out a heavy sigh. "I should probably get back to the crime scene," he said.

Lenore shrugged her narrow shoulders as she reached for the doorknob. She held a lock pick in her hand, the device pulled from deep in her jacket pocket. With the precision of a master locksmith, she seemingly opened the door with a simple turn of the knob.

King tossed an anxious look over his shoulder. "What are you doing?" he hissed between clenched teeth.

Lenore moved swiftly into the room, ignoring his question as he followed behind her and closed the door. She moved to the oversized desk at the front of the room and began to search through the drawers.

King peered through the door's sidelight before turning back toward her. "Are you serious right now?" he asked. "This is a violation of..."

"You are welcome to leave at any time," Lenore said, cutting him off. She began rummaging through the coach's desk. "I don't recall asking for your help or your permission."

King huffed. Although he was curious to know what she was trying to achieve, there were protocols, and rules, and she was breaking every one of them. That didn't sit well with him, but he made no earnest effort to stop her. "What are you looking for?" he whispered loudly.

"I don't know. But I'm sure when I see it, it will make sense."

"Why the coach's office?"

"I don't like that woman. There's something shady about her. Something tells me she knows more than she's saying." Lenore continued to flip through a stack of folders. Finding nothing, she reached for the bottom drawer and suddenly paused as she peered inside. Her expression changed, the color draining from her cheeks. Her eyes narrowed, and she bit down against her bottom lip.

"What?" King said, moving to her side. "What is it?" He peered over her shoulder to stare where she stared.

Tucked inside the desk drawer was a single woman's track shoe and a bright red hair bow the cheerleaders had all worn. Both had seen them before. It was the shoe missing from Tralisa's other foot.

"Don't touch it," King snapped as he pulled out his cell phone and took a series of photos.

Lenore resisted the urge to snatch the shoe up, but she knew without a warrant it would never make the evidence list if things ever went to trial. She slammed the drawer shut, the sound of it vibrating through the room.

King gripped her by the elbow and pulled her toward the exit. He peered out the door, looking left and then right, before the two stepped past the threshold and back into the hallway. As they navigated their way to the front of the building and the exit, he knew Lenore was pondering the same questions he was. What if that missing shoe wasn't Tralisa's? Then who did it belong to? And if it was Tralisa's, why was it in the coach's desk drawer?

Chapter 7

King found it disconcerting that he was comfortable with the lengthy moments of silence that rose easily between him and Lenore. It didn't bother him that she sometimes fell into a world of her own, leaving him hanging at the threshold of her thoughts. Nor was he bothered by the rants that would follow, everything she'd been pondering spewing like water from a broken faucet. She moved him to a level of solace that he'd not known before, and it was unsettling to his brain but serenity to his spirit.

They had left the crime scene, Tralisa's body having finally been claimed by the coroner's office. It would now be a waiting game for the autopsy results. Those items gathered by the investigative team were also being transferred to the state's crime lab with assurances their inspection would be pushed in front of the backlogged cases still pending.

Lenore had insisted on riding with him, leaving her car in the school's parking lot. Their first stop had been Tralisa's family home. Waking her stepfather to deliver the bad news had been delegated to Detective Christian Foret, who was still standing outside looking like a fish out of water when they arrived. Apparently the stepfather's reaction had shaken his nerves, but it was nothing compared to the mother's reaction. They could still hear the woman wailing like a wounded animal, her response gut-wrenching.

King wished he could leave all contact with the families to any other officer. He was grateful for those moments he could delegate to others on his team. Unfortunately, as the lead detective on the case, the task of dealing with the victim's next of kin almost always fell squarely on his shoulders. He'd tossed Lenore a quick glance, noting that her brow had furrowed and her eyes were misty.

Lenore had consoled the bereft mother, who'd fallen to the floor, her legs giving out beneath her. The young girl's stepfather had punched a sizable hole in the living room wall. In the other room, Tralisa's twin brothers cried from their cribs, no understanding of how their small worlds had suddenly changed. The family was broken, their hearts shattered, and there was nothing he, or Lenore, could do or say that could salvage the fragments of all they had been to each other. King took an inhale of breath, holding the air deep in his lungs before blowing it slowly past his full lips.

One of Lenore's rants suddenly broke through the

quiet, and he smiled ever so slightly. In another life, he might have called her moody. She was temperamental, short-tempered and prone to a level of rage that scared most. He found those moments amusing, most especially since he'd seen something in her eyes that told him Lenore's heart overflowed with concern and care for others despite her pretense otherwise. She had an innate ability to read a situation and say the right thing to calm an entire room. Despite her gruff persona, there was something about her that gave him pause.

King knew this case was challenging her, because it was also challenging him. He had to push through until it was resolved, but it wasn't a game she had any interest in playing. She wanted it solved yesterday, and if she could only get the rest of the world to move on her timetable, him included, things could finally be well with her.

"You need to do a background check on that coach. Her son, too. For all we know, he might be our guy, and his mother is protecting him. I'll have my people see what they can find, too. Don't forget to get that warrant. We need to get our hands on that evidence so you can drag her ass downtown for questioning. And I want to be there for that." She paused to take a breath, inhaling deeply.

King allowed the quiet to rise again, giving her a moment. Finally he said, "You done?"

Lenore cut her eyes in his direction. She didn't answer, instead shifting her gaze out the car's window.

"I'm a step ahead of you. Those files should already be on my desk. I'm looking at *all* the teachers *and* the principal. I also have a team pulling every minute of security footage from any camera in a twenty-mile radius."

She nodded. "That's good," she muttered. "That's really good."

King stole a quick glance to the digital clock on the dashboard. "Are you hungry? We should probably grab something to eat."

Lenore nodded her head a second time. "We need to make a stop first."

King eyed her curiously. "A stop where?"

"My father wants to meet you."

His eyes widened. "Josiah Martin wants to meet me?" General confusion and an air of awe and bewilderment seeped from his tone.

Lenore turned to stare at him. He could feel her eyes dancing over the lines of his profile as he stared at the road and the traffic slowing their pace. He wanted to return the look, but knew if he did, it would reveal his shock, and his sudden discomfort with the idea.

"Why does that surprise you?" Lenore questioned, still staring at him.

He shrugged his broad shoulders. "We have no business with each other. It seems like a strange request," he answered.

"He commanded, which means you have business with him that you don't even know about. Yet." She turned to stare back out the window.

Yet. King had nothing else left to say, feeling slightly dumbfounded. Of course, he'd heard all the stories about the notorious Josiah Martin. He'd even done his own research on the man who'd eluded the law more times than not. That Josiah Martin wanted to meet him wasn't anything he'd been expecting. King knew enough to know that the man didn't hobnob with law enforcement for the fun of it. King couldn't begin to fathom what his wanting to meet could mean for either of them.

"Please, don't go and get all weird on me," Lenore suddenly said. "It's not that serious. I had told him I didn't know if I'd be able to work with you, that I thought you were a jerk, and he said he wanted to meet you to form his own opinion. And don't try to make this about bringing my father to justice or whatever else you and your ilk like to do."

"My ilk?"

"Law enforcement. You wouldn't be the first cop who's tried to get to my father through me or one of my sisters. And I doubt you'll be the last."

"Is that why you and Captain Romero don't date anymore?" he asked out of the blue.

Lenore's head snapped in his direction. Her gaze narrowed as she studied him intently. "And what did Juan tell you?"

King shrugged. "Nothing, actually. Another officer noted that you two dated briefly. No one's said why it didn't work out. I was just asking out of curiosity."

"So, you're the nosy type."

A slow smile pulled at his mouth. "I just like to know what I'm dealing with."

Lenore's history with Juan Romero was as much a sore point for her as it was for him. She dropped into reflection as she allowed herself to go back in time. Their introduction had been happenstance, the two seated at the same table at a community event to honor her mother. He'd been easy on the eyes and extremely flirtatious. She'd been receptive to his charms, agreeing to share a meal with him weeks later. The friendship that ensued had been more than she had hoped for. Their future had seemed promising, but she'd held him at arm's length, wary of taking their relationship to the next level. She had wanted more than physical sex, excited for intimacy that was sustainable and would last them through any hard times. But something deep in her gut wouldn't allow her to relax long enough to savor the potential.

Introducing any man to her family came with its own set of challenges. There were rules, spoken and unspoken, and such a gesture wasn't taken lightly. Doing so required a level of vulnerability that many couldn't handle and opened the entire family to scrutiny. She'd been the one to open the door, handing Juan a key as she waved him inside their small world. Lenore had likened Juan's actions to the fox romping freely through their henhouse. He had showed his appreciation by trying to devour them all. When the relationship imploded, she'd been grateful that she hadn't shared her goodies with him, giving him access to her most private places.

What Lenore had never said aloud, and what few knew, was that she had really liked Juan. She'd liked him a lot and had begun to believe that she might actually be falling in love with him. Then he'd betrayed her. That moment had taught her everything she needed to know about Captain Juan Romero. What she knew was that Juan was a man she couldn't trust, and just maybe, there wasn't a man out there that she could.

Lenore shook herself from the recollection and rolled her eyes skyward. She gave her attention back to King.

There was a wealth of attitude in her tone. "Well, right now you're working with a woman who's really pissed off. I don't appreciate finding out that I'm the topic of discussion around the watercooler in the police station. Juan Romero needs to keep my name out of his mouth." That attitude painted her expression like bad makeup.

"Were things that terrible between you?" King questioned.

"There was nothing between us. He wanted another notch in his belt to put on his résumé. He thought that taking down my father would be easy if he went through me.

"Juan was welcomed into our home, and he used that invitation to violate my parents' privacy. We caught him on video rambling through my father's office and his papers. Days later, my father's office was raided by the FBI based on information Juan acquired, thinking he had the goods to take my father out. He was wrong, and he embarrassed himself. He destroyed our friendship, and I will never forgive him for, or forget, what he did to me and my family."

King's head bobbed slightly. "I'm sorry."

"No reason for you to apologize. Just don't make the same mistake."

"Do you really think I'm a jerk?" King questioned, amusement dancing in the look he tossed her.

The annoyance that had kissed her expression disappeared for the briefest moment, and Lenore actually laughed, her head waving from side to side. She made no effort to respond to his question.

A blanket of silence descended over them once again as Lenore pointed King and his car toward the

French Quarter. Minutes later he had parked his vehicle, and they stood in front of the Hotel Monteleone on Royal Street. Lenore led the way and King followed her through the doors of the grand entrance, not at all certain about his intentions, or her own. But he followed dutifully, seeming slightly amused by her commanding personality. Amused, and excited. Determination fueled her steps. Curiosity fueled his and she could tell by his expression that he was wondering exactly what he'd managed to get himself into.

The extraordinary Hotel Monteleone was a New Orleans treasure with a rich, decadent history. It had been the stomping grounds for a lengthy list of distinguished Southern authors that included the likes of Ernest Hemingway, Anne Rice and John Grisham. Lenore's father was drawn to the property for its Truman Capote connection, the American author of *Breakfast at Tiffany's* and *In Cold Blood* a favorite of his. He'd been living in its penthouse suite since vacating the family home after the divorce.

Lenore sauntered through the hotel's lobby as King followed on her heels. He paused to stare at the large grandfather clock that sat at the room's center, drawn to the extraordinary detail in the olive ash burl overlays and decorative carved appliqué. It was a stunning piece of furniture and one Lenore herself often admired whenever she visited.

She found herself fighting not to stare at the man. There was no denying his good looks, but there was something else about him that had captured her interest and was holding tight to her attention. It was something decadent and intimate and nothing like she'd ever felt before. Often guarded in the presence of most men, there was something about King that pushed her reservations aside and left her feeling vulnerable in a way that was more comforting than chaotic.

Lenore waved a hand toward the front desk staff as they greeted her warmly. She noted his interest in their familiarity, although he didn't say anything. His eyes, however were speaking volumes as he watched and pondered, seeming to stack his questions for a later time.

As they waited for the elevator, a family of five, two adults and three elementary-age children, joined them. King greeted them politely.

"Good afternoon," he said, his smile bright.

"It's hot," one little girl muttered as she swiped the back of her hand across her sweaty brow.

"Have you been exploring the city?" King asked.

The kids nodded. "We went to the aquarium and then Daddy let us get ben-yahs," another answered.

"I love *beignets*," King said, his eyes widening. He winked an eye at the family's patriarch.

The little girls giggled, and both parents gave them a smile.

They stepped into the conveyor, the family following. Lenore pushed the button for the penthouse and stepped into the rear corner. King moved to stand next to her. It was suddenly a tight fit, with bodies, a stroller and the assorted bags the family had accumulated.

Lenore found herself pressed against King, her body curving just so into his side. He was so close she could smell the scent of his cologne, the aroma unexpectedly familiar. Her father wore L'Homme À la Rose, too. It was his signature fragrance, and at least one of his daughters always gifted him a bottle for his birthday, or Christmas, or Father's Day.

She closed her eyes and took a deep breath, inhaling the fragrance that always represented comfort and safety for her. When her eyes opened, King was staring at her, his look mesmerizing. Something magnetic sparkled in his eyes. Something exceptional that felt as though it was hers and hers alone. It was unexpected and startled her. She took a quick sidestep from him, almost knocking into one of the little girls as the elevator doors opened to let the family exit.

As the conveyor doors closed, she attempted to ease into the opposite corner, spinning her body away from his. The elevator suddenly shook abruptly, and she stumbled, tripping over her own two feet. King caught her by the waist, stopping her from falling. A bolt of electricity coursed between them, energy that felt like an explosion of monumental proportions. She turned in his arms to face him, her fingertips pressed to his broad chest.

Concern washed over his expression. "Are you okay?" he questioned, his voice dropping to a loud whisper.

Lenore nodded, a slow up and down bob of her head, her eyes locked tightly with his. His gaze danced across her face, and she gasped, as he gently pulled her even closer. His touch was heated, and possessive, seeming to claim her where she stood.

Before she realized what she was doing, with no thought to the consequences, Lenore reached up and pressed her mouth to his. Her lips slid like butter over his lips, melting into a kiss that left them both breathless. Tongues tangled and her pulse synced sweetly with the beat of his heart. She stepped even closer as he pulled her body firmly against his. They fit like two pieces of a puzzle, her curves settling nicely against his hardened frame as his hands danced down her back and across her buttocks.

They were so lost in the moment that neither noticed the conveyor when it opened. Nor did they see Lenore's parents standing side by side at the entrance to greet them. And in that moment, neither one of them cared.

Chapter 8

King's cheeks still burned with embarrassment. When Lenore had pulled herself from him, turning to greet her parents as if nothing had happened, he was still standing wide-eyed and slack-jawed. He'd hesitated like a deer in headlights, and then Lenore clearing her throat pulled him back to his senses. As she stepped out of the elevator, he followed on her heels. Her father glared at him, and her mother's amused grin welcomed both.

"Detective Randolph, allow me to introduce you to my father, Josiah Martin, and my mother, Claudia Martin. Josiah, Claudia, this is Detective King Randolph."

He extended his hand politely. "Mr. Martin, Mrs. Martin, it's a pleasure to meet you."

Josiah eyed him up and then down, then turned abruptly as he waved a dismissive hand in King's direction. He tossed his daughter a look, visibly displeased with their earlier display of public affection.

King took a deep inhale of air and blew it out slowly. His whole body had tensed, and he was feeling uncomfortable.

Claudia rolled her eyes at her ex-husband, annoyance painting her expression. She smiled at King as she stepped forward and clasped his hand between both of hers. "Detective, welcome," she said softly. "It's always a pleasure to meet one of our city's finest." She gestured for him to follow. "Please, come in and have a seat."

King smiled back politely. "Thank you," he said softly.

As he followed, he noted Lenore had moved behind a mahogany bar. She grabbed a heavy-bottomed whiskey glass and a bottle of Jack Daniel's and poured two fingers. She tossed back the drink in one gulp, then poured herself a second. She let that next round sit on the polished bar top, her eyes lifting to meet his. Her head waved from side to side. Her expression said she would have offered him one but knew he would decline since he was still officially on duty. Lenore never wasted time on unnecessary niceties.

"It's a little early for that, isn't it?" her father bellowed.

Lenore shrugged. "Not after the morning we've had." She picked up the glass and moved to where her parents sat. She dropped down against the sofa beside her mother, leaning her head against the woman's shoulder.

King didn't miss the concern that swept between the young woman's parents. It filled the room, making the air thick and viscous. They had questions, but neither said anything, allowing Lenore the moment to collect herself. He suddenly felt her father's eyes boring into him, the man's gaze narrowed. His stare spoke volumes, questioning what he didn't want to ask his baby girl.

"My apologies, sir," King said. He shifted forward in his seat. "While investigating one murder, we discovered the body of a second student who'd reached out to Lenore for help this morning."

Josiah shook his head, turning his attention back to his eldest child. "You may be too close to this, Lenore. Perhaps your mother can find something else for you to work on." He lifted his brow toward his ex-wife.

Claudia rolled her eyes skyward. "We don't have the luxury of picking and choosing our cases, Josiah. We go where we're asked to help the people who need us most. Lenore knows what to do if it becomes too much for her. Not one of our girls needs to be coddled by you, or any other man." She shifted her gaze toward King with her comment.

"Expressing concern for my child's well-being isn't coddling," Josiah muttered.

Lenore shook her head. "Please, don't argue. I don't have the energy for it right now." She tossed back that second shot of Jack Daniel's and dropped the glass onto the glass coffee table. "Did you get my text?" she asked her mother.

Claudia nodded. "I did. We already have people there to help the family. When I spoke to your sister, they were taking the mother to the hospital to be checked out. She's having a difficult time."

"And Ms. Hattie?"

"She's made of strong stuff. She'll be fine, and we'll be there to help however she needs us."

Lenore nodded. For the briefest moment, King thought he saw a tear slide down her face. But with a swipe of her hand, it was gone as quickly as it had risen, her gaze dry. She began to share what she could about the case, filling her parents in on all that had happened since she'd risen that morning. King listened, his eyes closed as he too reflected on what they knew, and more importantly, what they didn't.

Josiah suddenly called his name, rising from his seat as he gestured for King to follow. King stole one last glance toward Lenore, who was eyeing them both with a raised brow. She gave him the slightest smile and nodded her head. Her mother chuckled softly, and King couldn't help but wonder where it all would eventually lead him.

As the two men moved into the next room, Josiah Martin shut the door behind them. The space had been converted into an office, and a wall of windows looked out over the street below. Family photos decorated one shelf of the bookcase, and an assortment of leather-bound books filled the space.

The patriarch moved to a glass-topped desk and took a seat in an ergonomic leather chair. He pointed King toward an upholstered wingback. The two men locked gazes as King took his seat, leaning back against the cushions.

Josiah Martin didn't waste time getting straight to the point. "People are becoming concerned. The bodies of our young people seem to be dropping on a daily basis, and the police aren't giving us any answers. What do you need, Detective, to solve this case?"

King hesitated, not at all certain it was a conversation he should be having with one more person not officially affiliated with the police department or the case. Josiah being a known criminal didn't help King with his dilemma either. He looked the man in the eye, his expression stoic. When he finally answered, his tone was confident.

"Respectfully, sir, I need you and your family to stay out of my way. I understand the community doesn't trust the police and they don't know me, but I'm never going to make any headway if your daughter continues to challenge my authority and make things difficult for me."

Josiah's brow lifted, surprise washing over his expression. His head bobbed slowly against his thick neck. His full lips lifted in a warm smile. "Consider it done. Rest assured you won't have any further problems. If someone refuses to answer your questions, just drop my name. That should open plenty of doors for you."

"Thank you, sir. I appreciate that."

"As long as you understand my generosity will endure only as long as it takes you to solve this case. Once you've caught your killer and they've been charged and convicted, I can't promise I'll continue to extend you that courtesy."

King smiled. "Hopefully, sir, I'll have earned everyone's respect by then, and I won't need you to intercede on my behalf."

Josiah paused to consider the other man's comment. He suddenly chuckled. "I like you, Detective

Randolph. In fact, I like you enough to warn you. The Martin women are not to be played with. Cross them and there will be hell to pay. Not one of my daughters is all peaches and cream. They're more like cacti and arsenic. Piss one of them off and all of them will make it their life's mission to destroy you."

King laughed, thoughts of Lenore crossing through his mind. "I appreciate the heads-up, sir!"

"It's the least I can do," Josiah said, laughing with him. He changed the subject. "How is your grandfather? It's been some time since I last spoke with him."

"He's doing well, sir. I appreciate you asking."

"Please give him my regards. Tobias is a good man. He always afforded me the best advice. Sometimes I took it, and sometimes I regretted that I didn't. I have great respect for him."

"As he has for you, Mr. Martin."

"Please, call me Josiah. Something about the way you were wrapped around my daughter tells me you might be around for a while."

Embarrassment warmed the color in King's dark complexion. He was grateful the other man couldn't see him blushing so profusely. He shook his head and apologized.

"I'm sorry about that, sir. We didn't mean to be disrespectful."

Josiah chuckled. "No apologies necessary. Lenore can be a handful! I could tell by your expression that you didn't initiate that kiss. My daughter caught you off guard. And I have no doubts she did it on purpose."

Still blushing, King shrugged his shoulders.

Josiah moved back to the door. Amusement covered

his face. "But I also didn't miss that you didn't do any-thing to stop it, Detective Randolph. So, let me give you another warning." The man paused, took an inhale of breath and grinned. "That's how her mother roped me in!"

"Why did Daddy want to meet King?" Lenore questioned, still leaning against her mother for support. "Daddy never wants to meet any man we're dating."

Claudia shifted her body from her daughter's, moving onto her feet. She lifted Lenore's whiskey glass from the table and moved it to the sink behind the bar. For the briefest moment, she stared at her daughter but said nothing. She sat back down beside Lenore, shifting her body to look directly at the young woman. "Are you and Detective Randolph dating now?"

"You know what I mean." Lenore was suddenly sputtering. Being called out on that slip of the tongue threw her off guard. "I didn't mean *dating* dating."

"There's another kind of dating?" Amusement danced in Claudia's tone.

Lenore rolled her eyes, hoping her own silence would shut down the topic. She was feeling out of sorts about the man she'd kissed in the elevator. Theirs was a business relationship first and foremost, and she'd broken the cardinal rule about not mixing business with pleasure. Kissing him had been reactionary. She was sad, and all she had wanted was to experience the nearness of someone who understood what she was going through.

Kissing King had also been necessary. She'd been thinking about it. More than once, actually. Curious to know how he might feel against her. The gesture had been selfish and purely egotistical on her part. She figured he would understand that as well. Because there was something about King Randolph that felt familiar. She was comfortable around him. He seemed to understand her despite all her eccentricities. She believed King understood because he'd seen what she'd seen. He wanted the same answers she did. He hurt like she hurt.

She hadn't deluded herself into thinking that her heart, or his, was in any way tied to her decision to press her mouth to his. She may have said *dating*, but she hadn't meant it in the traditional sense of the word. It had been a slip of the tongue that should be forgiven or ignored. She would have to make sure she was careful with her words in the future. Especially if she was talking about King Randolph to any of her family. She lifted her gaze to her mother's and shrugged her narrow shoulders skyward.

Claudia nodded, her head bobbing slowly up and down against her thin neck. "Figure it out, Lenore. And while you're doing that, don't forget you have a job to do."

King cut his eyes in Lenore's direction. The remaining time spent with her parents had been pleasant. They asked questions about his family, told stories about her and her siblings, and allowed the two of them time to collect themselves before heading back to their investigation. Claudia had ordered lunch, and they'd enjoyed plates of grilled catfish atop a salad of spring mix, banana peppers, shaved onions, dried cranberries and a strawberry vinaigrette. Lenore had said little, stealing an occasional glance in his direction to gauge his re-actions. Now she sat staring out the passenger window of his car.

He disrupted the silence with a question. "Don't you think we should talk about what happened?"

She feigned ignorance, turning to give him a dull stare. "What? Didn't you have a good time hanging out with my old people?"

"I enjoyed your parents. But I think we need to talk about that kiss."

Lenore sighed. "I kissed you. It didn't mean anything. There is absolutely no reason for you to make a big deal out of it," she said dismissively. "Besides, it wasn't that good."

King laughed. "You lie quick, don't you?"

Her expression was smug as she tossed him a wry look. "Who's lying?"

"You are. You know that was a good kiss, and only because I was good at it."

"Says you."

"Damn right says me! And I'd be willing to kiss you again just to prove it!"

This time Lenore laughed heartily. Her entire face glowed, and her body relaxed for what seemed like the first time since earlier that morning. She shook her head. "That's what we won't be doing," she said. "I'm not going down that road with you, King Randolph. This relationship is strictly professional."

"You've already broken that rule, Ms. Martin," he said with a wink of his eye.

She sighed softly. A moment's hesitation passed between them before she spoke again. "I'm sorry. I crossed a boundary that I shouldn't have."

"Not until we had talked about it, at least. Under different circumstances, I might feel slightly violated being kissed before you asked my permission." His eyes darted from the road to her face, and he smiled ever so slightly.

"I'd argue that the way you kissed me back would more than support permission having been granted. There was no resistance on your part."

"No, there was not. You're right. I actually enjoyed kissing you."

"Well, clearly, it's not something we should even consider again until this case is officially closed."

"I couldn't agree more," King concurred.

"So, we don't need to talk about it anymore."

"As long as you keep your lips and hands off me, we'll be good."

The moment of levity had lifted Lenore's spirit. She giggled, and Lenore was a woman who rarely giggled.

Chapter 9

The ride back to the high school was easier than they'd anticipated. Their conversations were casual fact-finding missions as they asked each other questions. Lenore learned he had a penchant for charcuterie boards, he detested jelly doughnuts and he considered himself somewhat of a master trivia pro. She shared her dislike of most things fried, chicken in any form and her love for decadent fabrics even though she didn't sew.

Taking just a brief moment to forget the case, they laughed and allowed themselves time to reflect on things that made them smile. And then, without warning, the moment was snatched from them.

Lenore saw the duo first, every one of her senses switching to high alert. She dropped her left hand against his forearm as she pointed toward the front of the school building with her right. King's eyes followed the line of her index finger. He nodded as his gaze fell on Coach Carmichael and her son, the duo standing in heated conversation. She was screaming in his face, waving her hands in exasperation. The young man said something back she didn't like, and she slapped him, hitting him with a backhand so hard that his head spun around as if it were on a hinge. He took two steps back, fists clenched tightly at his sides. He spat a litany of profanity over his shoulder as he turned, bounding down the steps away from the woman. Seconds later he was in his car, speeding off the campus.

As they stepped from King's vehicle, Coach Carmichael caught sight of them. Her gaze swept past King and rested on Lenore. Her brow furrowed, and her expression was pained. She was visibly shaking, and it was obvious that they were the last two people she'd wanted to see. The school's bell rang loudly, signaling the end of the day. Students began to pour out of the building. Turning an about-face, Coach raced up the short flight of concrete steps and inside the building.

Lenore and King exchanged a look, curiosity rising fiercely.

"What do you think that was all about?" Lenore questioned.

"I'm not sure, but I'm legally obligated to ask."

"And if she doesn't give you an answer?"

"I may need to flash my badge and threaten to hit her with an assault charge since we did witness her putting her hands on her son. The threat of jail is often a great motivator."

"Good luck with that. Something tells me her son

would never support charges being levied against his mother. No matter what issues the two have with each other."

"You never know."

Lenore shrugged, her expression nonchalant. She shoved her hands into the pockets of her navy blue blazer. "There are some things I need to go check on. The game starts at six thirty. We should probably be back here by six. I'll text you my address. You should pick me up at five."

King laughed, a robust guffaw that rose from deep in his midsection. "Are you always so damn bossy?"

"I'm not bossy. I just believe in getting straight to the point of things without all the fluff and bull crap. So, if five thirty works better for you, that's fine. I'm easy."

"I doubt that," King muttered. He shook his head, his mouth still pulled into the slightest smile. "I will see you at five."

Lenore laughed as she moved to her car. "See, that wasn't difficult at all!" she said, tossing him a look over her shoulder.

He grinned. "Trust me when I tell you," he answered, still staring, "that was harder than you'll ever know!"

She wasn't bossy, Lenore thought as she maneuvered her car toward her office. Not really. Okay, maybe a little. She muttered under her breath. "So what if I'm a *lot* bossy," she said aloud, warm breath melting in the cool temperatures of the car's air conditioner. Obviously, King didn't mind as much as he professed. She'd gotten her way with little argument, and Lenore usually got her way.

She was curious what King might be thinking about her. She wondered if he liked her. Or if her sometimes brash demeanor was a turnoff. It was a rare breed of man who could handle her personality. An even rarer breed that she allowed into her inner circle and let her guard down for. She was still very much in work mode with King Randolph and had yet to soften her ways. They still had much to learn about each other. Much she needed to know about the man before she would even begin to think about trusting him.

Not that they were trying to build a personal relationship. But they might become good friends, she thought. Maybe even good friends with privileges. Thinking about that kiss had her curious about what else the two might explore together. Because that kiss had been good. It had been better than good, leaving her with a wanton desire that she'd not known with any other man before him. She heaved a heavy sigh, her head shaking from side to side. She should never have kissed that man!

The office was quiet, each of her sisters lost in the stacks of work on their own desks. No one looked up as she moved through the office interior toward her own office. Only Piper, who was deep in conversation on the telephone, gave her a nod and the slightest smile.

Lenore dropped into her leather executive's chair and lifted her boots to the desktop. She needed to change before the football game, and she was quickly running out of time. But something about the entire day wasn't sitting well with her. Something about Coach Carmichael, her son and finding the body of poor Tralisa Taylor had her completely discombobulated.

On the surface, she liked Coach and her son for the crime. But it felt too easy to lay the blame on the duo. Tralisa's shoe in the teacher's desk, with her knowing they were coming to investigate and possibly search the premises, felt contrived and sloppy. Coach Carmichael didn't give her the impression that she ever ignored the details of anything.

Her son, Charles, had been too affable. When she'd asked about his connection to the students in his mother's classes, he was nonchalant, nothing about his answer raising any red flags. Nothing about him screamed serial killer. His mother gave Lenore psychotic personality vibes more than he did. Still, though, Lenore wasn't willing to take any chances just in case her instincts were wrong. She shot Cash a quick email to pull everything she could find on the Carmichael family.

Celeste suddenly stood in the doorway of Lenore's office. She didn't bother to knock before pushing her way into the room and dropping into the chair beside her desk. "Sorry about your client's granddaughter, and her friend."

"They were kids. They didn't deserve what happened to them."

Celeste nodded. "Our friend at the coroner's office reached out. There's something he needs you to see. He said he'll be there in the morning if you can come by."

"Did he say what it was?"

Her sister shook her head. "No. Just that he thinks it's important."

The two women stared at each other for a moment.

Celeste had dyed her hair a stunning shade of burgundy red that complemented the creamy tones of her complexion. Last week her lengthy curls had been a brilliant shade of green. She'd been able to pull that off equally as well. Lenore wasn't so brave, preferring to leave her natural red tresses as they'd been the day she'd been born. "I'm loving the hair!" she said, wanting to change the subject.

"I do, too! I might keep it this way." Celeste hesitated, and then she laughed. "That would be a lie," she said.

Lenore laughed with her, and in the blink of an eye, that laughter turned into an ugly cry, tears streaming down her face. She gasped for air, fighting the sobs that had risen with a vengeance. Her fists were clenched tightly, her entire body bristling with frustration.

Celeste allowed her the moment, sitting still in her seat as she watched her. Lenore sobbed as if her whole world had just crashed and burned beneath her. Every hurt and pain from the last two days spilled out with her tears. When she was finally cried out, gasping to catch her breath, Celeste pulled a tissue from a box on the desk and passed it to her.

"What's that saying about a good cry curing a heavy heart?" Celeste said softly.

Lenore shrugged. "I'm sure it was something our mother made up." She pressed the tissue to one eye and then the other. "Daddy always said tears were a sign of weakness."

"Daddy was wrong more than he was right. Most especially when it came to little girls and grown women and our crying when something hurt our feelings."

Lenore chuckled, still swiping at the moisture that dampened her cheeks. "Do you remember when we were all little and Mom had to go to Lafayette for the day, leaving us with Daddy?"

"Yeah! You and Alexis got into a fight with that Bradbury boy!" Celeste grinned.

"He punched her in the face, and she started crying! I think I hit him first, but we beat the fire out of that kid! When Daddy came to break it up, all four of us were crying."

Celeste laughed. "We weren't crying, we were wailing!"

Lenore nodded. "And Daddy left us there. I think it was Grandma Martin who finally came to get us."

"If we're honest, Daddy wanted boys. Boys didn't cry."

"Which is why I would never break down and cry in front of anyone except you, Sophie and Alexis."

"We'll always have your back, Sissy." Celeste smiled. "So, what's on your agenda tonight?"

Lenore stole a quick glance toward her Rolex. It had a black ceramic and stainless steel case surrounded by hand-set diamonds. It was just a few minutes after four. "Detective Randolph is picking me up in an hour. We're going to the football game at the high school."

"Is this a date?" Celeste's expression was smug.

"No." Lenore shook her head. "It's surveillance."

"Surveillance?"

With a roll of her eyes, Lenore stood up. "We're investigating a case, remember? I don't have time for dates. I need to find a killer."

"Just remember you're not doing this alone, please.

Let that man do his job. He'll get all the credit for it anyway. They always do."

"Well, I don't need credit. I just need justice."

"We need to get you a caped crusader leotard."

"Girl, please! I wear my Black skin and my crown daily. What more would any of us ever need?"

Celeste lifted her hand and gave her sister a high five. "Just be safe out there, please. If anything happens to you, your sisters and I would have to go gunning for someone. And that wouldn't be pretty!"

"It sure as hell better not be," Lenore said with one last chuckle as she moved toward the door. "Or I'm coming back to haunt you all!"

Detective Foret sat in the station's break room. His color was ashen, looking like the blood had been sucked from him. He lifted his eyes to King, his head waving from side to side like a flag beneath an easy fall breeze. Despite his best efforts to hide his emotion, King could see the man was past ready to be done with the day.

"Hey," Christian muttered, the two men exchanging a look between them.

King nodded. "What's up?"

"That girl's mother was still crying when I left. The whole house was having a meltdown. Mom, the babies, even the husband was having a hard time holding back his tears. It was a lot to take. Then when all those women from the church started to show up…" Christian tossed up his hands before folding his arms above his head. "I'm about ready to transfer back to traffic duty."

King nodded. "I know the feeling. We just have to take it all in stride."

"Well, there are times I'd rather hang out with the dead bodies down at the morgue over facing the victims' families."

King's gaze narrowed slightly. Although he understood the sentiment, he didn't know if he would have spoken it aloud. He changed the subject. "I'm headed back to the high school for the football game. I'm not sure anything will come of it, but Ms. Martin is convinced our killer might show his hand just to catch a glimpse of how his handiwork has impacted the community," he said, his tone snarky. "She thinks she can pick whoever it is out of a crowd."

"And what do you think?"

King paused for a quick moment before finally responding. "That she might actually be able to do it."

Christian laughed. "Well, that didn't take long!"

"What?"

"For you to be converted. You know she has a cult following, right? There are a whole lot of people who think she and her family can walk on water! Me included!"

"Well, I haven't fallen down that rabbit hole, but I do think she's good at what she does."

Christian eyed him with a raised brow. "Maybe so, but I wouldn't turn my back on her if I were you."

King laughed. "I appreciate the warning."

Moving into his office, King stared at the corkboard on the wall. The victims stared back at him, the images capturing happier times. Each had been young, full of potential, with bright futures ahead of them. Their light had been darkened in the blink of an eye, someone not caring that they were loved and cared for by family that now missed them.

He moved to his seat, still staring, hoping that something would jump out at him that tied the growing list of victims to each other. Minutes later, when the intercom on his desk buzzed, he was still drawing a complete blank, feeling less than capable of doing the job to stop any other bodies from dropping into his lap.

He depressed the talk button to answer the receptionist calling from the front desk.

"Detective, you have a visitor."

King was confused, not knowing who would be seeking him out or why. "A visitor?"

"Yes, sir. It's a woman, but she refuses to give me her name. She insists it's important. She says Josiah Martin referred her to you."

King jumped from his seat. "I'll be right there," he responded.

The older woman was named Janie Dunn. Mrs. Dunn was a Louisiana transplant originally from Durham, North Carolina. Her late husband, Riley Dunn, had lured her to Louisiana when she'd been in her late teens. She'd set down roots in New Orleans, raised five children here and now called the city home. Her Riley, who she referred to with adoration, had passed on years prior, pancreatic cancer stealing him from her. She was left with a small home in the Seventh Ward and four sons she professed should be doing more to care for her. She rambled, her thin voice sounding like a loud whisper in an empty room.

"My Riley couldn't tolerate no laziness, and my

youngest two boys is lazy as hell! Neither one of 'em wants to work, laying up with any girl that smiles their way and will pay their bills. Don't make no kinds of sense," she muttered as King led her into an empty interrogation room and pointed her to a chair.

"So, how can I help you, Mrs. Dunn?" King questioned, hoping to shift her focus.

"I'm here about my baby girl."

King's eyes narrowed, his expression confused. "Your baby girl?"

"Elaine. We lost her when she was fifteen."

"I'm sorry for your loss. What happened?"

"That's what I need you to figure out. Elaine went off to school like usual and never made it home. My baby girl went missing for two whole weeks. The police said she was a runaway 'cause she'd had some previous run-ins with the law. Just juvenile stuff. Nothing serious. But they didn't put no stock in trying to look for her. Just said she run off and would find her way back home when she was ready."

King nodded slowly. "But she never came home?"

"Hunters were out checking their gator traps and found her body down in 'dem swamps. I never got to see my baby. Undertaker said she was too messed up. That there wasn't much left of her for me to see. They ain't even open her casket at the funeral before they buried her away in that tomb."

"Did the police ever say what happened to her?"

"They said it was an accident. But my baby girl ain't take herself out in 'dem damn swamps! She ain't hang herself from no tree. Someone did that to her. Just like all them other young girls before Elaine, and them girls you finding dead now."

King bristled. "The girls *before* Elaine?"

Mrs. Dunn nodded. "Two little Black girls and a little white girl. Somebody's boy went missing, too, but y'all said that ain't had nothing to do with 'dem girls that got killed."

King's mind was suddenly racing. "Mrs. Dunn, I'm going to need some time to look into this," he said. "If you can give me a day or two, I promise, I'll get back to you."

Mrs. Dunn rose from the table. She was a frail woman who needed a cane to help carry what little weight she wore on her thin frame. Life had left deep remembrances over her face, frown lines deep and sadness seeping from her eyes. She carried her hurts and disappointments like a shroud, but wanting closure kept her pushing. Life hadn't given her many choices, and she was okay with that, continuing to put one foot in front of the other. Now she was trusting King to find the answers about a daughter she'd cherished. Those she had wanted to trust years earlier had disappointed her in ways that felt unfathomable. The woman grabbed his arm as he led her back toward the front of the building.

"Can you get home okay by yourself?" King questioned.

"Yes! Yes!" she answered. "My son Chauncy is waiting out in the car. He wouldn't come in 'cause he don't like no cops. That's 'cause he always doing something he ain't got no business doing!"

King smiled. "I promise I'll call as soon as I have some information," he reiterated.

"The Piper ain't never forgot about our kids. He said we could trust you."

Confusion washed over King's expression one last time. "The Piper?"

The old woman chuckled. "Mr. Josiah. Back in the day, folks would call him the Pied Piper 'cause everyone followed his lead. He took care of us. Still does. When he called and told me to come down here to tell you my story, I knew he trusted you. He knows you can find who killed my baby girl."

King nodded his understanding. Deep down, his gut was telling him that Josiah "The Pied Piper" Martin had already suspected a serial killer in the previous murders. Now he believed the cases were connected. Sending Mrs. Dunn in his direction was only meant to give King enough information to make the connection himself.

"You take care, Mrs. Dunn, and I will call you soon," King said as he helped her into the waiting car. He stood watching the taillights as her son lurched forward into a line of traffic.

Hurrying back inside the building and to his office, King called out for Christian. "See what you can find on a cold case from forty years ago. The victim's name was Elaine Dunn. I also need the files for any other unsolved cases involving missing high school kids. I want everyone that you can find!"

"On it!" Christian said, his expression grateful for something to do that could clear his head and take his mind off his earlier angst. "You headed to the game?"

King nodded. "I'll be back for those files right after."

As King moved toward the building's front lobby, he ran straight into his commanding officer. Captain Romero eyed him curiously.

"Heading home early, Randolph?"

"No, sir. I'm headed to the high school to observe the football game and the students' tribute to our victims. It'll give me a chance to set my sights on their friends… and hopefully an enemy or two. I'm hoping someone might tip their hand and give us a lead."

"I heard you connected with Ms. Martin?" There was a hard edge to his question, his tone shifting as he called Lenore's name.

King nodded, his own tone suddenly cautious. "I did."

"Was she able to give you anything?" Romero eyed him curiously, folding his arms over his broad chest.

King noted that Romero's fists were clenched, and his jaw had tightened as he gritted his teeth together. He shrugged as he answered. "Nothing I didn't already have. But Lenore has been instrumental in opening a few closed doors for me."

"I just bet she has," Romero mumbled under his breath.

"Excuse me?" King replied.

Romero cleared his throat. "Just watch yourself. You working with a private investigator is a slippery slope that could end badly for you if you're not careful. And we don't want it to reflect back on the department."

"Maybe I'm not understanding. I thought you wanted me to work with Ms. Martin?"

"I wanted you to find out what she knew and if it could help you close this case."

King's stare narrowed, his expression hardening like stone. The air between them chilled substantially.

Romero continued. "Lenore and her family are dangerous. No one's willing to say that out loud, but they can't be trusted. I wouldn't be surprised if she promises you favors she has no intentions of delivering on, just to sabotage this case."

"Is that what happened when you were dating her?" King suddenly questioned. "She promised you favors and didn't deliver?"

Romero bristled. His entire face hardened, and he reminded King of a concrete gargoyle that might adorn a graveyard. He was still and unmoving, and when he next spoke, there was an icy chill in his voice. "You're still figuring things out, Randolph. And what you need to know is that this job requires you having a few friends in high places if you're going to be successful. I can be that friend. Or not. I would watch myself if I were you."

King met the look Romero was giving him. A cold, steely glare that felt a bit threatening. It was on the tip of his tongue to ask if that was an order as well, but he didn't, biting back the snark.

"I need to run, Captain," he said instead. "But I will be back after the game."

"You plan on pulling an all-nighter?" Romero questioned.

"I'll do whatever it takes to solve this case!" King answered as he tugged on his blazer. Then he stepped past his superior and swept out the door.

Chapter 10

Lenore was waiting in the lobby of her apartment building when King pulled up out front. She didn't wait for him to exit his car before she was pulling the door open and sliding into the passenger seat.

"You're late," she quipped.

"I'm here," he snapped back.

They exchanged glares before he turned his gaze to the road, pulling back into traffic.

"Why are you always so damn disagreeable?" King questioned. He cut his eyes in her direction.

Lenore inhaled a deep breath of air. She didn't bother to answer, instead turning to stare out the window before asking him a question. "Did you get the warrant to search the school?"

"Is this what we're doing now? You get called on

your bad behavior and you change the subject to avoid accountability?"

Lenore's head snapped toward him, her mouth opening and then closing like a guppy out of water. Her eyes bulged, then darted back and forth across his face. A minute passed, and then she heaved a heavy sigh, her body deflating like a balloon popped with a pin. She lowered her eyelids, her head shaking from side to side. "I'm sorry," she finally said. "I didn't mean to take my frustrations out on you."

Surprise swept across King's face. Her apology was unexpected and not the conversation he'd anticipated. From the look she was giving him, it seemed to surprise her as well. "Do you want to talk about it?" he asked, his voice dropping an octave.

"Someone's out here killing our children, and we are nowhere close to finding out who's committing these crimes. I feel helpless, and I don't do vulnerability well." Her eyes darted in his direction and back. She took a deep breath. "Did you find out anything that might help?"

King understood her feelings, although he paused before responding. He felt as if his hands were tied as he thought about what he could share, and more importantly, what he couldn't. Suddenly there was a lot of gray area where things should have easily been black-and-white.

Their breaking and entering a locked classroom showed him how working this case with Lenore could easily go left, leaving him open to legal consequences. Constantly scrutinizing everything he might share with her was problematic at best, catastrophic at worse. The totality of his career suddenly flashed before his eyes.

As he sat thinking about it all, something about his last conversation with Romero felt off. King sensed his boss would probably shut down him giving her any details they discovered and penalize him if he did. Knowing he'd ordered him to work with Lenore left King conflicted.

He thought about the old woman who'd been sent in his direction by way of her father. Clearly Lenore knew nothing of Mrs. Dunn, or maybe she just wasn't being forthcoming, keeping certain details to herself. If her father hadn't shared that information with her, King couldn't help but question why. He suddenly felt as if he were back at square one with Lenore Martin, and it wasn't a feeling he was happy about. Nor one that he was willing to accept.

As if a lightbulb had been turned on in his head, it suddenly dawned on him that Romero was setting him up to be the scapegoat, willing to hang him out to dry if he weren't able to solve the murders that were piling up. Him being new made him expendable. In that brief moment, he realized he was on his own. And then, as if there was a flip of a coin, he understood he wasn't in this by his lonesome at all.

"We really need to talk," he said. He pulled his car into a parking space in front of the high school. "Before things get out of hand."

"What about?" Lenore asked.

He shook his head. "After the game," he said. "We both have some questions we need answers to, and we don't need to be interrupted."

He pointed to the principal, who was walking into the building, turning at the bottom of the steps to give them a look. The man paused, seeming to wait for them to exit their vehicle for a conversation.

Lenore waved a hand at the school's administrator before turning her attention back to King. She was staring at him, memorizing the line of his profile with her gaze. Whatever was on his mind was serious, and she sensed it was about more than finding their killer. She considered giving him a hard time, and in the blink of an eye, she changed her mind. This was bigger than her ego, or his. They were running headfirst into one dead end after another. Partnering with him was meant to capture a killer, and that wouldn't happen if she wasn't willing to cooperate with him and collaborate on the best way for the two of them to do their respective jobs.

"Dominate and devastate, we'll blow you away! We're the mighty, mighty Pelicans, and we're here to stay!" The Thomy Lafon cheerleaders were shaking pom-poms and body parts to electrify the crowd. Their smiles were canyon-wide as their ribbon-laced ponytails swayed in sync with their chants.

There had been a moment of silence for Michael-Lynn and Tralisa. The principal extended condolences to both families, reiterated there was support throughout the community for those in need, and extolled the virtues of both girls as if he'd been their very best friend. Their teammates had yelled out a military roll call, and when neither girl responded, the lead bugler in the band began to play a really bad rendition of "Taps." After, the cheerleaders had linked arms and done a tribute chant complete with leg kicks and fist pumps to their lost friends. The band jumped in when they were finished to perform the school's fight song. Kickoff happened precisely at seven o'clock, and between the football team and the cheerleaders, they had all been thoroughly entertained since.

"Pelicans?" King eyed her with a raised brow.

Lenore shrugged. "It's the state bird," she answered, as if that made it make sense. Her gaze was focused on the cheerleaders, and the crowd watching the cheerleaders.

The squad had their own personal fan club, but most of the audience were focused on the game and the players out on the field. Parents were cheering loudly, and save for one or two adult men who were leering at the girls salaciously, nothing in particular seemed out of order. King's gaze followed hers, and he gestured uniformed officers toward the more vocal perverts to shut them down and collect their personal information.

Together they moved slowly through the stands, Lenore pausing occasionally to speak to someone who recognized her and introducing King to members of the community she thought he should know.

The atmosphere was almost too staid until it wasn't. The cheer squad were yelling a chant for a touchdown when a fight suddenly broke out in the stands. Teens from the opposing high schools were throwing food and punches as King's police team jumped between them, ejecting a handful from the premises. Out on the field, Thomy Lafon scored their fifth touchdown, ending the game with their first win of the season.

As Lenore turned back toward the crowd, scanning

the many faces one more time, another heated disagreement caught her eye and grabbed her attention with both hands.

Charles Carmichael sat on the bleachers behind the cheerleaders. He was a few rows up and had a clear view of the football field. An elderly man sat beside him, and there was no missing the familial resemblance between them. Neither was happy, and Charles appeared to be lecturing the senior, who clearly had no interest in anything he was saying. Both were wading through a pit of frustration trying to get their point across to the other.

Coach was eyeing both intently, and if she could have run up to put a stop to their bickering, she would have. She waited until she was able to catch her son's eye, and then she gestured with a throat chop, signaling them to cut off whatever was going on between them.

King suddenly leaned in behind Lenore, turning his head just so in order to whisper into her ear. "They resemble each other. Father, maybe?"

Lenore shook her head. "I think he's too old. More like grandfather, maybe. And he's not happy."

"No, he isn't. I wonder what that's all about?"

"I say we go find out," Lenore said, sidestepping him to head in their direction.

Before she could push her way through the crowd trying to exit the stadium, the two men halted their conversation, moving down the set of bleachers to the field below. The older man made a beeline toward the cheerleaders, stopping directly in front of the young girl named Amber Gaines. Lenore's gaze narrowed ever so slightly as she watched. The girl visibly bristled, taking a step back from the old man's exuberance. His head suddenly snapped left when Coach called out to him, gesturing for her son to take him away.

"Looks like they might have some family drama going on," Lenore said, tossing the comment over her shoulder as King followed behind her.

"You think?" he answered sarcastically.

Lenore tried not to smile at his snark. His dry sense of humor was reminiscent of her own. She would have laughed out loud if the coach hadn't been eyeing her as she approached.

"Congratulations!" Lenore said as they came face-to-face with the instructor. "Everyone did a great job tonight. The girls were very impressive."

"They really weren't," she quipped, "but additional practice and we can get there. They did okay for the last-minute adjustments that needed to be made."

"That's kind of harsh, don't you think?"

"I think these girls need to be told the truth. No one needs to be coddling them."

Lenore felt King's hand gently grip her elbow. It was as if he were reading her mind, sensing there was something else about that woman not sitting well with her. His touch was purposeful, intended to pause the retort that sat on the tip of her tongue. On a different day, it would not have worked. On this day, she paused. She took an inhale of air and held it deep in her lungs.

"Detective! Ms. Martin! I'm surprised to see you again so soon!" Charles Carmichael greeted them both cheerily. Almost too cheerily, Lenore thought. But she was grateful for the interruption, the conversation with his mother having left the air around them feeling cold and slightly hostile.

King extended his hand. "Obviously we wanted to support the community and the families who've suffered devastating losses. It was only right we be here."

"That and they wanted to put eyes on the crowd and see if anyone looks suspicious!" the older man with Charles interjected. "It's how cops do!"

King smiled. "It is, sir." He extended his hand. "Detective Randolph of the New Orleans police department. And this is Lenore Martin."

The old man eyed them both from head to toe and back. Amusement painted his expression. "Carmichael. Richard Carmichael. Former police lieutenant Richard Carmichael!" The man's chest pushed forward, pride gleaming on his gaze.

Lenore's brow lifted ever so slightly. "You were with the police department?"

The man grinned. "Forty-two years of service. Longer than I was married to that witch I was cursed with."

"Grandpa!" Charles's tone was chastising.

"What? Everyone knows how your grandmother was."

"She's not here now to defend herself, so we're not going to speak badly of her."

"Well, I'm glad that witch is dead!" He leaned toward King. "Take my advice. Don't waste your time with a headstrong woman. They're always plotting behind your back to take you down." He shifted his eyes toward Lenore, who rolled her own dark orbs skyward.

"You'll have to forgive my father," Coach Carmichael chimed in, joining in the conversation. "He suffers from dementia and doesn't always know what he's saying."

The old man's face hardened. "I know exactly what I'm saying!" he snapped. He muttered a profanity, then turned from them, heading in the direction of the parking lot.

"I need to get him," Charles said, waving his apology as he hurried after the old man.

Coach Carmichael shook her head. "My father can be a handful," she said, her voice softening.

She seemed to fall into thought, and something neither Lenore nor King could recognize washed over her expression. In the blink of an eye, her face and her voice hardened. "I need to be going as well," the coach said. "You two have a good night."

As she scurried after her father and son, King and Lenore exchanged a quick glance.

"Something feel off to you?" Lenore asked.

King shrugged but didn't respond, moving toward the exit behind the last of the crowd. As they approached the entrance gate, Amber waved at Lenore, greeting her warmly.

Lenore grinned. "You guys did a great job!" she said. "You helped the crowd keep the team motivated. It was a good win."

"Thank you!" Amber responded. "I just wanted to ask if you had any information about what happened to Michael-Lynn and Tralisa. The cops searched the school today, and everybody's making up stuff, acting like they know something."

Lenore turned to give King a look. She hadn't realized he'd already served the search warrant, nor had he bothered to tell her what they'd found. A silent conversation passed between them, her eyes admonishing him for keeping her out of the loop. She shifted her gaze back to Amber.

"We're still investigating," King said. "And if you or any of your friends have any information that you think we should know, we'd appreciate your help." He handed the girl his business card. "Give me a call at any time."

Amber nodded. Before she could respond, a loud argument sounded through the evening air. They turned in time to see Coach Carmichael and her father standing toe-to-toe. The exchange was heated, and the old man had his hand wrapped around his daughter's neck. King moved swiftly toward them, leaving Lenore and Amber to watch from a distance.

"They're so weird!" Amber said. She folded her arms over her chest.

"Does Mr. Carmichael come to the games often?"

"No. Just every now and then. And they fight every time!"

"I saw him talking to you earlier. You looked uncomfortable."

"He's scary. He just blows up for no reason, and I've seen him swing on the coach before. I know he's old and Coach explained he has dementia, but I think he's always been like that, even before he became geriatric and sick."

Lenore smiled. "Some old people do get meaner as they age. They say their true personalities just become more intense."

"Exactly. I feel like he could hurt someone if they didn't keep his old butt in check! He listens to Charles, though."

"What did he say to you?" Lenore asked.

Amber shrugged. "It didn't make a whole lot of sense," she answered. "He just told me how pretty I was, and then he said my turn is coming."

Lenore blinked, the comment feeling like an arrow through her midsection. She repeated what she'd heard. "Your turn is coming? Your turn for what?"

"Beats me! But I didn't think he meant it in a nice way. He said the same thing to some of the other girls, too! It just freaked us all out, but Coach said to ignore him. She always says to ignore him."

"So, this has happened before?"

"The last time he was grabbing our asses and trying to pinch our boobs. The principal banned him from the games if there wasn't someone around to keep him in line."

Lenore paused, still staring as she watched King guide the patriarch to Charles's car, helping him inside. Coach Carmichael was gently rubbing her neck with her hand, her cheeks a flaming shade of embarrassed. Her eyes were darting back and forth at the crowd that had gathered, and then she turned, sliding into the driver's seat of her own vehicle.

"I have a question for you," Lenore said, shifting her attention back toward Amber.

"Yes, ma'am?"

"Do you know who Kevin is? It's my understanding he was a friend of Tralisa's."

Amber shrugged. "I only saw him once. He came to pick her up, and she and Michael-Lynn got into an argument about it. But you should ask the coach. She knows him. I think he might be a friend of her son's."

Lenore's head nodded ever so slightly as she fell into

thought. The coach had claimed no knowledge of anyone named Kevin. Why would she lie?

"How are you getting home?" Lenore asked, shifting her attention back toward Amber a second time.

"My brother. He's on the team. I was just waiting
for him to get out of the locker room. When I saw you,
I asked him to wait for me." She pointed to a stocky
young man whispering into some girl's ear. They stood
beside an older model Ford Explorer. The girl was giggling as he ran teasing fingers down the length of her
arm.

"Good. Until we close this case, I want you to stay
close to your friends and family. Don't be traveling
alone. I need you to do whatever you need to keep yourself safe."

"I will," Amber said. She took a step forward and
gave Lenore a hug. "Have a good night, Miss Lenore!"

Lenore hugged her back. "You, too, baby girl!"

King felt as if he'd just gone ten rounds in a heavy-
weight brawl. Trying to mediate the disagreement between Coach Carmichael and her father should have
come with hazard pay. The old man was angry, his ire
fueled by old age, his dementia and the crowd goad-
ing him on. The coach should have made the situation easier, but she too had wanted to prove a point
that wasn't worth the energy. They had actually come
to blows, and had the coach insisted her father be arrested, King would have had to put handcuffs on the
old man since he threw the first punch. Instead, she'd
pleaded with him, not wanting the police involved. She
proclaimed it an accident, wishing it would simply go

away. Charles had finally ushered the old man to his car, and after thanking King profusely, the coach had followed behind them.

Now King stood second-guessing his actions. Maybe he should have taken them both in. There was something about the family that was completely off, and he didn't know where to begin to figure them out. But they were not the first dysfunctional family he'd had to deal with and would not be the last. He had bigger problems than a daughter who barely liked her father and a father who seemingly didn't like his daughter at all.

His eyes walked the landscape, roaming over the few individuals still there. Most were parents and friends waiting for players to exit the gym's locker room. In the distance, he saw Lenore standing in conversation with one of the cheerleaders. The two looked comfortable with each other and the sight of her swept a calm breeze over his spirit.

He liked Lenore. He liked her more than he was willing to admit out loud. If anyone were to ask him about her, he would probably lie and pray that his interest in the beautiful woman didn't show on his face. Because mixing business and pleasure went against the grain of everything he'd been taught. But he couldn't get that damn kiss out of his head, still feeling the heat of her touch against his skin.

Chapter 11

"What did the search warrant find?" Lenore asked when they were alone, adding that she was a little irritated he hadn't told her. "Did the coach explain that sneaker in her drawer?"

King shook his head. "It wasn't in her drawer. They found it in the front office. In a lost and found box. Allegedly, someone found it in the hallway and assumed one of the students had dropped it. It was turned in to Coach Carmichael, and she took it to the office."

Lenore rolled her eyes. "Isn't that convenient!" She heaved a deep sigh of frustration. "Now what?"

"I need to run by the station to pick up some files," King said as he turned his car and headed in that direction. With the events of the football game behind them, they were moving on.

He'd left a patrol car at the school, two uniformed officers parked for the night. The crowd had dispersed with no further incidents, and things had been quiet when they'd pulled out of the parking lot.

"What kind of files?"

"The kind restricted to law enforcement."

Lenore cut her eyes in his direction, curtailing the urge to give him a piece of her mind. Instead, she changed the subject. "What was it that you wanted to talk about?" she questioned, still curious to know what had been on his mind earlier.

King shook his head. "Let me grab those files first, and then, if you're up to it, maybe we can grab something to eat before we have our conversation."

"This must really be serious. You're dragging it out like you're afraid to say what you need to say."

"No fear here," he said with a shake of his head. "And because it *is extremely* important, I need to know I have your full and undivided attention." He gave her the slightest smile as he continued to maneuver his way through traffic.

Lenore stared at him but said nothing. She was anxious to have a conversation with him. She was also excited to spend more time with the man. Even if it was only to profile a killer.

Their conversation continued to be easy and casual, an exchange of polite chitchat as they continued to feel each other out. Minutes later she sat outside the police station waiting for King to handle his business and return. He had promised to hurry, and she had promised to not call an Uber to take her home.

The sun had set hours earlier, and the sky was ominously black. A veil of fog was thick, teasing late-night showers, and the barest sliver of a new moon peeked from behind the caliginous clouds.

Lenore saw Romero before he saw her. Juan walked out of the building having a conversation on his cell phone. He appeared agitated and not at all happy. His posture was tense, and he seemed ready to throw a punch at someone.

When they had been together, he had always found it difficult to relax into a moment, forever on edge about something. The few times he'd allowed himself to just be, worry tucked away and out of sight, had been her favorite times with him, allowing her to also relax and be at ease. But those times had been few and far between. More moments between them felt like a bomb would drop if either one let their guard down.

His gaze turned in her direction, and he stared, suddenly realizing someone was sitting in the car. She assumed that he hadn't immediately recognized her, his view impeded by the cloak of darkness. Lenore opened the passenger door and eased her way out. She moved to stand beneath the dim light gleaming from the streetlight overhead, leaning her slim body against the car's front frame. She folded her arms over her chest, her chin lifted defiantly, as if she dared him to say the wrong thing.

He sighed, his entire body blowing out a gust of stale air. His steps were slow and deliberate as he made his way to stand before her. His eyes narrowed as they locked gazes. "What are you doing here, Lenore?"

"Hello, Lenore. Hello, Juan. How are you? I'm good, how about you?" She swung her head from side to side, feigning a conversation between them. She eyed him with a raised brow, and her voice was syrupy sweet to prove a point he wasn't interested in hearing. "I did meet your mother, Juan. I know she raised you to have better manners."

"I'm not in the mood for your games tonight, Lenore. Now, what are you doing here?"

"Waiting for my dinner date," she quipped.

He visibly bristled. "You're dating my new detective now? Is that your way of getting even with me?"

"Don't flatter yourself, Juan. Whoever I date doesn't have a damn thing to do with you."

"Are you working with him on this case?"

"You'd like that, wouldn't you? It would give you and the district attorney a reason to go after my license."

His jaw tightened as he continued to stare. The look he gave her was bitter, anger wrapped around it like tissue paper with a bow, He asked again. "Just answer my question, Lenore. Are you helping Detective Randolph work this murder investigation?"

Lenore shifted her weight from one hip to the other. "What murder investigation?" she responded, a wry smirk pulling across her face. "I'm only headed to dinner with a new friend. I don't know what investigation you're talking about, Captain Romero."

His temperature rose, ire bubbling over like a teakettle on high. "Like hell you don't," Juan snapped. He shook his index finger in her face. "If you, or any of your family, get in the way of our finding this killer, I will charge you as an accessory to each and every murder."

Lenore took a step toward him, closing the distance

between them. "Get out of my face, Juan. Before I press harassment charges against you. I'll have no problems showing you to be a bitter ex-boyfriend intent on revenge because I didn't want you anymore. And if you don't believe I will, you try me!"

Romero's head shook slowly. The hostility in his stare was palpable. For the first time, Lenore had no doubts that if he could hurt her, he would. The closed fist at his side and the vein pulsing in his neck were strained as if he were ready to throw a punch in her direction. She'd challenged him, and he was not a man who would take that lightly. He didn't like to lose and would ensure himself a win by any means. He pursed his lips as he chewed on the inside of his cheek. He sneered as he turned abruptly, storming off in the opposite direction. "Stay out of my way, Lenore," he shouted over his shoulder. "I mean it!"

Lenore watched him as he moved to his car. He gunned the engine as he pulled out of the parking space, speeding out of the lot. When he was out of sight, the sound of his vehicle fading in the distance, she pulled her cell phone from her pocket and dialed. Her mother answered on the third ring.

"What's wrong, Lenore?" Claudia answered.

"I might have a problem," she answered, filling her mother in on the conversation she'd just had.

There was the briefest moment of silence before Claudia responded. "I knew that young man wasn't going to just go away. He was a problem from the start, and I told you not to waste your time and energy on him."

Lenore chuckled. "Did you really just flip me off with an 'I told you so'?"

"I did no such thing. I simply stated a fact."

"Well, that lesson has been learned," Lenore said, a puff of warm air blowing past her lips.

"I hope so," Claudia said. "You can tell a good man from a bad one in a five-minute conversation if you ask the right questions. You and your sisters rarely ask any questions that you need to ask. Y'all always get scammed by the pretty faces and the smooth lines."

"That's not true."

"Who do you want me to start with?"

Lenore hesitated. Then she said, "Start with Detective Randolph."

Her mother laughed. "He's a perfect example. That man is giving you the same energy you are giving him. You push and he doesn't hesitate to push back. He's not going to coddle your bad behavior and will give you his best as long as you are doing the same for him. But you're all ready to turn tail and run because you're afraid he will try to dominate and control you. But that's the last thing he's interested in. He only wants to be your equal."

"And you garnered all that from an hour of conversation?"

"That doesn't begin to scratch the surface of what your father and I learned about that young man this afternoon. He wasn't trying to impress us. He was being himself, and he exuded confidence and decency. That first time we met Juan, he fell all over himself trying to do and say what he thought we wanted to hear. I trust Mr. Randolph. He is a good man. I would never turn my back on Mr. Romero. But I've already told you that. Multiple times!"

Lenore considered her mother's comments. Claudia had been right more times than she had ever been wrong. So maybe she had ignored her mother's previous warnings about Juan. It wouldn't happen again, and definitely not anytime soon. She changed the subject.

"So, what should I do about Captain Romero?"

"Nothing. It's already being handled."

"But what if…"

Claudia cut her daughter off, stalling the comment that sat perched on the tip of Lenore's tongue.

"I said it's being handled. Now, if there's nothing else you need, I have a date."

"You and Daddy doing dinner again?"

"I have no idea what your father is up to this evening. I am grabbing a late-night snack at Bouligny Tavern with a friend. Now I have to go. We can talk more in the morning."

"Yes, ma'am."

"Be safe, Lenore. And know that you are loved."

"I love you, too, Mother!"

As King exited the police station, Lenore was standing beside his car, her back turned toward him. As he sauntered to where she stood, he realized she was on her cell phone. When he heard his name being spoken, he came to an abrupt stop, shifting the box in his arms against his hip.

He quickly realized she was talking to someone in her family…about him…and he wasn't sure whether to walk away or continue to stand there and eavesdrop. Without giving it a second thought, he stood still, the package in his arms just a pound shy of being too heavy to carry. Curiosity planted his feet where he stood. He listened intently, only feeling slightly guilty for the intrusion, and then she wished her mother good-night and turned to find him standing behind her.

Startled, Lenore jumped at the sight of him. "What the hell…" she snapped, her eyes widening.

"Sorry," King replied. "I didn't mean to scare you. You were on the phone, and I didn't want to interrupt."

"So you stood there listening to my conversation?"

"Yes, I was eavesdropping, but only because you were talking about me." He grinned broadly, showcasing perfectly white teeth with the hint of a gap between his upper two incisors. He moved to the trunk of his car, lifted the hood and settled the box inside.

Lenore laughed. "You really are a piece of work!"

"You know you would have eavesdropped, too!"

"But I wouldn't have gotten caught."

King laughed with her. "I really didn't mean to frighten you, and I apologize for being rude. But I appreciate all the nice things your mother said about me, I'm even more grateful that you didn't contradict her."

"Don't read too much into that."

"It just sounded like you might actually like me."

Lenore laughed again, the sound billowing softly on the tail of an evening breeze. "I still think you might be a jerk. I haven't made up my mind yet."

King opened the passenger door and gestured for her to take a seat. "That's fair," he said. "I look forward to convincing you that I really am a great guy."

"Well, you'll need to start by feeding me. I'm starving."

"That's fair," King said as he slid into the driver's

seat. "How does a platter of forty-plus years of cold murder cases with the same methodology sound?"

Lenore paused, her head snapping in his direction. "Are you serious? Is that what's in those files restricted to law enforcement?" she asked, the question edged in sarcasm. She inhaled swiftly as he continued.

He nodded. "Allegedly, there's even an eyewitness statement for dessert."

Processing the comment, Lenore shook her head. Her eyes were wide, and it was something like shock that washed over her. She pressed a hand to her chest, her fingers clutched tightly as if she held on to a strand of pearls. She bit down against her bottom lip before she finally spoke. "You keep talking dirty to me, Detective Randolph, and I might actually have to be nice to you!"

King laughed as he cut his eyes in her direction.

The couple was headed back to Lenore's apartment, having decided to go there to work and filter through the box of files. King had offered to take them for a bite to eat before they started, but she had insisted they order in. She was anxious to get started and felt like they'd already wasted more than enough time.

"What tipped you off?" Lenore questioned. "How did you figure out this has been going on for years and they might all be connected?"

"Your father referred a woman named Janie Dunn to me. Her daughter had been killed back in the 1980s. The similarities are eerie, and she was the one who told me that her little girl hadn't been the only one."

"My father?" The news seemed to shift Lenore's mood. She suddenly went quiet, introspection washing over her face. She didn't say anything, and King realized the news had struck a nerve.

"What's wrong, Lenore?" he questioned, shifting his eyes from the road to her and back again.

"Nothing," she said, an icy edge to her tone.

"Oh, there's something wrong. Spill it."

The silence seemed to swell thick and full between them. He noted her furrowed brow and imagined she was struggling to understand her feelings and put them into words. He also imagined she had no interest in showing him an ounce of weakness or vulnerability. He circled the block around her apartment building, still waiting. When she finally spoke, there was something unexpected in her voice. Something that bordered on sadness, or disappointment. Something that actually pulled at his heartstrings.

Her voice had dropped an octave. "I was just wondering why my father didn't share that information with me."

King shrugged. "You're not a cop. I am."

"Please don't think that badge of yours gives you a leg up on anyone, and definitely not on me." The look she gave him was not quite as icy as her tone, but there was definitely a hint of chill in her eyes.

"You are so spoiled!"

Her eyes widened. "I am not!"

"Yes, you are! You're sitting there, all in your feelings, giving me attitude because your daddy told me something he didn't tell you. That's the epitome of spoiled!"

Lenore paused. She suddenly laughed. "So what if I am spoiled!"

"You're actually owning it?"

"And if you ever tell anyone I said so, I will hurt you, King Tobias Randolph!"

King grinned. "It must be serious. You used my full name and I don't remember giving it to you!"

"I'm dead serious and I always do my research. Please don't make me hurt you!"

He smiled. "I would never want to push you there. Because I like you, Lenore *Justine* Martin."

She shook her head, fighting a smirk that wanted to pull into a full grin. "Just park the damn car, please, so we can get some work done!"

Lenore had questions. Starting with why her father hadn't thought to share the tidbit of information he'd given King and ending with why her father hadn't thought to tell her what he knew. They had joked about her being spoiled, but truth be told, that wasn't far from the truth. Growing up, she'd been abundantly blessed. Spoiled didn't begin to describe her childhood. She and her sisters had wanted for nothing, their needs and wants met tenfold. She was very much her father's daughter. A die-hard daddy's girl, Lenore would never have imagined her father excluding her from something so important. Then she wondered if her mother knew. All that wondering had her already sensitive feelings on overload.

In the other room, glasses rattled as King loaded dishes into her dishwasher. They'd enjoyed a good meal and had begun to lay out the dust-covered files stored in the box taken from his trunk. Her dining room table would serve as office central for the duo as they tried to piece together the mystery of a killer who'd apparently been at it for longer than either had imagined. From what they were able to surmise from the statement Janie Dunn had given King, and the earliest dates on the files in the box, the killer had rained terror on the community for at least five decades, if not more. Fifty-plus years of bodies and no one had been able to catch him. Or her, Lenore thought. She refused to let any more time pass without justice being served.

She stared at her reflection in the mirror. She had needed a quick shower to rinse away the stench of death that had clung to her skin. She had slathered a thick layer of coconut oil against the warmth of her complexion and spritzed just a hint of her favorite perfume. She hadn't bothered to give King a heads-up before disappearing, but she heard him humming and plates were rattling. From the sounds coming from the living space, he had managed to entertain himself while she'd been gone. She pulled open a drawer in the oversized chest and pulled out a change of clothes. Once she was dressed, her thick curls pulled into a high bun atop her head, she felt ready to tackle whatever lay ahead of them. At least, that was what she wanted to believe.

King had felt a little off when Lenore had disappeared into her bedroom, staying longer than he'd anticipated. And when he heard the shower running, he'd been reluctant to stay. That moment passed, because he knew what they had planned was more important than him being uncomfortable about Lenore Martin being naked in the next room, beads of warm water glistening against her skin. He tossed back the last gulp of red wine in his wineglass and added it to the dishes he'd arranged in her dishwasher.

Minutes after they arrived, their evening meal had been delivered to her front door. The little boy carrying the insulated containers had surprised him, and it had been clear from the expression on the kid's face that he, too, had been surprised to see King. His name was Terrance, and his large dark eyes and thick Creole accent reminded King of everything he loved about Louisiana.

Terrance had chattered nonstop, asking questions about King and why he was there. He directed those questions toward Lenore, only giving King a skeptical side-eye. Lenore had laughed, telling him to mind his business. The boy had teasingly reminded the beautiful woman that she was his girl and had promised to wait for him to turn twenty-eight.

Responding that she wouldn't forget and that when he was twenty-eight, she'd be too old and he wouldn't want her anymore did little to sway his enthusiasm. She had tousled the jet-black curls atop his head and had pressed a kiss to his cheek. He'd blushed profusely, winking an eye toward King as if to say the man was hardly competition for him.

King still didn't know where the food had come from other than Terrance's grandmother had cooked it especially for Lenore. He only knew that it was the best meal he'd had in ages. They'd eaten at her kitchen counter, sitting side by side atop two high-back wicker chairs. She had plated jambalaya, a masterpiece of rice, crawfish, andouille sausages, chicken, bell peppers, sweet tomatoes and celery. Alone, it would have been sufficient, but the cook had added oven-warm cheddar biscuits and a creamy cucumber salad. He'd eaten like he was starved, helping himself to a second serving of that jambalaya.

He liked that they hadn't talked business, taking time to simply relax as they enjoyed each other's company. There was still much he wanted to discover about Lenore Martin, the good and the bad. What he did know intrigued him in one breath and gave him pause in the next. She was an anomaly compared to other women that had been in his life—cantankerous, moody, argumentative and difficult for no obvious reason. She was also funny, devilish, playful and compassionate. He couldn't begin to explain it if he had to, but everything about her brought him a level of joy he had never known before.

King moved from her kitchen to her living room, easing over to stare out the wall of windows. The sun had set hours earlier, and the dark sky was peppered with brilliant clusters of flickering stars. The view was exceptional.

Time passed as he stood lost in thought. A noise from the other room suddenly interrupted his reverie. He wasn't sure how long he'd been standing there, and he was surprised at the time when he stole a quick glance toward his wristwatch. Moving from where he'd planted his feet, he stared down the length of hallway. The door to Lenore's bedroom was cracked just enough that he could see her reflection as she stood before an oversized mirror above a dresser. She wore a black lace bra and matching panties, and she was simply stunning.

King felt a ripple of heat course through his groin, igniting a low flame between his legs. He gasped loudly, sucking in a mouthful of air and filling his lungs with it. Every muscle in his body pulled taut, his reaction to the sight of her visceral. His southern quadrant lengthened with an intensity that surprised him, all control seemingly lost. Despite his best efforts, he could not tear his eyes away, and he knew he should not have been staring. When Lenore finally slipped a cotton T-shirt over her head, King blinked, taking two steps back and spinning around on his heels. He hurried back into the dining room and dropped down onto one of the upholstered chairs. His breathing was labored, and he was feeling completely out of sorts.

Moments later, Lenore entered the room, her nonchalant expression putting him slightly at ease that he hadn't been caught peeping. The exhale of air that blew past his lips was a full-on sigh of relief.

"I'm sorry that took so long," Lenore said, a hint of contrition shimmering in her eyes. She paused, eyeing him intently. "Is everything okay? You look flushed."

King nodded his head. Words caught in his chest as he tried to gather himself. He cleared his throat before he spoke. "I'm good," he muttered.

Lenore didn't look convinced, still staring at him.

"Really," he said. "I appreciated the break. How are *you* doing?"

Lenore nodded. "Ready to get to work." She pointed toward a closed door. "If you'll look in my office, there's a large corkboard resting behind the console. We can hang it here on the wall and use it to organize ourselves. I need to see everything laid out."

She reached for the large painting that decorated the space. It was an abstract portrait of a young girl exploding out of a cloud of color. There was an ethereal quality about it that made him want to sit and stare for a moment to explore the little details within the composition. Lenore seemed to read his mind.

"It's by an Israeli painter named Yossi Kotler. It was a gift from my mother after a trip to Tel Aviv."

"Interesting," he murmured, still staring at the piece.

She smiled. "I'll go put on a pot of coffee while you go grab that corkboard." She turned and headed toward the kitchen.

King watched her, trying not to focus on the sway of her hips as she exited the room. He suddenly thought that him staying would prove to be a mistake, and he couldn't afford to get things wrong with this investigation. Or with the beautiful woman who had suddenly become a distraction that he surely didn't need.

Lenore wasn't sure how she felt about King being in her home. The shower had helped, allowing a blast of cold water to cool the rise in her body temperature. The nearness of him had her lost in a wealth of emotion that was unexpected and inconvenient. She needed him to take her seriously, and planting a kiss on him in the elevator truly hadn't helped her cause. Now to have him so close that she could take two steps and press her body against his...*damn*!

Lenore cursed and shook the provocative thoughts from her head. She needed to stay focused, and in that moment, all she could think was King being in her personal space was opening the doors to something decadent, and dangerous.

As the Keurig coffee maker spewed water through

a large coffee pod, filling the carafe with a rich, dark roast, she took a deep breath and called his name.

"Do you like bread pudding? I have a slice or two left if you're interested. And rum sauce to go with it."

King sauntered into the kitchen, leaning against her counter. "I'd love some bread pudding! Thank you." He took a seat on one of the stools and watched as she prepared two plates of dessert, sliding one in front of him.

"Cream and sugar?" she asked, gesturing with the coffee carafe as she poured the beverage into a mug.

"No, thank you. I drink my coffee black."

When she was finally seated beside him, sipping on her own cup of coffee to wash down the sweet bread pudding, King cleared his throat to speak.

"There's something important we need to talk about."

"You said that earlier. Is it about the case?"

"Yes. And no." King shrugged, his eyes skating from side to side as he seemed to be choosing his words carefully. "I've got some concerns. I don't think Captain Romero is interested in me solving this case, and he's definitely not interested in you being anywhere near it." He relayed the conversation he'd had with the man, sharing his thoughts about his superior wanting him to fail.

Lenore nodded her head slowly as she took another sip of coffee. "I had my own run-in with Juan this evening. He kept asking if we were working together."

"After he told me to reach out to work with you. Now, apparently, that's a problem."

"It was always a problem. Every police department nationwide is protective when it comes to sharing their cases with other parties. Not only are there the legalities surrounding them doing so, but cops are greedy bastards! They don't like to share if it means someone else might get credit."

"We're not all that bad."

"Yes, you are!" She rolled her eyes skyward.

"Why do you think Romero ordered me to reach out to you?"

"To see what I knew. My guess is, he thought I had information you didn't have. And he didn't want the agency closing this case and embarrassing the police department."

"So, how do we make this work, Lenore? Because I'm not going to pretend that I can solve this case alone, and they're already dismissing it. They'll be tossing the file in a cold case box before the week is out."

"That's why all those other cases weren't solved. No one cared enough to keep fighting for the victims. I can't tell you what to do, but I can tell you I have every intention of getting justice for Michael-Lynn and Tralisa and all the other kids this monster has murdered."

"Then I hope you'll want to continue to work with me. I can't ignore the fact that you and your family have access to resources the police department can't even begin to imagine. Why wouldn't I want your help? I also know you want to solve this as much as I do, and we'll get far more done together than we will separately."

"I agree," Lenore said, her eyes darting quickly across his face.

He continued. "Obviously, we'll need to keep it between the two of us, but I'm game to get this done, if you are."

"Why would that be obvious?" she said, shifting her

weight against the seat as she crossed her arms over her chest. She didn't look amused as she stared at him.

"It's not obvious?" Consternation seeped from his eyes as he suddenly wondered if he'd gotten things all wrong. Maybe he had misread the situation with Romero and with Lenore.

"What?" Her hand went to one hip as the other rested on the counter.

"That your ex-boyfriend is trying to get to you through me."

Lenore laughed. "My ex is being a complete and total ass, because that's who he is. This has nothing to do with me. It's you he doesn't like."

"Maybe so, but he liked me until I started asking questions about *you*." King fought the smirk that wanted to pull across his face.

"I wonder why?" Lenore said, her own smile like a sweet breeze through the room.

"He probably knew that once you met me, you'd be totally smitten."

She laughed again, the wealth of it gut-deep. "Aren't you full of yourself, King Randolph."

He laughed with her. "So, we're good with each other, Ms. Martin? Because it's my ass and my job if they find out I shared classified information with you."

She nodded again. "We're better than good, Detective Randolph. Now let's get to work," Lenore said, lifting herself from the stool. She grabbed her coffee cup and headed toward the dining room.

Hours later, the couple had read through some fifty-plus cold cases, a number of the file folders faded from boys disappearing from their homes and later found murdered and mutilated. All the kids had gone to local high schools in the city. They'd ranged in age from fourteen to nineteen, a few having graduated a year or so before their disappearance. Some had played sports. Others had preferred the sciences or literature. One or two had just been biding time until they could leave the city for bigger and better, prophesizing the grass had to be greener anywhere else. There was no file in the year Hurricane Katrina had decimated the city, and not a single death that fit the profile for almost five years after. When they started up again, it had been business as usual, and no one in the New Orleans police department had been able to make sense of what little they did know. There were more similarities between the cases than not and still nothing to point them toward their killer.

What was consistent with each case was the manner in which the bodies had been disposed of. All left in or near the swamps. For most of the bodies, time and nature had left them with little evidence to process. The killings had always happened during the school year and then nothing over the summer holiday. Every few years, five to six high school students had gone missing, their disappearances thought to be random. Notations on a few of the cases had labeled them possible accidents, and over half had been labeled runaways. Only the notes on a single case had suggested a connection between that death and two previous killings. Just one.

Lenore sighed softly. "I was hoping something would

ing for."

"That would have been too easy," King answered.

"How long can we keep these files?" Lenore questioned.

"As long as it takes. Why?"

Lenore reached for her cell phone and began to text a message. She paused, waiting for a response, and when it came, she sighed again.

"I have someone who can go through these for us." Lenore said. "Cash Davies. She's our tech guru. If there's anything these cases have in common, she'll find it. Full disclosure, though, she may hack the police department's computer system."

"That's illegal, Lenore. There's no way I'd be able to sanction that."

Lenore shrugged her narrow shoulders. "No one asked you to give permission for something you'll know absolutely nothing about. I think they call that plausible deniability."

"But you just told me!" King tossed up his hands, chuckling lightly.

"If I need to lie about our working together on this case, you can lie about what that may take. It's a mutual washing of backs."

King paused. "I'm going to hell. Or worse, jail!" he muttered.

Lenore laughed. She rose from her seat at the mahogany table. "Coffee?"

"Do you have anything stronger?"

"Aren't you worried about getting in trouble with the department?"

"Officially, I'm off duty. And at the moment, I could use a drink."

Lenore smiled. "Coffee with a little extra something coming right up!"

age. It was too many years of young girls and a few

Deborah Fletcher Mello

163

Chapter 12

King woke with a jump, startled out of his sleep by the low ring of a cell phone. For a brief few moments, he had no idea where he was, and then he remembered. He lifted his head slightly to look around the room. He was lying sprawled across Lenore's sofa. She was lying beside him, her body curled tightly against his. They were both fully clothed, and the round of her buttocks fit snugly against his pelvis. He suddenly realized his hand was lost beneath the T-shirt she wore, and he snatched the appendage away as if he'd been burned. The abrupt movement pulled Lenore from her own sweet dream.

"You okay?" she asked as she slowly sat upright, rubbing at her eyes with her fists. She seemed oblivious to the fact that he was just molesting her as they slept soundly beside each other.

King nodded. "What did you put in that coffee?" he asked.

A full smile lifted, every muscle in her face like a beam of light pointed in his direction. She giggled. "It was just bourbon. I told you that."

His eyes darted back and forth as he tried to recall everything that had happened after he'd asked for something strong. He remembered the laughter and the easy conversation. After a few hours of work, they'd tabled the research and had simply enjoyed each other's company. By the third cup of bourbon with just a shot of coffee, he realized he was too intoxicated to drive, and she had told him to stay. Everything after that was a total blur, although memories of her skin beneath his palm as his hands had trailed the lines of her torso were slowly coming back to him.

Lenore rolled her body from his and stood up. She tossed him a look over her shoulder as she headed toward her bedroom. "You're welcome to take a shower if you want," she said. "The guest room is that way." She pointed toward the other hallway. "You'll find everything you need in the linen closet in the bathroom."

He nodded. "I appreciate that. I need to grab my gym bag out of my trunk. I think I have a change of clean clothes inside."

She pointed toward the front door and the oversized duffel bag that rested on the floor. "You grabbed it last night," she said as she tossed him a wink of her eye.

King shook his head. "Is there anything else I need to know about last night before I completely embarrass myself?"

Lenore laughed. "I don't remember," she said as she

turned back around, sauntering easily into the other room and closing the door behind her.

Lenore couldn't stop grinning, the smile across her face pulled so tight that she was amazed her face didn't break. She hated to think that her time with King would soon be coming to an end. She knew he couldn't stay forever. But the night they'd shared had been one of the best she'd ever had with a man that hadn't ended with the two of them in her bed.

There'd been little they hadn't talked about. She'd shared things with King she'd never shared with anyone else. Opening up so freely had been a breath of fresh air that she hadn't anticipated. He listened, shared his own stories and made her laugh. Not polite giggles to seem as if she were listening, but soul-stirring laughter that brewed deep in her midsection before exploding like fireworks on the Fourth of July. Laughter that pulled tears from her eyes as her stomach cramped with glee. Laughter that cemented a friendship born from trust, and openness.

They'd both had too much to drink, although it hadn't seemed like it at the time. The bourbon mash she'd spiked the coffee with had been handmade by the friend of a friend of her father's. The concoction, made from an age-old recipe, was considered a precious commodity, and only a few were allowed a bottle or two during the year. Had it been legal, it would have been one of the silkiest, richest formulas on the market.

The best moments had been before they'd overindulged, when they had been super relaxed and lost in the moment. He'd teased and she'd made jokes, and they had curled up on her sofa side by side, the warmth of their two bodies blending sweetly together. He never once asked anything about her father, and had been focused on her hopes and dreams, listening intently as she shared her truths about her life.

Sleep had hit her first, her eyelids so heavy that it took every ounce of effort to keep her eyes open. She'd stretched her body along the length of the sofa, snuggling against him. She'd wiggled her buttocks against his pelvis, and he'd laughed, calling her a tease. He'd pressed a gentle kiss against the back of her neck, nuzzling his face into her hair. As she'd allowed herself to savor the sensation of his touch, slumber pulled her into the sweetest dreams.

She'd opened her eyes one last time, listening as King's breath slowed, deep exhalations of warm breath blowing against her skin. An arm eased around her waist, drawing her closer against him. His fingers had tapped gently against her abdomen, and sometime in the middle of the night she felt his hands flitter over her breasts, cupping one and then the other as he'd snored softly.

As she stood in reflection, the memories fueling the smile across her face, her cell phone rang. Shaking the reverie from her head, she pulled the device into her hand. She read the caller ID before she answered the call.

"Hey, Cash! Where are you? Did you get my message?"

"Downstairs. And I did get *all* your messages. What's going on?"

"I need you to work here today. We're going to need your skills to help us solve these murders."

"Who's we?"

"I have company, so please don't embarrass me!"

"Company? What kind of company?"

"The kind where I expect you to be on your best behavior."

"I have questions! Who is he, and was he good?"

"Really, Cash?" Lenore shook her head as if her friend could see her.

Cash laughed. "I'm going to tell!" she chimed, her singsong tone ringing over the line.

"Get focused!" King hissed to himself. His teeth were clenched, and every muscle was taut. He stood beneath a spray of hot water, allowing the flow of moisture to rain down over his head. It felt good, and the tension through his body was beginning to ease.

Despite the clarity that was pushing out the earlier clouds in his head, there were still moments from the previous night that were foreign to him. It almost felt like an out-of-body experience as he thought back to his time with Lenore and what they had shared.

Lenore had been pure joy. She'd brought levity to their time together, and being able to simply laugh had been the best experience. Despite the magnitude of their situation, she wouldn't allow him to take himself, or her, too seriously. He hadn't known how much he had needed that relief until it was given.

Waking up beside her wasn't something he would have ever fathomed, and now he couldn't imagine himself not falling asleep beside her. Or holding her tightly against him as he slept. Seeing her beautiful smile when he opened his eyes in the morning would be a dream come true. And the fact he was even focused on those thoughts had him completely discombobulated.

He stepped from the shower and wrapped a plush white towel around himself. He needed to think. Needed to get thoughts of Lenore out of his head. More importantly, he needed to find this killer and close this case so he could put some distance between himself and the beautiful woman.

When King returned to the living room, Lenore and a woman he didn't know were reviewing the oversized corkboard he and she had started the night before. A stack of files lay between them. It was clear the two women were comfortable with each other, the camaraderie feeling familial. The other woman was tall and muscular, clearly comfortable in a gym. She donned a button-down khaki shirt, oversized matching khaki pants and leather brogue Dr. Martens. She wore her hair in a platinum-blond buzz cut that complemented her tawny complexion. She grinned as he moved into the space, giving her a slight wave of his hand.

"Hi, I'm King Randolph."

Lenore pointed at her friend. "Detective, this is Cash Davies. Cash, Detective King Randolph. Cash is our techie at the agency. She's family to us, and I trust her implicitly."

King nodded.

Cash looked him up and then down. "Ooh! He is cute!" she murmured, winking an eye in Lenore's direction.

Lenore looked from the file she was holding to him and back. "He's okay," she responded, amusement dancing across her face.

"I'd do him," Cash said with a deep laugh. "If I were interested in men, of course."

"You like men," Lenore said.

Cash shrugged. "True! I just like women more." She held out her hand in greeting. "It's a pleasure to meet you, your highness!"

King shook his head. "The pleasure's all mine, and you can just call me King. Or Detective."

Cash laughed, then shifted her attention back to Lenore. "My therapist says my inability to make an emotional connection with a man has much to do with my choice of life partners. That and their arrogance gives me a rash. But I would definitely do him. Did you do him?"

Lenore tossed King another quick glance. "Nope! I'm not sure if I like him."

"You like him! If you didn't like him, he would never have crossed the threshold of your royal abode. The fact he spent the night says you like him a lot!"

"I don't recall asking for your opinion, Cash."

King lifted his hand as if he were a grade school student afraid to get the teacher's attention. "Excuse me," he said. "I'm standing right here."

The two women exchanged a look and then burst out laughing.

Lenore was smiling as Cash and King chatted comfortably together. Cash was asking him questions, and she was awed by how easily King answered them. She'd moved from the dining room to the kitchen and returned minutes later with a carafe of hot coffee and three mugs. She poured a cup for King and passed it to him.

"There's nothing in this, is there?" King asked, sniffing at the hot brew.

Lenore laughed. "Do you want there to be something in there?"

He shook his head. "No. I've definitely had more than my fair share already, I think."

He looked at the board and the changes she'd made. He immediately saw a pattern that he hadn't seen the night before. "What's this?" he asked, his gaze roaming over the photos of the victims that had been grouped together.

"Cash has spent the last hour filtering out those things that didn't connect the students. It'll make it easier for us to figure out what does. Right now, we know they were all honor roll students at their respective schools. They were all socially active, participated in extracurricular activities and, with the exception of Tralisa and Michael Lynn, they all had a police record."

King bristled. "Police record?"

"Juvie stuff. Shoplifting, loitering, driving while unlicensed," Cash said. "Just stuff you overzealous cops needed to ticket and charge to get your numbers up. Most of them paid a fine or did community service to satisfy the state. And the majority of them eventually had their records expunged."

"So why not Michael-Lynn and Tralisa? Why are they the only two that don't fit the pattern?"

"Actually, both girls were picked up for underage drinking about three years ago," Cash said. "Because of COVID restrictions, they never made it to trial, and all charges were eventually dropped."

Lenore watched as the information settled over King like a wool blanket. His body tensed, and something she couldn't recognize crossed his face. She couldn't begin to fathom what he was thinking, but imagined he, too, wasn't taking that tidbit of info lightly.

"Before I forget," Cash said, typing swiftly, "I ran that background check on Maxine Carmichael."

"What'd you find?" Lenore asked.

"Where do I start?" Cash said, a hint of exasperation in her tone. She pointed at King. "You might want to sit down for this."

He was already sitting, and he looked from her to the cushioned seat his rear end had imprinted on, then back toward her.

Cash smiled and shrugged.

King's head swayed from side to side, his expression stoic. "My brain already hurts," he said. "What's one more thing to make my skull explode?" He chugged the last swig of his morning brew.

"She's been teaching here in New Orleans since receiving her teaching credentials after graduating college. She was an only child born to Peggy Carmichael and her husband, Richard Carmichael. Peggy was a stay-at-home mom. Richard Carmichael is a former police lieutenant who has a nasty record of misconduct. He was investigated multiple times for the use of excessive force, the misuse of public funds, assault on a minor, child abuse and a host of other really bad doings. But nothing stuck."

"Nothing?" King asked, incredulous.

Lenore shrugged. "Let me guess. He has friends in high places?"

"Either that or he was giving the police commissioner private lap dances!" Cash joked. She laughed, finding her own humor hilarious.

"What about her mother?" Lenore said as she took the empty seat beside King.

Cash continued. "Her mother died under mysterious circumstances when Maxine was nine. Allegedly, Peggy jumped from the Lake Pontchartrain Causeway in Metairie and drowned. Her body was never recovered. There was a witness who claimed she saw someone throw a woman's body off that bridge. The witness mysteriously disappeared a few weeks later. After that, Maxine was raised by her single father, and according to her records, at the age of twelve she spent one year in foster care when her father was being investigated for sexually assaulting her. He was cleared of all charges, and she was returned to the family home. From what I can tell, things went downhill from there."

Cash took a deep breath before she continued. "Multiple complaints were filed against Lieutenant Carmichael during his tenure with the police department, but most were labeled nonactionable."

Lenore tossed King a look. "What's nonactionable?"

"It's a polite way of saying the powers in charge didn't care because he was doing his job. They claimed insufficient evidence or some other bullshit to give him a pass."

Cash continued. "Maxine gave birth to twin boys her senior year in high school. Charles and Christopher Carmichael. She has never identified their father on any public record."

Lenore sat up straighter. "Twins?" She met King's eyes. "Didn't Charles say he was an only child?"

"He did say that."

Cash typed away again, her head bobbing to a beat in her own head. She paused to read something on the screen, and then she typed a second time. When she had found what she was looking for, she looked up. "The family moved from Labadieville to New Orleans shortly after the twins were born. Charles was registered in the local schools. Christopher was not, and I can't find a death certificate for him."

"Any other family members that might have taken custody of him?" King asked.

Cash shook her head. "No, sir, Detective Cutie. None that I've found, but I can keep looking. Once they moved to N'Orleans, little Christopher fell off the family tree."

King sat back in his seat. He fell into thought as he processed everything he'd just learned about the coach and her family. How that all connected to his murder case was still a mystery. If their family drama connected at all. He couldn't help but think that he might be chasing threads that would inevitably lead him nowhere. At least, he thought to himself, there was something that they could chase.

He lifted his eyes toward Lenore. "I have questions, and I think it's past time I went looking for answers." He stood up, then gestured toward her front door with a nod of his head.

Cash grinned, winking an eye at him. "See you later, Detective Hottie!"

He chuckled. "It's been my pleasure, Ms. Davies."

Lenore followed behind him as he led the way toward her foyer. "Where are you headed?"

"I need to run by the station, and then I want to have a conversation with the former lieutenant. I need to pay a visit to the Carmichael home."

"Let's catch up later this evening," Lenore said. "Right now, I have an appointment with the coroner."

"Something I need to know?"

Lenore shrugged. "He requested an audience. There's something he says I need to see."

"Keep me posted, please."

"I will. Let's plan on meeting back here later." Lenore pressed her manicured fingers to his chest as she took a step toward him. She tossed a quick look over her shoulder, then lowered her voice an octave. "Thank you. I'm glad you stayed. I had a good time last night."

King smiled. Aware that Cash was eyeing the two of them keenly, he responded with a wink of his eye, not saying anything aloud. He wrapped his arms around her torso and pulled her to him. Then he pressed a damp kiss against her forehead before he turned and exited out the door.

Chapter 13

Lenore's emotions were all over the place. On one hand, she was riding a monumental high after her time with King. On the other, her frustration level was strangling, making her reconsider whether she should be working his murder case.

After King had left, she'd sat down with Cash while she finished her morning coffee. Her bestie had teased her unmercifully about being enamored with King, threatening to tattle to her sisters. It had been a good time, but the more questions Cash had asked about her and King, the more Lenore began second-guessing her actions.

She hated to admit it, but there was something that had her feeling a tad guilty. Like she had trod into forbidden territory and eaten from the illicit fruit tree.

She'd crossed a boundary she had known full well didn't need exploring. Although she really hadn't done anything wrong…yet…the night on her couch with King, fully clothed, with a few easy caresses, a pinch, and a tickle or two had left her reeling.

Piecing together a whodunit puzzle always came with its own set of unique challenges. This case was more than either had anticipated, and they were going nowhere fast. Despite the information they'd uncovered with Cash's help, nothing they'd learned put them any closer to finding Michael-Lynn and Tralisa's killer.

She pulled her car into the parking space down at the city's morgue. Truth be told, she was in no mood to see the aftermath of someone's devastation, a life snuffed out maliciously. She'd had to view more than her fair share of dead bodies, and she wasn't in the mood to have her good day ruined. She should have canceled, she thought, despite knowing such hadn't been an option.

Dr. Mayhew greeted her at the lower-level elevator. "Good morning, Lenore," he said, giving her a nod of his head.

She smiled politely. "Dr. Mayhew."

"I'm sorry to bother you, but there was something I thought you needed to see. I would have pointed it out yesterday, but…well…" He shrugged, giving no real reason for withholding information when she'd been with King. He turned, guiding her back to one of the autopsy rooms. Both Michael-Lynn and Tralisa lay on tables positioned next to each other.

"You haven't released the bodies yet?" Lenore questioned, her mood shifting like an unexpected rainstorm.

"The funeral home will be here to pick them up this

afternoon. It's my understanding that your father made all the arrangements."

Lenore nodded. For the briefest moment, she stared at the two bodies. Both were covered by white sheets, index-card-size tags looped around their big toes. One's arm had fallen off the side of the table. Their once warm complexions were now an ashen white. Despite her best efforts, Lenore began to shake, her legs responding with a mind of their own. She shifted her weight from one hip to the other and took a deep breath to catch her balance.

"What did you find?" she asked, forcing her gaze back to Mayhew's face.

He moved to Tralisa's body first and lifted the left arm that hung awkwardly. He gently laid her hand in his palm and parted her fingers. "This," he said, as Lenore moved to his side. He pointed to the side of the girl's middle finger. On the proximal phalanx was a mark, and it took Lenore a minute to realize it was a tattoo. The minimalistic design appeared to be a simple cross above a small triangle. He tucked the arm back beneath the sheet and moved to where Michael-Lynn lay. Lenore followed, her brow rising as he pointed out the same tattoo also on the middle finger of her left hand.

Lenore felt like she'd suddenly been sucked into a vacuum. The room seemed to be closing in on her as Mayhew's voice echoed in the distance.

"They aren't the first two bodies to come in with that tattoo. In fact, I'd venture to say all the high school students had similar markings and in the same location on their bodies. Those that still had their hands, anyway. But everyone I checked did so I went back to previous cases just to be certain. I thought you would want to know."

His tone was devoid of emotion, sounding mechanical and hollow. It was an irritation, and Lenore wanted to push her way out of the room and run. Instead, she took another deep inhale of air. "Did you get photographs of them all?" she questioned.

He nodded, moving to a corner desk in the room. He reached for a manila folder and turned an about-face to pass it to her. "I made copies for you. And a set for your detective friend. I'd appreciate it, though, if you didn't mention my name when you give them to him. I'm taking a lot of risk here sharing this information with you first. But under the circumstances..." He hesitated, innuendo trailing in his silence.

"Don't worry," Lenore said. "And thank you. It's much appreciated."

Dr. Mayhew gave her a slight smile. "Give my regards to your mother, will you?" he said, an edge of hope vibrating in his voice.

Lenore gave him one last look. She didn't bother to respond as she spun toward the door and hurried from the room.

Rushing from the building to her car, Lenore battled with the lock on her cell phone. She dialed King's number as she slid into the driver's seat of the vehicle and started the engine. The call went instantly to his voice mail, and she left a brief message. "Hey, it's Lenore! I need you to call me. It's urgent."

The second number she dialed was the office of Sorority Row Detective Agency. Piper answered on the second ring. "Thank you for calling..." she started before Lenore interrupted her.

"Hey, Piper. It's Lenore. I need to speak with my mother." There was an air of urgency in her pitch.

"Hold on," Piper said.

Elevator music began playing in Lenore's ear. It was an instrumental rendition of something familiar, but she couldn't immediately identify the tune. She depressed the button to transfer the phone's audio to her car speakers as she pulled out of the lot and into traffic.

When her mother finally answered, she was more than halfway to her destination.

"What's wrong?" Claudia Martin said as she answered the call.

"I need you to meet me at Daddy's. I'm almost there now."

"What's going on, Lenore? You sound frantic."

Lenore suddenly hit the brakes, coming to an abrupt halt in the middle of the road. The driver in the car behind her blew his horn as he barely missed hitting her bumper. She took a deep breath as she eyed him in her rearview mirror, flipping her his middle finger as he cursed profusely. Shaking her head, she waved apologetically as she pulled her own car off the road into a parking lot.

Claudia called her name. "Lenore! What's going on? Are you okay?"

"I need you to meet me at Daddy's. I think these murders may somehow be associated with *Symmetry*," she said, spitting the last word out of her mouth as if it were poison.

There was an uncomfortable pause on the other end. Then the phone line went dead. Lenore closed her eyes, her entire body shaking with something that felt like fear. When she was able to calm herself enough to drive again, she pulled back onto the road, headed for her father's penthouse. She knew her mother would probably beat her there.

As children, the Martin girls had been sheltered and protected from the bad things in the world. Their parents had gone to great lengths to give them a perfect childhood. But that perfection had sometimes been fractured, the intrusion of other people's crap upsetting the balance Claudia and Josiah worked hard for.

Lenore had just celebrated her sixteenth birthday. Celeste had been fourteen. Alexis had turned thirteen the month prior, and their baby girl, Sophie, had barely been eight years old. They'd been running around on Decatur Street while their father finished up a meeting at Café Du Monde. No one gave any concern for them running around the building and jetting across the roadway to steal glimpses of the great Mississippi. They were the children of Josiah Martin, and there were protective eyes around them wherever they went. Lenore had also been in mama-bear mode since Claudia had declined the invitation to join them. Sophie had her full attention as she held the child's hand, pointing out the tourists and entertainment in the market square. She should have been paying more attention to Alexis and Celeste.

When the two girls had disappeared from her sight, she'd thought nothing of it. They often played impromptu games of hide-and-seek for Sophie's amusement. When she'd found them talking to the handsome stranger, she'd barely given that a second thought either. If he didn't know any better, he would soon, she'd mused. Bodyguards often jumped out and walked up on them when they were least expected. Men her father paid handsomely to keep them safe were always lurking around every corner. Intimidating figures who'd have you contemplating all your life choices or peeing in your pants.

This young man had been tall and slender with ocean-blue eyes and Elvis Presley's hairstyle in a cool shade of corn silk blond. His porcelain complexion made him seem angelic, but even then, there'd been something in the depths of his stare that Lenore had found hauntingly demonic. Alexis had been instantly enamored with his soft-spoken persona. Like she predicted, their conversation was cut short when a hulking brute of a man called them by name, saying their father wanted them back at the café.

Lenore pulled into a parking spot in front of her father's hotel. Thinking back, she couldn't even remember what they had been talking about, just that he'd focused all his attention on Alexis. Not her, or Celeste. Just Alexis. That had been their first encounter with the nightmare named Stefan "Symmetry" Guidry, and it had not been their last.

She undid her seat belt, still sitting in the car as she reflected back. Weeks after their initial meeting, Stefan Guidry entered a classroom at Academy of the Sacred Heart, the private Roman Catholic girls' school they attended. Imagine their surprise to discover he was the new math teacher, this his first assignment after graduating college.

He'd become a popular figure at Sacred Heart, building a cult following of sorts. Staff and students loved him. By the time anyone realized what was going on, it was too late, the harm already done. Guidry had made preying on children an art form, the destruction he left behind damaging multiple families.

During this time, Alexis had honed her own skills, lying and sneaking off to follow after the charismatic instructor. She'd taught her and Celeste a thing or two about shaking their parents' security team. Not even she had questioned Alexis's antics, the wealth of it feeling like normal teenage behavior, sometimes mischievous and most times not. Lenore had always battled blaming herself for not paying closer attention to her sister. Back then, though, she'd been more focused on the boys at Brother Martin High School.

Things came to a head the day Alexis disappeared, running away from home to be with Mr. Guidry. Her parents had been manic, Josiah calling in every favor that was ever owed to him to find her. Her sister had been missing for almost two months when out of the blue, Alexis had called home, begging her parents to come get her.

To this day, no one had ever spoken about everything that had happened to Alexis. Lenore and her sisters had been shielded from the details of their sibling's trauma, but it hadn't been hard to piece most of it together. The man who called himself Symmetry had eventually been arrested. His charges had run the gamut from child pornography and prostitution to sex trafficking. His victims had been easy to identify, each of them marked with the same tattoo Lenore had seen earlier on the bodies at the morgue. The same tattoo Alexis still wore on her middle finger. Symmetry had been out on bail when he suddenly disappeared, never heard from again. Until now, no one had dared to even say his name.

Alexis had gone through years of therapy before her beautiful smile had returned and her life seemed normal again. After she'd returned home, only Lenore and Celeste had been allowed to finish their education at the Catholic high school. Alexis and Sophie were home-schooled, and rarely, if ever, let out of their parents' sight for any length of time.

Those years had been hard. Lenore had always felt like it was the beginning of the end of her parents' marriage. Instead of drawing closer to each other, they'd drifted apart, her father seeking solace with other women. That the two were still friends was a miracle in and of itself. That they'd managed to hold them all up, together, getting their daughters to adulthood as un-scathed as possible, had been a blessing none of them took lightly.

Lenore lifted the folder Dr. Mayhew had given her from the passenger seat. She slowly sifted through the photographs inside. The multiple images of that damn tattoo were terrifying. She slammed the folder closed, tossing it back onto the seat. Lenore felt like she'd been kicked in the gut. She folded herself forward, leaning her head on the steering wheel. She couldn't begin to explain how their tragedy from the past was connected with what was happening now. And it broke her heart to think that her little sister would be made to relive that past all over again.

"Is he alive?" Alexis asked as she hurried off the elevator and into the penthouse apartment. "Is Symmetry alive?"

There wasn't a hello or any other greeting as Alexis Martin moved to Lenore's side. She tossed her purse onto a cushioned chair, then turned toward her father. "You said he was dead! Why isn't he dead?" Her voice came out in a high pitch, her anger palpable.

Josiah stood behind the bar. He held a bottle of bourbon in his hands, filling a shot glass. He passed that glass to Claudia, who tossed it back abruptly. Dropping the glass onto the bar top, the matriarch stood and moved to her daughter's side. She wrapped her arms tightly around Alexis's shoulders and held her close. Lenore watched as her sister melted into the embrace, deflating as if she were a balloon and the air had just been sucked out of her.

"He's supposed to be dead!" she muttered into their mother's shoulder.

"I assure you," Claudia said, "that man cannot hurt you. He will never again be able to cause you pain."

As King headed toward his office, Christian jumped from his seat, racing after him

"Good morning, Christian," King said.

"Enjoy it while you can," Detective Foret responded. "The captain is on a rampage, and he's been calling your name for the last hour."

King rolled his eyes and released a heavy exhale. "So, it's going to be that kind of day, is it?"

Christian lowered his voice. "Rumor has it that he's not happy about you and Lenore Martin. Not that he would say it out loud."

"I'm sure he wouldn't," King said.

"But he will make your life as miserable as he can."

"I don't doubt that either."

Forct chuckled. "So, what's going on? Anything good from those files?"

"More questions than answers, although it looks like the same killer from forty-plus years ago has struck again. Or we might have a copycat. I'm not sure yet."

"That's not good!" Foret exclaimed.

"No, it's not." King paused. "What do you know about a former police lieutenant named Richard Carmichael?"

"Haven't heard that name in a long time!"

"Do you know him?"

"Just by reputation. He ruled the police force before my time. Him being older and all." His expression was smug, his tone sarcastic.

King smiled. "Well, I knew you two didn't serve on the force at the same time. I was just hoping you might have worked with someone who worked with someone who worked with him."

"What do you need to know?"

"What kind of cop was he? What kind of cases did he work on? Just anything really."

"He was a dirty cop. He only worked on cases he wanted to work. The ones that didn't involve a lot of effort and he could manipulate the outcome. From all I heard, he also liked those cases that involved pretty women. I don't think many people liked him."

King nodded. "You interested in meeting him? I need to go ask his grandson some questions."

Foret grinned. "I thought you'd never ask, partner!"

The ride to the Carmichael home took no time at all. Christian chatted about everything from the blister on his toe to his thoughts about the candidates running in the midyear election. King found him entertaining and appreciated that if he had to be partnered with anyone, then Foret was his guy. He was open and genuine and content with his position in the squad.

The property on Allen Toussaint Boulevard sat on a neatly manicured quarter-acre lot. The house was a stunning Second-Empire-style two-story masterpiece with meticulous architectural details, gorgeous medallions and a second-floor balcony. Both men eyed it with raised brows, thinking the same thing. How did a teacher and her retired cop father afford the lavish home?

The grass was pristine, and great care had been given to the landscaping. King noted the one car sitting in the driveway, recognizing it from the football game. He half expected Charles to answer the door and was surprised when a young girl, no more than fourteen, pulled the entrance open.

King flashed his badge. "Good morning. I'm Detective Randolph, and this is Detective Foret." He gestured toward Christian, who nodded his head in greeting.

"Is Charles or Richard Carmichael available?"

The girl looked from one to the other. She was chewing on a large wad of gum and blew a pink bubble that nearly covered her entire face. When it popped against her chin, she slid her tongue out to recapture the sticky substance so that she could chew on it some more.

She turned her head slightly, tossing a quick glance over her shoulder. Then she screamed at the top of her lungs. "It's police! He says he needs to speak with you."

She turned her attention back toward King, her gaze sweeping from his head to his toes and back.

King smiled. "What's your name?"

The child eyed him dismissively. She didn't bother to answer.

"Shouldn't you be in school, young lady?" Foret asked.

The girl took a step back, then slammed the door closed in their faces. From where the two stood, they could hear her screaming a litany of profanity, her voice fading off in the distance.

Foret muttered under his breath. "Do you want to take the demon spawn down or do you want me to take her?"

King chuckled as he rang the doorbell a second time. This time Charles answered, opening the door ever so slightly.

"Detective! This is a surprise. What brings you here?"

"Good morning, Charles. I was hoping to speak with you and your grandfather."

"What's this about?"

"We just need to ask a few quick questions to help us clarify information we received. It won't take very long. May we come in?"

There was a moment of hesitation that King noted, Charles's reservations dancing across his face. He took a deep inhale of air.

"My mother isn't here," he said. "She's at the school."

"We're not here to see your mother," King reiterated. "We'd like to ask you some questions and possibly speak with your grandfather."

Pausing a second time, Charles looked decidedly

nervous. Then, just like that, he opened the door fully
and waved them inside.

Christian entered first, King following on his heels.
As he stepped over the threshold, his phone chimed, a
message ringing for his attention. He took a quick look
at the screen, noting Lenore's name and number. Taking a quick glance at his watch, he made a mental note
to call her as soon as he was finished with the Carmichael family.

Chapter 14

The interior of the Carmichael house didn't meet the expectations of the home's outside. The rooms were a hodgepodge of colors. Olive green in the hallway, red in the dining room, sapphire blue in the family area and a strange salmon color in the kitchen. Each room was piled high with boxes. Discarded clothing rested on every surface. Paper and trash littered the floor, and the air was rank, something sour scenting the air.

Richard Carmichael sat in a recliner in the family room. He was focused on an episode of *Family Feud*, shouting answers as he played along with someone else's family. The little girl from earlier was nowhere to be seen, but music played loudly from the floor above them. The heavy bass of someone's rap song swept harshly down the stairwell.

"Is today a holiday for students?" Christian asked.

Charles raised his brow, looking confused.

Christian pointed an index finger skyward. "The kid. Did she have a day off today?"

Charles's confusion vanished, understanding washing over him. "That's Linda-Gail. She lives next door. She had a fever and sore throat this morning, and her mother didn't have anyone to watch her. Personally, I think she just wanted to skip school, but my mother volunteered us to keep an eye on her until her grandmother comes to pick her up." He looked at the clock on the wall. "Hopefully, that's in the next hour. She's a pain in the ass. We would never have gotten away with being so rude."

"You and your twin brother?" King asked, studying him intently.

Charles visibly bristled. It was a moment before he answered, seeming to choose his words carefully. "I wasn't raised with my brother. I don't know what he got away with. Like I said, I was raised as an only child. If you need to know anything about him, you'll have to ask my mother."

Richard suddenly shouted from his chair. "That kid has problems. That mother of his is his biggest issue. He was better off in that home she found for him. We should have just kept the good one!"

"The good one?" Christian said, taking it all in.

"The one that didn't cry like a girl all the time. That brother of his never did anything but cry. He was a pain. I gave his mother a choice. Get rid of him or I was going to drown it!" Richard laughed, like the thought of harming his infant grandson amused him.

King focused on the old man's words, not quite sure which brother he was referring to. The man's explanation felt disjointed, flooded with confusion, like he, too, wasn't certain about the topic of conversation.

Charles gulped air like a guppy out of water. His cheeks were flushed a deep shade of red, embarrassment like a wool blanket wrapped around his shoulders. He opened and closed his mouth as though he wanted to chastise the old man but thought better of it. King sensed that drawing attention to the bad behavior would only shift the former police lieutenant into another gear. Finding the man's behavior deeply disturbing, he too didn't bother to respond.

"Forgive my grandfather," Charles said, his voice dropping. "It's the dementia. He has good days, and he has bad days." He sighed, hoping that was enough to excuse the behavior.

The old man grunted. He rolled his eyes skyward but turned his attention back to the television. Steve Harvey was batting his eyelashes at one of his contestants, the game show host eliciting a laugh out of the old man.

King nodded. "Do you know where we might find your twin brother?"

Charles shrugged. "No," he said, clearly not offering any information to make things easier.

"Does your mother keep up with his whereabouts?" King questioned.

"I don't know. You'll have to ask her."

"Where were you yesterday morning, Charles? I don't know that we got an answer the last time we saw you."

"I don't recall you asking," Charles said, snark tinting each word.

"Well, I'm asking now," King responded.

Charles blew a heavy sigh. "Class. I had a quantum physics exam. I was nowhere near my mother's school until I came to pick her up to take her to lunch. Nor was I anywhere near where they found that little girl's body. You can check."

"Oh, we will," Christian chimed in, his tone a little too eager.

"That one almost got away," Richard muttered under his breath. "She almost got away, damn it!" He suddenly jumped from his seat and rushed toward the television. He yelled, "You're letting the bitch get away!"

"Who's getting away, Lieutenant Carmichael?" King asked.

The old man spun around on his heels, his gaze narrowing as he met the look King was giving him. "What?" he snapped.

"You said she was getting away, Lieutenant. Who's getting away?"

Richard stared at him. King felt like he was trying to remember who he was and then it clicked, a slow grin pulling across his face. "You young cops think you're so good. But you'll never be as good as me. I've had more years of experience than you've been alive. You can't trip me up! Plenty have tried, and no one could catch me." He hawked up a clot of phlegm and spat it to the floor as if to punctuate his point.

King gave his partner a side-eye. He wanted to ask the patriarch about his time on the police force, but something told him he wouldn't get any answers that would make an ounce of sense. Today was not one of the old guy's good days. He glanced back toward Charles and extended his hand. "I appreciate your time."

"Glad to cooperate however we need to, Detective. Stop by anytime."

Upstairs, the little girl named Linda-Gail squealed with glee, sounding every bit her age. But as King and Christian made their exit, Richard Carmichael screamed at the television again, and King could have sworn he heard another voice also coming from upstairs.

"My aunt Trudy had dementia," Christian said.

The two men were headed back to the station, still reeling from their encounter with the former police lieutenant and his grandson.

"But she was always sweet. I don't remember her ever getting angry at any of us. The worst she ever did was try to kiss her daughter's boyfriend. You know, they sometimes get frisky," he said.

"I did not know that," King answered, his attention elsewhere.

"Yep! They can get pretty frisky. That's why they don't let them socialize too close in those nursing homes."

King chuckled, amusement allowing him to relax if just for a quick minute.

"And who was the old guy talking about?" Christian questioned. "He had me confused!"

King nodded his head. "Me, too!"

"I don't think he's our guy. But that younger one is a little too squirrely for me. He makes me nervous."

"When we get back to the station," King concluded, "I'm going to need you to double-check his alibi. Maybe head over to the school and snoop around. See what his teachers and friends have to say about him. And see what you can find out about his twin brother." King didn't bother to mention that Cash Davies had already claimed the twin named Christopher had dropped off the Carmichael family tree, unable to be found. He couldn't help but wonder if maybe Richard had done more than threaten to harm the child. He sighed.

"Will do. And I want to meet the mother who thinks it's okay to leave her preteen daughter with that lot. That child should not be there!"

King smiled. "Something tells me we should be more worried about what she might do to the two of them. I got the impression they have met their match in that little girl."

Christian's head waved slowly from side to side. "Like I said, demon spawn!"

Their mother had flipped the switch from mommy dearest to boss bitch without blinking an eye. After calming Alexis and reassuring her everything was fine, she ordered her daughter back to the office and an assignment that would keep her sufficiently distracted. Lenore was less accommodating as she glared in Claudia's direction.

"How can you be so certain about Symmetry? Someone's out here tattooing young girls the same way Alexis was tattooed. The difference is these little girls are dying. No one knows what happened to him. He could very well be back."

"He's not," Claudia said firmly. "He is never coming back."

"But you don't know that…"

"Yes!" her mother snapped. "I do! I know beyond any doubt that Stefan Guidry will never again be a problem for anyone."

"But how…" Lenore persisted.

Her mother stomped across the room, coming to an abrupt stop in front of her. Her tone was rift with emotion, the words coming like a sledgehammer against concrete. "Because I pulled the trigger that ended his pathetic life!" Claudia spat, her jaw tightening. The lines in her face hardened, and daggers of ice shot from her eyes.

Lenore couldn't remember ever seeing her mother so angry. Her brow lifted, a hint of fear washing over her face.

The matriarch suddenly doubled over, her palms pressed against her pants legs. She gasped, sucking in air as if oxygen was in short supply. When she stood up, she swiped her eyes with the backs of her hands before composing herself. When she next looked at Lenore, her expression was blank.

Lenore's father had moved from the bar and now stood in the doorway. He eyed the two of them, looking from his daughter to her mother and back. He shook his head as he read the room, unhappy with the story unfolding. He moved slowly to his ex-wife's side. He carried a fresh bottle of Woodford Reserve and poured another shot of bourbon into her glass, then poured one for himself before resting the glass container on the table. He trailed a large hand across Claudia's back until she pulled herself from his touch. She moved back to the sofa and took a seat.

Lenore tried to hide the shock she knew painted her expression. Her father's gaze was disapproving. Her mother stared toward the floor, refusing to look at her. The air in the room was suddenly stifling, and something heavy cramped her stomach. For a brief moment, Lenore thought she might vomit, but it passed, leaving her feeling empty. She moved to the sofa and sat down beside her mother. Reaching for the matriarch's hand, she pressed the older woman's fingers between her two palms.

"I'm sorry," she said softly. "I didn't mean..."

"Yes, you did," Claudia said, cutting off her comment. She drew the length of her manicured fingers down the side of her daughter's face. "You have never done anything you didn't mean to do, Lenore Justine Martin. It's one of your best attributes. You set a goal, and you become as determined as a pit bull with a bone to reach it. Your mind is always evaluating best-case scenarios, and you rarely ask a question you don't already have the answer to. I'm your mother, and I know you better than you know yourself." Claudia pushed her daughter's hands back to her own lap.

"I just needed it to make sense," Lenore said.

"You needed your mother to say it out loud. If you say it needs to make sense, you also need to be honest about what that means to you," Josiah quipped.

Lenore tossed her father a look. She threw up her hands as if she'd been caught with them deep in the cookie jar. "Fine. It's what I suspected, but I was never certain. In all honesty, I actually thought you did it."

Claudia shook her head. "Of all you girls, Lenore, you are probably more aware of your father's shortcomings than your sisters. And because of that, you are also most aware of the rules we follow."

Josiah nodded. "We don't talk about what I do or don't do. You do as you're asked for your own safety and the safety of this family. And I don't do anything that puts our family in direct harm."

"And we never allow your father's business to cross over into mine," Claudia interjected. Her tone was staid, the words feeling sharply edged. She cut the air with each enunciation as she continued. "Together, our business, first and foremost, is to protect you and your sisters. Even if that means protecting you from yourselves. It also means ensuring that anyone who causes any of you harm never gets the opportunity to do so again. Your father and I will wage war to protect you and your sisters. After everything that monster put Alexis through, he's lucky that me pulling that trigger is all I did."

"What happened to him?" Lenore asked, looking from one parent to the other. "They've never found his body."

"That's not something you need to know," Josiah said matter-of-factly. "Now you're treading into my business. Because after you girls, it's my business to protect your mother. Now, we never had this conversation, and you are never to speak of it again. Not to anyone. Not to your sisters, and not to your cop boyfriend. Is that understood, Lenore?"

Her father's voice was a loud whisper, but it felt like it was booming, vibrating straight through Lenore's heart.

He repeated himself. "Is it understood?"

She nodded, suddenly feeling like she was twelve years old again. "Yes, sir."

Josiah continued. "I've made some calls. I asked around about those tattoos. I put the word out that I'm looking for whoever is responsible. If there's a copycat out there, we will find them."

Claudia stood, straightening her skirt and blazer. "I need to get back to the office." As she passed by Josiah, she pressed her palm to his chest. The two stood staring at each other, the silent conversation something only they understood. He nodded his head as he leaned to kiss her cheek.

The matriarch came to a standstill as she reached Lenore's side. She wrapped her arms around her daughter's torso and hugged her tightly. "One day, hopefully," she whispered into Lenore's ear, "you will have a child of your own. What I did might not make sense now, but it will when you're responsible for your own little person."

Lenore hugged her mother back and kissed her cheek. "I get it. You don't have to explain. He hurt Alexis. That tells me everything I need to know."

Lenore stared after the matriarch, watching until the elevator doors closed behind her. She stood in reflection, so lost in thought that she didn't hear her father calling her name. The third time Josiah uttered it, his voice was raised. He waved a hand for her attention.

"Where'd you go? You drifted off on me," he said.

Lenore shook her head, no words to explain everything spinning through her thoughts. Finally she asked,

"Is this how you imagined our lives when you and mom first got together?"

Josiah paused to reflect on her question. "No," he eventually responded. "Back then I couldn't fathom it being this damn good!"

Chapter 15

As teens, Lenore and her sisters had often debated whether their parents were good people. Heated conversations where they argued the pros and cons of their father's illegal dealings against their mother's philanthropic ventures. They had always known the boys in blue with big shiny badges would have gladly carted Josiah off to jail before tossing away the key. Just like they knew their socialite mother was highly trusted and respected in the community. Where sometimes one outweighed the other, what often balanced the disagreements and their perspectives about each parent was the love between them. And the love shown to each of their daughters. Not one of the Martin girls could argue about them being loved.

The affection their parents had for them was irrefutable, so much so that there had been moments when they'd felt smothered by it all. Love that had weighed them down as they had struck out on their own, determined to conquer the world. That love had overshadowed everything else.

Lenore had always suspected her parents of being involved in the disappearance of Symmetry. She'd known her father had often made bad men disappear. It was something that had been understood, even if never spoken about aloud. After Alexis had come home, things had seemed even more strained. They hadn't immediately returned to their happy, joyous selves. Alexis had been withdrawn, and paranoid, always biting her nails and looking over her shoulder for things that weren't there. But mostly she'd been sad, and depressed.

Her parents had always been whispering, huddled together to the exclusion of everything and everyone else. Security drove them to school, stayed through their classes and escorted them home. Then Symmetry failed to show up for court, unable to be found, and her parents had acted as if the weight of the world had been lifted from their shoulders.

Lenore suddenly wondered about the other families. Had they been glad to see him disappear, too? Did they wonder what had happened to him, or did her father's assurances that it would be handled bring them comfort? And what about the new cases? Would those mothers want to see the killer destroyed when he was found? Would any one of their fathers be willing and ready to pull the trigger?

Would she have done what her mother had done? Could she be that strong if she were in that position?

If someone harmed a child of hers, would she be ready to wage war against them? Without a doubt, Lenore suddenly thought to herself. Without a single, solitary doubt. She would wage war and drop bombs until she destroyed everything in their wake.

King had heard something in Lenore's voice that gave him pause. When he'd finally been able to return her call, she had only asked him to meet her at her apartment, unwilling to share what was wrong over the phone line. His anxiety rose slightly as he considered what could possibly have gone wrong.

He had a headache, and he hated admitting it, but once again his caseload felt as if it were going nowhere fast. They had bodies and few clues to point them in the right direction. It felt slightly disingenuous to be paid for detective work and not detect anything.

He thought back to his visit to the Carmichael home. Something in his gut told him there was more there with the family than just the dysfunction that played out in public. Something they didn't want anyone to know about. Something more than an old man obsessed with the dynamics of his past. Or a twin son who no one talked about.

Coach Carmichael was next on his list to speak with. A mother would know about her child, he mused. Or at least, he hoped. But what was their secret? That Christopher Carmichael was killing students to satisfy some perversion, and the family was protecting him by keeping it secret? And why hadn't the two boys grown up together? Was there a father somewhere who'd been responsible for one and not the other? He had questions. Now he needed some serious answers.

Minutes later he stood in front of Lenore's front door. He felt anxious and excited and frustrated, a deluge of emotions tap-dancing with his spirit. He was about to ring the bell a second time when Cash snatched it open and gestured for him to enter. Her cell phone was pressed tightly to her ear.

"What's this about?" Cash questioned. She listened to the explanation being given on the other end, her head bobbing easily. "Okay...yeah...right...okay..." she muttered before hanging up on the caller.

King lifted his hand in greeting, a bright smile pulling from ear to ear.

"Hey!" she said in greeting, tossing her hand up to wave back.

"Hi," he answered. "I didn't mean to interrupt."

"You didn't. That was Lenore. She needs me to look something up for her. She said to make yourself comfortable. That she's on her way and she's bringing dinner."

He nodded. "What does she have you researching?" he questioned.

"She needs me to pull information on an old case. She thinks it might be related to the killings now."

"What's the old case?"

Cash spun around on the toes of her Adidas sneakers, but she didn't answer. When King asked a second time, she tossed him a look as she sat back down in front of her laptop.

"Look here, Detective Stud Muffin. I like you. Lenore likes you a lot to have let you into this inner circle. Which means she trusts you. I don't necessarily have the same warm and fuzzy feelings yet. Now, like I said, she's on her way. You can ask her all your questions when she gets here."

"You're protective of her."

"So are you," Cash countered nonchalantly. "We do that with people we have love for." She lifted her eyes to his, seeming to punctuate her statement with her stare.

For reasons King couldn't begin to explain, he found her comment unsettling. He changed the subject, wanting to ignore the emotion that had welled up in his midsection.

"How long have you been working with the agency?" he asked. He moved to the dining room table and took a seat. The stacks of files they'd left on the tabletop earlier had been pushed around and restacked on the other end.

"Over eight years. I've been with Claudia since the beginning, even before the younger two girls came on board."

"Were you two friends?"

"Not at first. I had done some prison time for penetrating a business's firewall to access their private servers and cloud storage systems. I forgot to get their consent." She chuckled.

"You were a hacker."

Cash grinned. "That's what the feds called me. Anyway, my daughter was going through a hard time and needed help with my two grandbabies. Claudia stepped in to be that help, and when I got out, I wanted to repay her generosity. We struck up a deal, and I've been here ever since."

"Grandbabies! You don't look old enough to have grandbabies!"

"Don't let my youthful complexion and spirited personality deceive you, Detective Dreamy. My daughter is the same age as Lenore, and her twin boys are twelve years old now. The key to youthfulness is not to act your age as you grow old. That, good booze and great sex!"

King laughed heartily. "I'll have to remember that."

Cash leaned back in her seat. She closed the lid of her laptop then folded her arms over her chest. "I'm sure you've already figured out that the Martins aren't your typical all-American family."

He nodded and gave her a slight shrug.

Cash continued. "It hasn't always been easy for them. They've been through some things. And men don't always date the girls for the right reasons. Don't you make the same mistake. We will all come for you if you hurt her. And we will come when you least expect it."

Before King could respond, Lenore came barreling through the front door.

At the sight of King, Lenore blew a sigh of relief. A single tear ran over her cheek. She didn't bother to wipe it away. King stood, concern like bad makeup on his face. He took a step toward her, closing the gap between them. She instinctively walked into his open arms and laid her head on his chest. The moment felt as natural as breathing. As he wrapped his arms around her torso, holding her tightly to him, she allowed herself a minute to settle into the feelings that were suddenly consuming. It was only when the bathroom door slammed closed, Cash making a not-so-quiet exit from the room, that Lenore stepped out of the embrace. Contrition furrowed her brow, and she was slightly embarrassed.

"Sorry about that. I've just had a hard day," she said, hoping that would be enough to explain her mood.

"Want to talk about it?" King asked.

She shook her head. "We need to talk about the case." She dropped her purse to an upholstered chair, then moved toward the kitchen with the bag of Chinese food she'd purchased for their dinner. She was grateful when King didn't push for more of an explanation, purposely shifting the conversation to what he'd accomplished on their to-do list.

"I visited the Carmichael home," he said as she pulled plates from an upper cabinet.

"How'd that go?"

"It didn't answer any questions for us. Charles did acknowledge he has a twin brother but says they weren't raised together, and if I had more questions, I need to speak with his mother."

Lenore frowned as she prepped three plates with food. "I would really like to be in on that conversation."

"I thought you would. That's why I didn't rush over to question her."

"What about the grandfather? Did he know anything?"

"He was ranting about one being good and the other bad. The conversation with him was difficult at best. How'd you make out at the morgue?"

Lenore moved back into the other room, returning with the folder of images Mayhew had given her. Back in the kitchen, she passed it to King.

"What's this?" he asked as he began to flip through the papers.

"Pictures the coroner took. It looks like all of the victims were tattooed on their middle finger. The victims from the current cases *and* the victims from the past cases. From what I can determine though, the tattoos were done well before their disappearances and their murders."

"And the coroner is just now sharing this information?"

Lenore shrugged slightly. "I didn't have an opportunity to ask. I recognized the tattoo, and all I wanted was to get out of there." She took a deep breath, holding the air tightly in her lungs.

King looked up and met her stare. He studied her intently, noting her body had tensed, and something that looked like distress crossed her face. Lenore put a hand to her stomach, her palm pressing against the fabric of her shirt. Her fingers trembled ever so slightly.

"Where do you know them from?" King asked, his tone dropping an octave. His voice was low and even, calming her nerves. "What do you know about these tattoos?"

Lenore blew out the breath she'd been holding. Before she could answer, Cash suddenly appeared at King's elbow, looking over his shoulder at the file he held. She looked and then she cussed, snapping her gaze in Lenore's direction.

"Is this for real?" Cash asked.

Lenore nodded at her friend, then she turned an about-face to pull a serving spoon from the drawer.

King's brow lifted questioningly. "What am I missing?"

Neither woman said anything, the silence in the room suddenly disquieting. His eyes darted back and forth between the two, and his nerves felt frazzled. He inhaled his own deep breath and patiently waited for one of them to answer the question.

Lenore set a plate of food in front of him as she passed a second plate to Cash. When she'd plated her own meal, she sat down and began to explain about the tattoos, and her sister, and the criminal that had destroyed the lives of so many young people. He had left their families debilitated, including her own, and King instinctively knew rehashing it all was painful for her.

"And this guy was never caught?" King asked when she'd finished.

"He was caught," Lenore said. "He was captured and charged."

"Then a judge actually allowed him out on bail," Cash interjected.

"Was he ever convicted?" King questioned.

Lenore's face was blank. She bit into an egg roll, having nothing else she wanted to say.

Cash answered for her. "He disappeared. To this day he has never been found, and is presumed dead."

That awkward silence seemed to grow even thicker between them. King made a mental note to pull the case file, curious to know if anyone on the force was still looking for the suspect.

The air was still, scented with the aroma of Kung Pao shrimp and pork fried rice. Lenore imagined she could actually hear King's heart beating as he processed everything he'd just learned. The detective took a bite of a Crab Rangoon and swallowed. "So, you and your sisters were in your teens when this all happened. And this teacher was what...? Twenties or thirties?"

"Midtwenties. It was his first teaching position. It's what made him so popular. He was closer to our age, not old like the other adults," Lenore said. "He was also nice-looking, and very charismatic. The girls obsessed over him, and the boys idolized him."

King nodded. "Then that would put him somewhere in his mid- to late forties now." He turned toward Cash. "You think you can work your magic and maybe see if you can get a hit on his prints? In case he was ever arrested elsewhere?"

"Probably," she said.

Lenore shook her head slowly. "That would be a waste of time," she said. "We're never going to find him."

King didn't miss the look Lenore gave Cash. Nor did he miss the way Cash's eyes dropped to her plate, her fork following. He took a moment to consider what that might mean before he responded.

"Well," he finally said. "If this Symmetry person is dead, then I imagine he got exactly what he deserved."

"I know that's right," Cash muttered.

Lenore's eyes locked with King's and held the gaze tightly. Something in his tone told her he would never again mention Symmetry to her if she didn't bring it up first. She nodded in his direction, blessing him with the sweetest smile she could muster.

"So, what now?" Cash asked, pushing her plate across the counter.

"Can you tell me who the investigating officers were on those old cases?" King asked. "Someone might still be around who knows something," he said.

"That's an easy one to look up," she answered.

"Can you also get me everything you have on this Stefan Guidry? I'm most interested in any known associates or friends. If it's not him doing this, we need to consider that it might be someone who was affiliated with him."

"I remember them telling my parents that he acted alone," Lenore said.

"I doubt that," King said. "Men like that always manage to find like-minded friends. These days the internet makes it easy for them."

"And that is why being able to do a deep dive in the dark web comes in handy," Cash said with a sly grin. "Just tell me what to look for, Detective Hot Stuff!"

As Cash headed back into the dining room and to her computer, Lenore excused herself and headed toward her bedroom. King sat in reflection for a hot minute, and then he rose from his seat and followed after her. He knocked on the closed door, but he didn't wait to be invited inside.

Lenore was sitting on the edge of her king-size bed when he cracked the door open and peeked inside. She appeared defeated, and her expression pitched a ball of energy through his midsection. He entered the room and closed the door after himself.

"I was worried about you," he said as he moved to sit beside her.

She shook her head. "I'm fine," she said softly.

The two sat side by side, neither speaking. King listened to her breath, the soft exhalations beginning to slow as she allowed herself a moment to relax.

Her voice was a loud whisper when she finally said something. "My parents...they're not bad people. They're just...well..."

King nodded. "They do what their conscience leads them to do. Good and bad. And only they have to live with the consequences of their actions."

She shot him a look.

"I'm not here to judge anyone else," King said. "I don't have a heaven or a hell to put anyone in. When my turn comes, I'll have to stand at that pearly gate and defend my own actions just like they will. Just like you will."

Lenore fell back against the mattress, pulling her arms up and over her head. She stared at the ceiling and the crystal chandelier that hung above their heads.

King glanced around the room. The design was simple, but welcoming. She'd chosen calming shades of green for the decor, with gold-and-white accents. Behind the massive bed, the wall was covered with a custom-designed tufted panel in white silk. An assortment of pillows rested at the top of the bed. The coverlet was forest green with a hint of embroidery along one edge. The wall in front of him showcased a montage of ornately framed gold mirrors. The space was soothing.

He lay back on the bed beside her, his own hand folded atop his midsection. He stared where she stared.

"Are we dating?" Lenore suddenly asked.

After a moment's pause, King chuckled. "I was just

about to ask you the same thing. We've gotten very comfortable with each other in a very short time."

"It's not lust. If it were lust, I would have slept with you by now and been done with you."

"There's some lust," King said. "But there's something else, also. Something deeper."

"You like me. You like me a lot."

He smiled "You're feeling yourself. I don't like you that much."

"Yes, you do!"

"Okay, maybe a little. But you like me more."

"Now you're reaching."

"Not at all. Lenore Martin is falling in love with me. Why can't you just admit it?"

Lenore laughed heartily. "I'll admit it when you do," she said.

King shifted his body toward hers, rolling onto his side as he lifted himself up and propped his head atop his hand. His fingers teased the outer curve of her breast and trailed across her tummy. Her nipple hardened like rock candy, tight against the brassiere she wore. She reached out to press a palm to his cheek, and he kissed the soft flesh.

Lenore stared into his eyes, searching for something that belonged only to her. When she found it, relishing her reflection in his gaze, she reached up to press her mouth to his.

The kiss was sweet, tasting faintly of sugared vanilla. Her lips danced easily across his, feeling like layers of silk gliding against each other. She slipped her tongue past her lips and then past his to dance a slow, sensual drag with his tongue.

Throaty breaths sounded through the room. She moaned and he gasped as the kiss became more intense. His hand trailed down her side and across her back, pulling her closer as he rolled her above him. King wrapped his hands around her torso, gently cupping her buttocks as he pushed his pelvis into the soft apex of hers.

Both were ready to tear away each other's clothes when Cash suddenly knocked on the bedroom door, calling out their names.

"Just a minute!" Lenore called back, stalling the harsh rap against the wood structure. She rolled her body from his and pulled herself upright.

King shook his head. He pressed a palm to the hardened flesh between his legs, the appendage displaced by the rise of nature. "We are breaking all kinds of rules," he said.

"Rules are made to be broken," Lenore replied.

"I don't think that's how that works," King said.

There was another knock, Cash hammering impatiently at the entry. "You really need to hear this!" she shouted through the door.

Standing, King adjusted his clothes and leaned to give Lenore one last kiss. As he moved to the door, pulling it open, Lenore had straightened her own clothes. She stopped short when she reached his elbow.

Cash stood grinning on the other side. "I hate to interrupt your little love fest, but I knew you'd want to hear this."

"What did you find?" Lenore asked.

"What do you want first? The good news or the bad?"

"Does it matter?" King said, his eyes narrowing slightly.

"Nope!"

The couple followed after her as she headed back to her computer.

"This better be good," Lenore said. "Just tell us!"

"One officer signed off on all the cases for a thirty-year period. Most of the cases were labeled suicides or accidents, and no one ever connected them to each other."

"Who was the officer?" King asked.

"Detective Richard Carmichael!"

Lenore gasped, her eyes widening. "So, he was involved!"

"And that's not all," Cash continued. "Two other names came up when I searched Stefan Guidry."

Lenore cut her eyes toward King as they waited for Cash to drop the other shoe. "Go on," she implored.

"First on the list was high school principal, Dr. Morris Brandt. He and Stefan Guidry were in foster care together. They were housed in a group home under the supervision of Richard Carmichael and his wife, Peggy. It seems that the Carmichaels became foster parents before Richard started police training, and once he got his badge, they were considered the model foster family."

"Well, I'll be damned," King said. His hands rested against his waist and Lenore could already see his mind racing to put the pieces together.

"That's not all," Cash continued. "And you're not going to believe this one."

"What?" Lenore asked, her face twisted anxiously.

"They also had a third foster son until he aged out of the system. Someone you're both acquainted with."

"Who?" King questioned, his eyes wide. He took a breath, the air in the room feeling charged, like a current of electricity firing on all cylinders.

Cash shifted her gaze toward Lenore as she answered. "Police captain Juan Romero!" she said, the words falling out of her mouth like bricks being slammed against a concrete floor.

Chapter 16

The makeshift board on Lenore's dining room wall had been switched out and updated. They were no longer focused on the victims, but on what had become of a growing list of potential suspects. Cash had finally left them, headed home to have dessert with a friend. King had started to ask about this *friend*, but Lenore had shook her head, waving him off the subject. "You really don't want to know," she'd said as Cash had laughed.

Cash had hugged him, leaving him with a wink of her eye before kissing Lenore's cheek and disappearing out the door.

Lenore headed toward the kitchen, readying herself to prepare a pot of coffee for the evening. She called out to him from the kitchen area. "What lies did you tell Cash to have her so enamored with you?"

King laughed. "I don't have to lie! I'm just that kind of guy! Everyone loves me!"

"No, you definitely did something," Lenore said. "Cash has never liked anyone I'm interested in as quickly as she liked you. For that matter, neither have my parents."

"What about you?" King asked. "Have you ever fallen for anyone as quickly as you've fallen for me?"

"Who says I've fallen for you?"

King could hear her giggling in the other room. The sound of her laughter made him smile, and it warmed his spirit to have her mood shift from that dark place she'd been in earlier.

She poked her head through the door to stare at him. "Cookies with your coffee?" she asked.

"No, thank you."

Minutes later she moved back into the space, two cups of coffee and a plate of chocolate chip cookies on a serving tray.

"You have a sweet tooth, don't you?"

"It's horrible!" Lenore answered with a chuckle. "I could eat cookies and candy all day long. So where are you?" she questioned after taking a sip of brew and the bite out of her first sweet treat.

King leaned back in his chair. His legs were stretched out in front of him and crossed at the ankles. He crossed his arms over his broad chest. "I'm still trying to figure out how everyone plays into this. Right now, I would be willing to bet a dollar to a dime that they're all involved. But I couldn't tell you who's running the show or how they all play into the scenario."

"We can tie the old man back to the older cases. He

may have been your perpetrator and covering up his own crimes, or he knew Stefan and the other boys were committing the crimes, and he was covering things up to protect them."

"That's one scenario, but Stefan was never charged with a murder, or even connected with one."

"That doesn't mean he wasn't involved. Maybe exploiting his victims for profit was his only thing and then he passed them along after the fact to his foster brothers, who were even more perverse."

King jotted a note onto the yellow lined pad that rested on the table. "I need to reach out to the local FBI office. We can check to see if any of these guys show up in their database of violent crimes against children. That might tell us something. For all we know, they might already be subjects of interest."

"Cash can do that for you," she said as she reached for her phone, pushing Send on a text message seconds later.

"We're going to get Cash sent to jail."

Lenore shrugged. "Maybe they can give us all cells beside each other."

He shook his head. "That's not funny, Lenore. That's not funny at all."

She laughed.

King continued. "Let's say Richard Carmichael started them down this path. He was responsible for the initial deaths and the cover-ups. He taught them the tricks of the trade, and when they grew up, they stepped out on their own. Stefan Guidry expands their sick business for profit. But he gets caught and goes down. When he disappears, everything stops for a while."

"How long is a while?" Lenore asked.

King pointed his index finger in her direction. "Good question. We need to pinpoint exactly how much time passed with no killings and then figure out where each of them was during that time." He jotted another round of notes on the pad.

"Juan hasn't been in New Orleans long. He was actually hired just before the first bodies started turning up."

"Where was he before this assignment?"

"The police department in Plano, Texas. Allegedly he had a good tenure there. He wasn't happy about leaving."

"So why did he?"

"He just said the job opened here and it was an opportunity he couldn't pass up."

"Interesting..." King muttered, jotting notes one more time.

"You're going to need a confession. One of them is going to have to put this together for us. For all we know, they could be taking turns. With no physical evidence to tie any of them to the actual murders, there's not much else to go on, and what we do have is purely circumstantial conjecture."

"And I thought this was going to be easy," King said facetiously.

"What if we start with Tralisa's murder first and work backwards? She wasn't part of the plan. Something went wrong. She discovered who killed Michael-Lynn, and they had to stop her from telling."

"And that happened at the school, which points us toward Principal Brandt."

"And possibly one or both of the Carmichael twins,"

Lenore interjected. "Because in all honesty, I don't see Brandt chasing down any of the kids to murder them."

"Or Richard Carmichael's daughter. You can't say definitively that the coach didn't have anything to do with this. Or that she doesn't have any knowledge of what's going on. She was raised in the home with all of them."

"Did you get anything from the security cameras at the school?"

"You mean the security cameras that were conveniently down for maintenance the day Tralisa was murdered?"

"Damn!" Lenore shook her head. Frustration seeped from her eyes.

"So," King continued, "maybe Brandt shuts down the security feeds on purpose and gives one of his brothers free rein in his school to hunt his students."

"Or he is able to chase them down, and he kills them himself," Lenore said with a shrug of her shoulders.

King sighed, his headache quickly sliding toward migraine status. Talking it out, he realized Lenore was right. Unless someone dropped the killer, or killers, in his lap, he was going to have to get one of them to talk and give up all the others.

Lenore seemed to read his mind. "I say we start with the coach. She may be the weak link in their little boy's club."

"And it might explain why her father has so much animosity toward her," King said. "She might not be the team player he needs her to be, and he knows it."

For another hour, the duo forecasted every possible scenario they could imagine. As time ticked by and both began to feel weary, reasoning began to devolve into something close to nonsensical.

Lenore rose from the table and gathered the dirty dishes. She sauntered into the kitchen, mumbling something under her breath.

King shook his head. "I didn't get that," he said, calling after her.

Her voice rose. "I said at this rate it could have been a damn swamp monster for all we know!"

King moved into the kitchen behind her. "It's late, and we're drowning in coffee. Let's call it a night and get back to it first thing in the morning. I need to officially interview Coach Carmichael."

"That might be a challenge."

"Why would you say that?"

"You can't trust anyone at the station, especially if Romero is involved. He can be an ass, but he has a loyal following. You cops don't usually play well when someone is going after one of your own. You pull her in for questioning, and if he's involved, then you've tipped all of them off."

King pondered her statement. After a minute he asked, "So what do you suggest?"

She shrugged. "I suggest we table this discussion until later. I need a shower."

He watched as she placed the last coffee mug into the dishwasher. She grabbed a dishcloth and took one last swipe at her granite counters. He nodded. "I should be going. I'm sure my grandfather is wondering where I am."

Lenore smiled. She crossed the room, strolling slowly past him. She paused in the doorway. She pulled her sweater up and over her head, tossing it aside as she exposed a black lace bra that looked as if it had been painted on. "You could call and check in," she said. "Let your grandfather know you're tied up, and then you can join me in that shower. Or, not."

She turned, her slacks falling to the floor beneath her feet. She stepped out of them and continued toward the primary bedroom. King's eyes slid to the round of her buttocks and the matching lace G-string she wore. His eyes trailed after her, and before he could change his mind, the rest of him followed.

There was no denying that the shower in Lenore's primary bathroom was a thing of sheer beauty. Inside the glass enclosure, the stainless steel ceiling was a rainfall showerhead that poured a magnificent waterfall or the gentlest spring shower over one's head. Six additional showerheads were placed strategically around the shower walls to ensure that no matter where you stood, you were completely enveloped in water. It was the epitome of luxury, and King imagined it had to be one of her favorite places in her home. He knew it would be his.

Lenore stood with her eyes closed. Her palms were pressed against the tiled wall as she settled into the warmth of wetness. King hesitated as he stared, completely enthralled by the sight of her. She was exquisitely beautiful, and he imagined the feel of her warm brown skin beneath his hands would be a dream come true. A quiver of energy rippled through his midsection and out into each limb. He suddenly felt as if his whole body were on fire, flames shooting through his lower quadrant.

He had left his own trail of clothes, dropping them from her kitchen to her bedroom. If there were any doubts about what would happen between them, those doubts would be all hers. Because King couldn't imagine himself ever doubting how he was feeling for Lenore. Walking away from what he knew they could have was no longer an option. As he pulled open the glass door and stepped inside, King prayed that she was feeling the same way, too.

When King finally entered the bathroom, suddenly coming to an abrupt halt, Lenore thought her legs might give out from beneath her and send her to the floor. Leaning against the tiled wall was the only thing that kept her standing. She knew the invitation had been bold. Just like she knew them crossing that threshold in their relationship could potentially end badly. But in that moment, all she could think of was making love to King. She wanted him in her bed, and she was determined to get what she wanted.

He had taken longer than she'd thought he would, and for the briefest moment, she'd imagined the worst. She'd been afraid that he hadn't been interested, heading out her front door instead of following her. And then, in the blink of an eye, he'd been standing there watching her, and every muscle in her body quivered with excitement.

King stepped into the shower enclosure. He eased his naked body against her backside, skin searching hungrily for skin. Lenore heard herself moan as he pressed his lips to her neck, his tongue lapping at the water that rained down over them. His fingers burned heat against her skin as he slowly caressed her, eager to know her body with each pass of his hands. She turned around in his arms and lifted her face to kiss his lips. Kissing King had become her new favorite thing in the world to do.

He moved against her, easing an arm around her waist to pull her closer. Lenore knew there'd be no going back as her body screamed his name, every nerve ending eager for his touch. His kisses had her dizzy. The wanting was so intense she thought she might combust. She eased her leg against his hip, hooking the limb around his waist as he lifted her off the floor, pressing her back against the wall. She suddenly felt desperate, want becoming a need.

His breathing was labored, and they both gasped for air, sucking in oxygen. Steam swirled in large undulations, a thick and warm blanket wrapping around them. She pointed toward the foil-wrapped prophylactic resting on the soap dish, and he pulled himself from her, easing her back onto her feet as he sheathed himself quickly.

Seconds later, her legs were wrapped tightly around his waist and locked tightly behind his back. He eased himself into her, pushing forward slowly, a gentle push and pull that made her whisper his name in a quiet mantra. He held her up, the wall helping to support her weight, and she clung to him, determined to never let him go.

They loved each other sweetly, moving from the shower to the bed, the living room floor, the kitchen counter. He claimed her in every corner of her home, marking every square inch of her body with his own.

Lenore had never loved any man before, she thought, the elusive emotion nothing but a distraction. She'd mastered the art of ignoring those feelings that weren't necessary for her to be successful. Her whole body quivered, and the heat that had risen puddled moisture in places she had never imagined. And then his orgasm hit, fueling her own erotic explosion. As King yelled her name, falling over a cliff into a chasm of sheer bliss, he pulled her along with him. Tumbling down into a vat of pure ecstasy, Lenore knew beyond any doubt that what she was feeling had to be love. So she allowed herself to completely let go, trusting that love would cushion their landing.

Chapter 17

Lenore lay perfectly still. Her eyes were closed, and her breathing was meditative, the inhalations slow and even. She listened, hoping to hear some sign of life coming from her living space. But there was nothing. Not a pot rattling, no clock ticking, no man breathing.

She lay completely still, trying to decide if she was going to rage or not. After the previous night, she hadn't expected to wake up to an empty bed, King nowhere to be found. After hours of the best sex she'd ever had, he'd slipped out of her bed like a thief making his getaway. He hadn't even bothered to say goodbye.

She wanted to kick herself. She'd done what her parents had warned her against since she'd discovered boys. She'd given up her goodies without making him work for it. She could already hear her mother chastising her because until this case was solved, the encounter wasn't a hit-it-and-quit-it moment. She'd left the option of walking away, once they were done and over, off the table. She couldn't wish him well and plan to never see him again. Because they still needed to focus on the case and work together. But the good detective had seen her in all her glory. He'd tripped through the private garden only a select few had ever had access to, and he hadn't allowed her the opportunity to throw him out of her bed. He'd done what too many men tried to do. He'd bested her at her own game, and now her heart hurt.

Lenore was pissed. Where had he gone? she wondered. Why hadn't he blessed her with a kiss and a smile and some hint that he'd gotten as much joy from their encounter as she had? Why had he left her doubting her own emotions?

Rising from the bed, Lenore glanced toward the digital clock on the nightstand. She was late, and that pissed her off even more. She knew she should call him, but that's not how their encounter was supposed to have played out. Lenore Martin didn't chase after any man. For any reason. If one left, he left, and good riddance to him. But King wasn't supposed to leave. She'd been emotionally invested in him, which meant he should have been invested in her.

Damn him, Lenore thought. She headed toward the shower, determined to wash the memory of her night with King from her. But she couldn't begin to reason why she was letting it play with her head. Or why she was reacting so irrationally.

The morning shift security guard at the entrance desk had given him the third degree. King had been annoyed at first, until he realized they were not accustomed to random men coming and going from Lenore's apartment. After he'd flashed them his badge and showed that he also had a key to gain entry, they let him pass, but not before taking down his information and making him sign the guest book.

He had slept well for the little time that they had actually closed their eyes. Wrapping his body around Lenore's had felt like home, and he knew it was a place he would fight to return to over and over again. Rising early, he hadn't wanted to disturb her sleep. Tiptoeing from the bedroom to the kitchen, he wasn't surprised to find that there was nothing in her pantry or her refrigerator to prepare them breakfast. Initially he'd thought about ordering something to be delivered, but changed his mind. He wanted a fresh change of clothes and needed to check on his grandfather. The ride to his home hadn't taken as long as he'd imagined, and he'd been able to get there and turn around in no time at all. Now he just wanted to get back to Lenore and be in her presence, enjoying her company.

Together, they had made a long list of things that needed to be accomplished and people who needed to be interviewed. Truth be told, he worried that another body might drop if something didn't bring them closure soon. There was information that needed to be searched out, and time wasn't on their side. First on that list was a conversation with Coach Carmichael. But Lenore was right. Bringing her in could tip them all off that they were being considered potential suspects, especially if he didn't have enough to actually arrest her. The whole lot could go into flee-or-fight mode. And if his own captain was somehow involved, either actively or as part of the cover-up, the investigation could get shut down fast. King couldn't let that happen.

King exited the elevator and rounded the corridor toward Lenore's apartment. He used her key to let himself back in. In the distance, he could hear the water running, and he smiled. For a brief moment, he thought about joining Lenore in that shower. But he knew that if he did, they wouldn't get anything accomplished.

The previous night had been everything. Even more than he could have ever imagined it being. She had moved him in a way no other woman before her had ever tried. He had to admit that Lenore Martin had successfully managed to take hold of his heart. He had no intentions of ever letting her go as long as she wanted him as much as he wanted her.

He moved into the kitchen and emptied the grocery bags that he had carried upstairs. He had managed to score freshly baked muffins, crispy bacon and one of the prettiest fruit salads he'd ever seen. It was enough to get their morning started. All that was needed was a cup of coffee that he was about to brew in her fancy coffee maker.

When Lenore finally made an entrance, he was seated at the dining room table, just a few short pages from the conclusion of her sister's case. Reading about her trauma had been a punch to his gut and left a bad taste in his mouth. He could only begin to imagine what the details had done to her father. A review of the court transcripts confirmed Symmetry's involvement was more financially motivated than anything else. But it also made it clear and evident that he had no soul, and his heart was ice that had shattered when he'd been a boy born to abusive parents and lost in the foster care system. King found it interesting that most of the girls he had preyed on had revered him as a god despite the atrocities he had rained down on them. They had fallen for the lies that he'd sold them, desperate for his attention. He'd promised to help them manifest every fantasy they imagined. Most had only wanted someone who supported their dreams. Someone they trusted and who believed in their aspirations. Symmetry had played that role well until his games became their own personal nightmares. The shining prince who'd ridden in on the white horse had become a monster from hell.

During his trial, those that had survived couldn't explain their obsession with him, just that he needed them to protect him from the enemies determined to take him down. Even as they detailed the horrific abuse, and the multiple rapes, some of their stories so devastating that a few members of the jury had become physically ill, they'd had no answers that made an ounce of sense. The prosecution had even brought in a psychiatrist to explain Stockholm syndrome and how hostages develop a psychological bond with their captors during captivity. The news had likened him to Charles Manson, calling him a psychotic cultist.

He had yet to be officially declared dead. No one had come forward to verify his death, and with no body, it was assumed he was still on the run, drinking piña coladas on a tropical island. The case had gone cold, filed away to be forgotten. The investigative officer, Detective Juan Romero, had been dismissive, ruling Symmetry had acted alone.

King looked up as Lenore hurled herself into the room. At first glance she looked like she had just lost her best friend. From the expression on her face, he realized she was surprised to see him. She stared, her mouth agape. Then she began to fuss. He couldn't help but smile.

"I thought you were gone," Lenore snapped.

"I was. I went to get some food for breakfast, and then I ran by my house to change into a fresh suit and check on my old guy."

"You could have said goodbye," Lenore quipped.

"You were sleeping soundly, and I didn't want to disturb your rest. I knew it was going to be a long day for us. And I borrowed your key. I put it back on the table. In case you were looking for it."

She folded her arms over her chest. "Oh," she muttered.

King laughed. "You actually thought I just left! You thought I was that kind of guy."

"Don't flatter yourself."

"That's not flattering at all. And I would never have pegged you for being so emotional."

Lenore rolled her eyes skyward. "I am not being emotional. I just had a moment."

King's expression was smug. "I can't believe your confidence was shook. Women have told me that happens when I put it on them like that."

"What women?"

"No one you'd know."

"You've been with that many women?"

"Dozens!" King said, the word wrapped around a laugh.

"Now you've got jokes!"

"Just a funny ha-ha to start our day."

"I'm not laughing."

"Well, you don't ask me about my past, and I won't ask you about yours."

"Like hell I won't! We will be having this conversation later," Lenore said, attitude flooding every word. "And for the record, my confidence wasn't shook. Don't get that twisted."

King tapped his thigh, gesturing for her to come take a seat. She slowly eased her way in his direction until she was close enough for him to reach his hand out and pull her to him. "I didn't mean to worry you," he said.

"I wasn't worried."

"Yes, you were. You were scared that I'd gotten the goods and taken off on you. You were shook. I can see it on your face."

Lenore feigned a pout, pushing her bottom lip out. She dropped her head against his shoulder and nuzzled her face into his neck. "I hate feeling vulnerable," she whispered. "And I hate that you're being so damn smug about it!"

King laughed. "Now I'm smug!" He wrapped his arms around her and kissed her cheek.

Lenore finally gave him a smile, laughing with him. The tension in the room dissipated like a morning mist beneath a bright summer sun. She was actually surprised that he could read her emotions so well. Not many men had ever been that intuitive when it came to her moods.

"My feelings are caught up in whatever this is between us, King. I know I acted irrationally, but this relationship actually scares me. I don't like worrying about my heart being hurt. And whatever this is has happened so fast! I just need it to make sense."

He nodded. "I know exactly what you're feeling. But if I'm willing to trust you with my heart, I'm going to need you to trust me with yours."

Lenore stood and turned until she was facing him. She straddled his legs and the chair as she settled in his lap. She cupped his face between her palms. "I do trust you, but you're on notice. Mess up and I will hurt you!"

"I swear, that has been the second or third threat I've gotten from you or someone in your family. I can't say that I'm not a little scared." He pinched his thumb and forefinger together for emphasis.

"Good," Lenore said, her mouth lifting into a bright smile. "Fear will keep you on your toes."

"Then we both need to be afraid," King replied as he captured her lips with his own and kissed her intently.

As King plated their morning meal, they played another game of what-if, trying to fathom everything that could go wrong and how they would need to handle it. He appreciated Lenore's ability to put their personal issues aside and to focus on the business of the investigation.

The relationship between the Carmichael family, police captain Romero, school principal Brandt and the late Stefan "Symmetry" Guidry was too significant to be ignored. For all intents and purposes, they were more family than not. Richard Carmichael and Romero having both worked multiple murder cases of students involved with Symmetry's cult following and never connecting any of them to each other couldn't be coincidental. Was it a cover-up or conspiracy to commit those crimes? Nor could the significance of those tattoos be ignored. And how did Carmichael's daughter and grandson figure into the equation?

There still wasn't enough evidence to point a finger at any one individual, and both were frustrated by that fact. They were proceeding on the hopes of tripping one or more of them up. Tasked with making the pieces to the puzzle make sense wasn't what either would have wished for. Attacking the responsibility with everything in them was what King and Lenore did best. Individually, neither liked to lose. Together, they were a formidable team.

"Although I have concerns," King said, "your plan might actually work."

"We really don't have a lot of options, right now."

"I agree. I'm just concerned about your safety."

Lenore gave him a sultry side-eye. "I am perfectly capable of handling myself."

"I don't doubt that, but I still need you to be safe."

"I have a black belt in tae kwon do and learned how to fire a gun when I was nine. I'm going to be fine."

King smiled. "Still, I'll be there to back you up!"

Chapter 18

Outside of Lenore's building, the couple kissed each other goodbye and headed in opposite directions. King knew Lenore had as many concerns and doubts as he did, but she wasn't going to allow him or anyone to see her sweat.

Minutes later, he pulled into the parking lot of the police station. He sat in his car as it idled, noting the other vehicles parked around him. Captain Romero was there, and most of the others he had expected to see. He took a deep breath as he shut down the engine. Things could play out perfectly, or not, but he knew it was a risk they needed to take. As he stepped out of the vehicle, sweat beaded across his brow. The morning air was already hot and humid. He couldn't help but think it was a prelude to the type of day they were going to have.

Inside, he waved a hand at Foret, who rose from his seat and followed him into his office. "Good morning," King said as he moved back to the chair and took a seat. "What did you find out about Charles Carmichael?"

"I ran down his alibi for the morning Tralisa Taylor died, and it's legit. He was at school taking an exam. In fact, he was there most of the morning. Left for an hour or two at lunch but came right back. His classmates didn't have a lot to say about him. There's no one person or persons he appears to hang out with. One or two of them said he's standoffish and not very friendly. One girl said he was weird."

King leaned back in his chair, surprised by the comments. Charles had always seemed pleasant and likable. He had to wonder which personality was true to who Charles really was. More importantly, was he capable of torturing, butchering and killing young teens who crossed his path?

"Captain Romero is looking for you," Christian said. "I think he's ready to shut this case down. He thinks at least two of these deaths were accidental or maybe suicides. He sounded like he's ready to close the files," he repeated.

King didn't bother to respond. Instead he said, "Did you get anything on the grandfather, Richard Carmichael?"

"Not really. There's no one still around that worked with him. I did pull his employee records, though, and clearly, he was problematic. Then Captain wanted to know why I was wasting time and asking how Carmichael played into the murders."

"What did you tell him?"

"Nothing. I don't know enough to tell him anything. That's when he started screaming for you. He said he wants you to come see him the minute you get here."

King nodded. "I need a favor," he said, reaching for a file that he'd placed on the desk. "I need you to hit all the tattoo parlors. See if anyone has ever seen this tattoo before or if they can identify who the tattoo artist might be." He passed Christian a photo. "We're on the clock, so the sooner you can find anything the better."

"Consider it done. I got you!"

As Christian made his exit, King reached for the phone. He dialed the number he had written down for himself earlier and waited for it to be answered.

A woman with a pleasant voice greeted him warmly. There was the slightest Southern drawl attached to each word. "Plano police department! How may I direct your call?"

"Yes, good morning. My name is Detective King Randolph. I'm calling from the New Orleans police department. I'm investigating a murder here in New Orleans and was hoping to speak with one of your detectives."

"Yes, sir, Detective. Hold on a moment and I'll transfer you."

"Thank you."

The hold was brief. There was a quick moment of elevator music, two clicks, and a male voice with little bass in his tone answered. "This is Detective Radisson. How may I help you?"

King introduced himself again. "Our victims are in their teens, and the bodies were brutalized. They were also branded or tattooed with similar markings. We believe our suspect spent time in the Dallas area. Specifically in Plano. We were wondering if you had any unsolved murders with similarities to my case."

"Let me put you on hold a minute," Detective Radisson said.

King dropped his elbows on the desktop as he waited, that elevator music playing in his ear. From where he sat, he could see Captain Romero pacing in the outer room. He was chastising a rookie for some infraction, and like always, he didn't look happy. King knew it was only a matter of time before the man would be headed in his direction, and he needed to be ready. He turned his attention back to the call, Detective Radisson returning to the phone.

"We have three unsolved cases similar to what you described. What can you tell me about your suspect?"

"Nothing just yet, but as soon as I'm able, I'll pass the information along to you. One more question. Can you tell me who the investigating officer was? And maybe put me in contact with him?"

There was a moment of hesitation before the detective answered. "The investigating official was Detective Juan Romero, but he's no longer with the department."

"Thank you for the information!" King said. "I'll be in touch."

Just as he disconnected the call, Captain Romero flung himself into King's office, bellowing for his attention.

Lenore's nerves were completely frazzled. She worried for King. She didn't trust Juan, and now, knowing all they did, she trusted him even less. Sticking to their

plan came with challenges. They might not have predicted everything that could go wrong and what would
happen if something surprised them that wasn't expected. She knew what King needed from her, where
she needed to be and when she needed to be there.
But she couldn't predict that everything would go as
planned, and not having that control left her feeling
discombobulated.

Her phone chimed, and she quickly read King's incoming message. Things were good on his end, and he
promised to keep in touch.

The second call to come in was Cash, and her anx-
iousness only served to fray Lenore's nerves a little
more.

"What's going on?" Lenore questioned.

"I think I found Christopher Carmichael. I just texted
you the address."

"How'd you swing that?"

"I followed the mother's phone records. Tracked a
single number that she called regularly, and the rest
was history."

"Do me a favor and stay close. We may need you."

"How close is close?"

"If King or I fall off the grid, you can find us if no
one else can."

"Done!"

There was a moment of disquiet, and Lenore sensed
that Cash had something else to say.

"What's going on, Cash? You don't sound good."

"I'm going to send you a link. It's encrypted, so
you're not going to be able to open it."

"What is it?"

Cash took a breath. "Remember when I told you I was going to do a deep dive on the dark web?"

"Yeah."

"Well, I found something. It's a video posted of one of the victims."

"Cash!" Lenore exclaimed. "Just one video? Can you tell who posted it?" Lenore suddenly had a ton of questions.

"I'm sure there are more, and no, you know how the dark web is. It's called dark for a reason. But I think someone else was doing what I was doing. And not one of the perverts they're being marketed to."

"You think it was law enforcement?"

"Yeah, I do, and I couldn't risk them trying to get past my firewalls to identify me. No footprint on the internet is ever really undiscoverable. The right person, the right equipment, and secrets fall like paper walls!"

Lenore nodded as if Cash could see her. "So, what do you need me to do?"

"Email the link to King. Send it from that blind account I created for the agency. Anyone he passes it on to won't be able to identify where it came from without some serious effort."

"I can do that."

"Tell King to call in a favor at the FBI. I'm sure he knows someone. Or he knows someone who knows someone. But he needs to get that tape to Vera Burgess in their Violent Crimes Against Children division. They may already be looking for these freaks."

"Vera Burgess. Got it!" Lenore said. "Thank you, Cash. I don't know what we'd do without you."

"And one more thing, Lenore," Cash said, taking a

deep breath. Her voice quivered ever so slightly as she continued. "Once King's able to open the file, promise me you won't look at the video. Ever. Or any of the other videos that they might find."

"Is it that bad?"

"It's worse. It's much worse."

Lenore's phone signaled incoming messages, and she scrolled through the short list. Cash had come through as promised, reiterating one more time her admonishment for Lenore to pass on the video and never, under any circumstances, watch it. If anyone else had told Lenore not to do something, she would have done just the opposite. Cash's warning hit home in a way Lenore would never be able to explain. Nothing and no one would move her to watch that video and break her promise. She just hated that Cash had been made to see whatever was so disturbing.

She dialed King's number and waited for him to answer. He picked up on the third ring.

"Is this a good time?" she asked.

"I'm here in a meeting with my police captain. Is it important?"

"It is. Don't talk. Just listen. Cash found a video with one of your victims. She didn't tell me which one. I'm emailing it to you now. She says you need to get that video to the FBI for their help with this. I've included the name of the agent she said you need to get it to. She said it's bad."

"I appreciate that information," he said politely.

"And she found Christopher Carmichael. I'm headed to his place now."

"That might not be a good idea."

"I'm going. I'll stay in touch and let you know what I find."

"I shouldn't be much longer," he said. "I would prefer you not make any life-altering decisions before we can chat. I'll give you a call back when I'm done."

"I love you, too," Lenore said as she disconnected the call.

King dropped his phone back to the desk and turned his attention back to Captain Romero. "Was that something I need to be aware of?" the man asked as he pointed toward King's cell phone.

He shook his head. "No, just some family stuff," King said. "Where were we?"

"Exactly! Where are we with this case? Do you have anything I can pass on to the mayor? Can we give the press anything to calm down public fear? You've been at this for a minute now, and it doesn't look like you're getting anywhere."

"That's not true. We are following up on some very valuable leads. We hope to close this case in the next day or so."

"Who's we?"

King gave him the slightest smile. "Detective Foret and I have been working very hard."

"Foret asking questions about a police lieutenant who doesn't work for the department anymore isn't a lead."

"You'd be surprised," King said.

Romero dropped both palms to the desk and leaned forward. "I would be. Carmichael was a good officer.

I will not have you disparaging one of our own without good reason."

"Did you know him personally?" King asked. His gaze narrowed ever so slightly.

Romero bristled as he straightened himself back up. "I'm sure we've met once or twice at a police function." He suddenly looked at his watch. "I have a meeting. When I get out, I want to know exactly what you do or don't have. Is that understood?"

King nodded. "Yes, sir, Captain. I'll be here."

Lenore was surprised by the Nashville Avenue home. She checked and double-checked the address Cash had sent her just to verify she was in the right place. As she pulled into an empty parking spot in front of the property, her phone rang, King making that return call as promised.

Lenore knew if she answered it, he would try to sway her from going forward on her own, so she sent the call directly to voice mail. She sent him a quick text message that she was fine and would call him back as soon as she'd completed her task.

She exited her car and moved swiftly to the front door of the early 1900s Grand Dame property. It was an architectural beauty with a gallery porch and a huge front yard. She rang the front doorbell and then waited patiently for someone to answer.

It was a nice neighborhood of older, well-maintained homes on a tree-lined street that harkened to another era. Lenore imagined it had made a wonderful family home for those who had occupied it.

As she took in the sights around her, the front door

suddenly opened. The older woman who stood on the other side was the poster child for grandmother of the year. She sported a head full of lush white curls that complemented her porcelain complexion and the most welcoming smile that lifted from her eyes. She was petite in stature, and at first glance one might have thought her fragile. She eyed Lenore curiously.

"Yes? May I help you?" Her voice was melodic, sounding like spun sugar.

"Yes, ma'am. My name is Lenore Martin. I was hoping to speak with Christopher Carmichael. I was told he lived here."

The elderly woman's eyes widened. "What is this about?"

"I'd prefer to discuss it with Mr. Carmichael. I'm a private investigator, and my client wants to ask him some questions about his grandfather and his twin brother."

"He won't be able to answer them."

"Excuse me? I don't understand."

"Chris doesn't have a relationship with his twin or that grandfather."

Confusion washed over Lenore's face.

The older woman seemed to read her mind. She pushed open the screen door and gestured for Lenore to cross the threshold. "Come in, dear."

"Thank you. I'm sorry, but I didn't get your name."

"Jeanette. Jeanette Picou."

Lenore followed Mrs. Picou through the foyer toward the rear of the house and the large kitchen. She was impressed with the cypress paneled doors, hardwood floors, ceiling medallions and exquisite chandeliers. The home was tastefully decorated and painted in a warm shade of gray with white trim. "You have a beautiful home."

"Thank you, dear. It was my dream home. My late husband, Alonzo, gifted it to me for our thirtieth wedding anniversary."

"It's very nice!"

"Can I interest you in a cup of ginger tea? It's very soothing for the stomach. I find it also calms my nerves."

"Thank you. That would be nice."

Mrs. Picou gestured for her to take a seat at the expansive kitchen table. She lifted an enameled kettle from the counter, filled it with tap water and placed it on the stove. Lenore watched as she pulled two teacups with matching saucers from the cupboard above her head.

"I also have these wonderful lemon cookies that I baked yesterday," she said as she lifted the lid on a cookie jar and placed a handful onto a plate.

"As I was standing outside, I couldn't help but think that this was a wonderful neighborhood to raise a family."

"Oh, yes, it is! It's a very nice community. Unfortunately, Mr. Picou and I were unable to have children of our own. But the good Lord blessed us with Christopher, and he brought us much joy despite the hardships we had to face."

"Hardships?"

"You really don't know anything about Christopher, do you?"

Lenore shook her head. "No, ma'am. His family hasn't been very forthcoming about him."

The older woman visibly bristled. "They are hardly what anyone would call family. Their connection may be genetic, but there's very little else they shared."

Mrs. Picou filled both cups with hot water, then dropped a teabag into each cup. She moved the cups to the table, going back to grab the cookies before she sat down beside Lenore.

"It's not often we get any company. This is such a pleasure," she gushed, that bright smile widening.

Lenore smiled back as she took a sip of the hot beverage. She eased the cup back to the table and sat back with her hands in her lap. "How long has Christopher been living with you?" she queried.

"He was a toddler when he arrived. Just the sweetest little thing. It was horrible what that man did to him."

Lenore's brow lifted. "That man?"

"His mother said the grandfather was responsible for his injuries. It was just wicked what he did to that child. Martin said it was better for him to be with people who would love and take care of him. Obviously we didn't know the full severity of his condition back then, but we loved him with every fiber of our being from that moment on."

"What did his grandfather do to him?"

"When he arrived here, they had just released him from the hospital. Child services should have been called in, but that grandfather being police, he was able to intervene. But that man ruined that baby's life. Christopher still has the scars, and he was just a beautiful boy!" She seemed to drift back in time as she took a sip from her own cup.

Lenore sat patiently as she waited for the matriarch to continue.

"His mother said he was a colicky baby. He cried constantly, and there was little she could do to comfort him. The night it happened, she was at work and had left both boys in her father's care. Well, that man shook that baby so hard that his little eyes rolled back in his head. The doctors say it's a wonder it didn't kill him. Then, to add insult to injury, he doused that baby with boiling water. Peeled the skin from half his little body. Took months for him to finally heal. He was never the same after. They say the shaking gave him brain damage."

Lenore closed her eyes and shook her head at the thought. Her stomach churned, and for the briefest moment, she thought she might vomit. She took a big inhale of air. "Did the police not do anything?"

"His mother claimed it was an accident. That he pulled the pot of water down on himself and that her father only shook him trying to revive him. But if you knew Richard Carmichael, you'd know that was a lie. The police barely questioned him since he was one of their own, and his mother preferred to give Christopher away rather than protect him from that monster."

"That's horrible!" Lenore muttered.

"Mr. Picou and I vowed to give Christopher a good life for as long as God saw fit to breathe life into us. He has wanted for nothing and has been given the best of everything. We have loved him like he was our own."

"What a blessing!" Lenore said. She blew a soft sigh. "Has his mother ever contacted you to check on him?"

"She calls quite regularly. Usually just to ask if anyone has been asking about her or her father. And we've always gotten a monthly stipend for his care. Mr. Picou invested all of it in a money market account to ensure there would be funds to care for him after we're both gone. We didn't plan for my husband to leave us so early," she said softly.

Lenore sipped her tea, sensing there was nothing she could really say to give her any comfort. Mr. Picou had been the love of her life, and she missed him. The woman suddenly jumped from her seat. "Would you like to meet my Christopher?"

"I would. Very much."

She grabbed Lenore's hand and pulled her along. Tapping at Lenore's fingers, she guided her to a bedroom directly off the kitchen. The space would have been considered the servant's quarters or maid's room.

Entering the room, there was no denying the Picous had gone above and beyond caring for Christopher Carmichael. The young man lay in a queen-size adjustable bed surrounded by state-of-the-art medical equipment. He was hooked up to a ventilator and a heart monitor. At first glance, Lenore thought he was sleeping, but his eyes opened, and he eyed her curiously.

"Hello, my darling! You have a visitor! This young lady is Lenore. She's here to check up on you and to see how you are doing!" Mrs. Picou cooed as she adjusted the blankets around his body.

Lenore gave him a wave of her hand and smiled. There was no denying the resemblance to his brother Charles. They both had the same thick head of hair and their grandfather's bright blue eyes. The resemblance ended there. The left side of Christopher's face looked as if it had been melted, the skin void of elasticity, its coloration a bright red. The burn extended down the side of his neck and over his shoulder and chest.

"He doesn't need the ventilator all the time, but he's been having respiratory issues for the last month. At first, they thought it was COVID, but it was only bronchitis, thank the good Lord!" She leaned to kiss his forehead. "He's been a tad warm today. I worry that he may be coming down with something. He's so susceptible to every little bug and virus!"

Christopher never took his eyes off Lenore. They followed her around the room, and at one point he lifted his hand and pointed his fingers in her direction. Suddenly both hands were dancing in the air.

"Yes, son, that is our new friend Lenore."

Mrs. Picou smiled at her. "He's nonverbal, but we taught him sign language so that he can communicate."

Lenore lifted her hands and began to sign. "My American Sign Language is a little rusty," she said softly.

Christopher clapped his hands together gleefully.

"It's very nice to meet you," Lenore spoke aloud and with her hands.

His adoptive mother smiled. "The nurse will be here soon, and we'll be able to unhook you from the machines," she said to the young man, although Christopher hadn't asked.

"Has he ever visited with the Carmichaels?" Lenore asked, shifting her gaze toward the matriarch.

Mrs. Picou drew a deep breath. "Once. It didn't go well. Something happened while he was there, and he came home traumatized. No one has ever told me what happened to him or what he saw, but after that, just mentioning them would send him into a panic. So we stopped talking about them altogether. As time passed, he got better. Now he barely blinks if we speak about them."

"Would you mind if I ask him a question or two about them?" Lenore asked. "I assume he remembers who they are?"

"He knows who they are."

Lenore signed to explain why she was there, and Christopher responded swiftly that he was open to a question or two if it was okay with Mrs. Picou.

"Well, then," Mrs. Picou said. She clasped her hands together in front of herself. "I need to get his lunch. Why don't I give you two a minute alone."

"Thank you, Mrs. Picou," Lenore replied.

When the woman had exited the room, Lenore moved closer to the bedside. She sat down against the edge of the mattress and began to sign.

"I was hoping you could tell me something about your mother, or your brother. That you think could help me with my case."

Lenore watched as he signed back. *Jeanette Picou is my mother.*

She nodded. "Mrs. Picou is a blessing. You are lucky to have her."

Christopher signed back. *That other family is evil!*

"Did they do something?" Lenore asked.

There was a split second of hesitation before Christopher answered, manipulating his fingers with apt precision. *The old man will hurt you. Be careful.*

"What about Charles? Can you tell me anything about your twin?"

That monster trained him well. He does whatever he's told to do.

"Thank you, Christopher," she said.

His fingers and hands danced again. *You are very pretty!*

Lenore smiled. "Thank you. That's very sweet of you to say."

Be careful. They like to hurt the pretty ones.

Lenore was prepared to ask another question, but Christopher closed his eyes, signaling he was done with her. She quietly exited the room.

In the kitchen, Mrs. Picou was humming softly to herself. She gave Lenore that big, bright smile as she entered the room. "He tires easily," she said.

"I appreciate you allowing me to speak with him," Lenore replied. "May I ask you one last question?"

"Of course, dear! What else can I help you with?"

"How did you know the Carmichaels? Were you close to the family?"

"My husband and Richard Carmichael were acquainted. When Maxine became pregnant with the twins, she spent some time here with us before the babies were born. She was very young, the poor thing! Barely old enough to know where babies came from! After they were born and Christopher was injured, she asked us to take custody of him. She said she was afraid her father would do him more harm."

"Did you ever consider legally adopting him?"

"We wanted to, but Maxine said their father refused to give his consent."

"Did she ever disclose who their father might be?"

Mrs. Picou shook her head. "No. She's never said

anything about him other than he wasn't interested in being a parent, but he also wasn't willing to give up his paternal rights."

"Were you not afraid that they might come and try to take him from you?"

"Not at all. Mr. Picou had insurance. Something he said would keep the wolves at bay if ever I needed it."

"Can you share what that was?"

Mrs. Picou pulled open a drawer in the lower cabinet. She pulled a large manila envelope from inside. "Take it," she said. "They're never going to bother us. Christopher is more work than they're willing to take on. They have no love for my sunshine!"

"Are you sure?" Lenore asked.

"I'm very certain. I believe there's a reason you dropped in on us today. And if you're asking about them, then I'm sure trouble will soon follow. My instincts are telling me that this is the right thing for me to do. Besides, I'm almost certain that if I have need, you'll come right to my rescue. I'm a great judge of character."

Lenore reached out to give the woman a hug. When Mrs. Picou hugged her back, Lenore was ready to cry, tears misting her eyes.

Mrs. Picou walked her to the front door. She chatted about the greenery outside the home and asked Lenore about a landscaper, not at all happy with the one she had. She wished her well, extended an invitation for her to return, making her promise to make it happen sooner than later, and then she closed the door, disappearing back inside.

When Lenore was safely tucked away in her car, she took a moment to collect herself. Christopher Carmichael was a victim of his own family's misdeeds. Clearly he'd had nothing to do with any of the murders. With one suspect eliminated, the list they still had to go through was shortened.

She reached for the envelope she had tossed onto the passenger seat. The seal was broken, indicating she was not the only person to see what might be inside. She pulled a stack of black-and-white photos from the interior. Photos of a teenage Maxine Carmichael. Photos of Maxine and her father and random men Lenore didn't recognize. Photos of Maxine naked and vulnerable. Maxine pregnant. Maxine being abused by the man who should have been protecting her. Photos that should have kept Maxine's baby boys as far from her abuser as possible had anyone discovered the truth.

Chapter 19

King was not happy about Lenore ignoring his call. He knew he'd been sent to voice mail, the woman refusing to answer her phone. He was worried for her but knew there was nothing he could do until she called him back. He'd left the office before Romero had concluded his meeting and could resume their conversation. The next discussion he planned with Romero needed to happen on his clock, and not the captain's.

Vera Burgess had answered his call at the mention of Cash Davies's name. She'd listened intently before requesting he meet her at the FBI office at Leon C. Simon Boulevard. As he drove in that direction, he tried to reach Lenore, growing frustrated that she was out there, running amok and putting herself at risk. He could just imagine her response to the conversation he planned to have with her about being reckless. He knew he would say what needed to be said, and then he would duck before she threw her thoughts back at him. He laughed.

Clearly, King thought, he was going to have to make some adjustments if he and Lenore took their relationship any further. She was not a woman who would be controlled by any man, and he would not be the first. He also suspected that she wouldn't be receptive to much criticism. He wasn't accustomed to relinquishing control. He would need to learn how to step back and allow her the space to do things her way. He recognized theirs would be a relationship of growth and compromise, things neither thought they had need of.

She had told him she loved him. Had he been able to, he would have said it back. Because King knew beyond a shadow of a doubt that Lenore Martin had his heart. He would never be able to explain to anyone how he was so certain, after such a short period of time, that they were meant to be. He just knew that he couldn't foresee any kind of future without her. All he wanted was to ensure her happiness and her safety, and to be able to grant her every wish imaginable.

As he approached the federal building, he tried to reach Lenore one last time. When there was no answer, he left a text message telling her where he was and promising to catch up with her as soon as he was able.

The New Orleans home of the Federal Bureau of Investigation looked more like a prison with its wrought-iron fences and drab brick building. King entered the parking lot and pulled his car into an empty spot. Once inside, he was greeted by a young man in a nondescript gray suit. He was pointed to a cushioned chair in the lobby as that young man contacted Vera over an inter-com to announce his arrival.

Vera Burgess was a four-foot-tall spitfire running on all pistons. King was both in awe of and intimidated by her level of energy. She was wearing a black pantsuit, and her vibrant red hair was closely cropped in a short pixie style. She extended her hand in greeting.

"Detective, it's a pleasure."

"I appreciate you agreeing to see me," King re-sponded.

"That's some file you sent us." Her voice dropped to a loud whisper. "Do I dare ask where Cash found it?"

King shrugged. "Dark web?"

"And you believe this video is connected to a case you're working on?"

"It's my understanding the video is of one of my vic-tims. I just don't know which one."

"First, let me tell you it's a difficult video to watch. You may want to pass if you've just eaten something."

"I'll be fine," King said. "I'm just anxious to catch this killer."

Vera nodded. "I understand completely," she said. "We want to shut down the individuals out here mak-ing these films," she said. "The video you forwarded to me has been traced back to a network of criminals who were once selling child pornography. Recently they've amped up their offerings with snuff films."

King's head snapped as he turned to look at her. "Snuff films!"

She nodded again. "You have some depraved indi-viduals out in this world that pay well for that kind of content. They get connected with psychopaths willing to make that kind of content for their own personal gratification, and you have disaster colliding with disaster."

"Were you able to identify anyone in the video?"

"We could not, but that doesn't mean you won't be able to. Perpetrators go to extreme lengths to keep their identities hidden."

She pointed King to a conference room at the end of a second-floor hallway. Inside, multiple computers lined the conference table, all connected to large thirty-two-inch monitors. Two men sat in front of them. Both paused as they waited for Vera to take the lead.

"Detective Randolph, this is my team. Team, Detective Randolph."

Both men gave him a nod, neither bothering to introduce themselves. King didn't bother to ask, already feeling queasy about what he might have to witness.

"Did you get through the encryption?" she questioned.

One member of the team nodded. "She installed a hatch that leads back to the source site. She pointed us in the right direction and literally opened the door. We're already downloading the files."

"How many are we looking at?" Vera questioned.

The other team member typed on his keyboard. "Almost fifty thus far."

King's eyes widened. "Fifty?"

"Are you ready to see the file Cash sent?"

"No," King said as he nodded his head. He inhaled, sucking in air until he felt as if his lungs might burst.

Vera pointed toward the center monitor. The first team member punched buttons, and a video began to play on the large screen before them. King took a step forward, crossing his arms on his chest. As the video began to play, King noticed the lighting was purposely dim. The setting was cluttered, trash and boxes piled high against the walls. Walls he had seen before. Walls painted a strange shade of salmon. The camera was focused on a steel surgical table. Michael-Lynn Jeffries was strapped to that table. The camera zoomed in on her face. Tears rained down over her cheeks, and she was shaking with fear.

Despite the mask and costume she wore, King recognized the woman who stepped into the frame. Coach Carmichael barked obscenities at the young girl and then she punched her over and over again until the poor child was sobbing. The abuse continued as Richard Carmichael cheered his daughter on as he stood off camera, laughing gleefully.

The abuse continued for what felt like hours. The young girl's body was assaulted and stabbed over and over again as she screamed for mercy. The cameraman captured every minute of hurt and pain Michael-Lynn had been made to endure. Her blood flowed like water from a faucet. An eye was gouged out. Her innocence was violated with foreign objects. Only when she stopped screaming, when there were no more tears, and she'd gasped her last breath, did the brutality stop.

King turned abruptly and moved toward the door. He'd had more than enough. When Vera joined him in the hallway, he was doubled over, desperate to catch his own breath. The woman said nothing, allowing him the moment to collect himself.

King finally released the breath he felt like he'd been holding since forever. He had stopped shaking, shifting rage to necessary energy. He apologized, tossing Vera a look. "How do you do this?" he asked as he stood upright.

"After a while, you become desensitized to it. Now I focus solely on gathering evidence to catch the perpetrator. I don't focus on the crime, but on the clues."

"I recognized my suspects in that video. I know who the killers are, and I know who is running this snuff film operation. Now, correct me if I'm wrong, but the FBI will have jurisdiction over this case since it's crossed state lines. I know of three murders that happened in Texas and I have no doubt there are others between here and there. If they documented all their crimes, then that will be icing on the cake."

"If that's the case, then we will definitely take point. For the time being, we can call it a joint operation that I will gladly give you credit for solving." She gave him a slight smile. "Now, what do you need from me?"

"Search warrants, arrest warrants and a stiff drink. One of our perpetrators is my commanding officer."

Vera's eyes widened. "Well, warrants aren't an issue. I've got all the warrants you want. But that drink will have to wait. Let's head over to my office."

Lenore answered her cell phone on the second ring. "Hello?" She could hear the relief in King's voice when he responded.

"Are you okay?" he asked.

"I've been better," Lenore responded. "How about you?"

"I know the feeling."

"I met Christopher Carmichael," Lenore said. "He's not the killer."

"Could he be involved with them?" King asked.

"No. There's no possible way he could be involved."

"Finally, some good news."

"And now for the bad news," Lenore continued. "Coach Carmichael was molested by her father. He photographed her and his abuse. I have those images. I also think if there was a DNA test, it's going to show that he possibly fathered her twins. Lieutenant Carmichael was also responsible for an assault against his grandson that left him incapacitated."

"Where are you now?" King asked.

"Sitting outside the school," Lenore responded.

"I'm going to need you to head back to your office or go home. We're about to execute a series of raids on the school, and the Carmichael house."

"You watched the video. How bad was it?"

"Cash was right. It's not something you ever need to see. Bad doesn't begin to describe it. It's horrific, Lenore. But there was no mistake about who was participating."

"Who's the victim?"

King hesitated. "Michael-Lynn Jeffries," he said finally. "Coach killed her as her father cheered her on. The murder was taped, and apparently they've been selling the video footage."

"I'll be damned." Lenore gasped as if she'd been sucker punched in the gut. Suddenly everything hurt, her body, her head, but mostly her heart. She took a breath. "What now?"

"I need to know you're safe, Lenore. Please go home."

Silence greeted him and he called her name. "Lenore? Lenore? Are you still there?" He shouted into the receiver. "Lenore! Answer me, damn it!"

It felt as if a lifetime had passed before she finally responded. "Something's going on, King," she stated. "Principal Brandt and Coach Carmichael just exited the building and are arguing here in the parking lot. I'm not close enough to hear what they're saying, but they're not happy."

"Damn, Lenore," King snapped, "you just scared the hell out of me!"

"Sorry about that," Lenore replied. "They're both leaving. Do you think someone's tipped them off?"

"Just let it go, Lenore. We will get them."

"I'm going to follow her. She's not getting away with this!"

"Lenore! Do not engage that woman! Please! We've gotten a judge to sign the warrants, and there are tactical teams en route."

"I'll be fine," Lenore snapped back. "If anything happens, Cash can track me."

King's frustration was palpable. "I swear, woman, when I get my hands on you!"

"Promises, promises," she quipped. "I'm hanging up now so I can focus. I'll call you when I see where she's headed. I love you!"

"I love you, too," King said as the phone disconnected in his ear.

Vera stood in the doorway watching him. "Is everything okay?"

King shook his head. "No, it's not."

"Well, we've gotten all our signatures, and the warrants are ready. The teams should be in place within the next hour. Do you want to ride?"

Chapter 20

Lenore drove two cars behind, never taking her eyes off the back end of Coach Carmichael's automobile. Traffic was moderately heavy, people making the most of their lunch hour. Despite King's efforts to dissuade her from trailing after the woman, Lenore refused to risk her getting away. She'd taken the life of a young woman who hadn't deserved what had happened to her. The whole family were sick and twisted, and they needed to pay for their sins.

As she drove, playing everything over and over in her head, she understood why her father sometimes did the things he did under the cover of darkness. Why he enacted vigilante justice on those who deserved to be buried under a jail instead of being caged in one. She knew it wasn't right to feel that way and that her father was wrong for his actions, but she had no trust in a system that would sooner put the most degenerate lot back on the streets at the first opportunity.

The coach suddenly turned onto a side street and then made a quick left into a driveway. Lenore followed, but she drove past the house with her head down. Watching from her rearview mirror, she eyed the woman as she bounded up the steps and through the front door. Her son Charles stood in the entrance, waiting for her. When the door closed, Lenore made a U-turn at the corner and parked her car.

What now? Lenore thought to herself. She considered just walking up to the door and ringing the bell. She had questions that hadn't been asked yet, she thought. She could play dumb to stall them from running, buying time for King and the tactical team to get there. Or she could just sit right there in her car, waiting patiently to follow after them if they took off before backup arrived. What she wanted was to go to the door and drop-kick that bitch for all the pain she and her family had caused. Lenore took a deep breath.

She needed to let King know where she was, she thought. Her cell phone had slid to the floor on the passenger side when she'd made that U-turn. She undid her seat belt and leaned over to reach for the device. As her driver's side door suddenly swung open, Lenore realized her mistake. She'd been so singularly focused on enacting revenge that she hadn't paid attention to her surroundings.

Juan Romero grabbed her arm and snatched her out of her seat. She was just a split second from striking out when he pointed his service revolver in her face and called her name.

"Don't make a scene," he said as he wrapped a tight arm around her shoulder and pushed the weapon into her abdomen. He pushed the car door closed with his hip and began to walk her toward the house.

"What are you doing, Juan?" Lenore whispered loudly. "You don't need to do this."

"I told you to stay out of my way. But you…" He tilted his head as if it hurt. "You always have to do what you want to do and all else be damned."

"Go to hell, Juan," Lenore snapped.

"I'm sure I'll make it there one day, but I promise you'll get there long before I will."

Entering the Carmichael home, Lenore was taken aback by the smell. The air was stale, and it felt as if death had painted the walls a noxious shade of dank and musty.

"What is she doing here?" Charles snapped when Juan pushed her through the door and into the kitchen. The gesture was abrupt, and she was thrown off balance, landing on the floor. The linoleum was slick, a nasty film coating the surface. It was only as she moved to stand that Lenore realized she'd fallen into a puddle of blood that had not been cleaned properly and had left a stain. She swiped her palms against her pants legs as she stood up. Taking a step back until she hit the wall, Lenore's gaze swept around the room, meeting the eyes that were staring at her.

"I found her parked outside," Juan snarled.

The coach took a step in her direction. "We need to get rid of her."

Behind her, their father clapped his hands excitedly. "I want to play with this one! I want to play with this one!" he squealed as if he were a toddler asking for a toy.

Charles moved into the room. "We don't have time for that. We need to get out of here. Put a bullet in her head and let's go."

Richard suddenly threw a tantrum. "I want to play with her!" he screamed at the top of his lungs. "You said I could play with her!"

Juan moved to a window to peer outside. "Make some decisions, people! We're running out of time!"

"Shoot her!" Charles yelled. "Shoot her and let's get out of here!"

"What happened to you people?" Lenore asked. She locked eyes with the coach. "I know what your father did to you. I know it wasn't your fault. He made you like this, but you don't have to…"

"Shut up!" the coach snapped. "You don't know a damn thing."

"I saw the pictures. I met your son Christopher."

The coach's eyes widened, then darted back and forth as she considered the ramifications of Lenore's comment.

Lenore continued. "He's a nice young man. Decent and loving. Even after everything that happened to him, he still has a kind heart. You know that. You care about him. That's why you continue to call. To check up on him."

Charles suddenly slammed his mother against the

side of her head. The blow was unexpected and threw her across the surgical table. His teeth were clenched, his jaw tight, and he hissed in her direction, "I told you to stay away from him. He's not your family! You never listen!"

Tears sprang against her lashes, pressing hot against the woman's eyes. She shot Lenore a look as she struggled not to cry. Instead, she pushed herself up and onto her feet and slapped him back, throwing the full force of her weight into her backhand. Charles's head snapped back on his neck, the sound of the strike vibrating through the room. Richard laughed, seemingly entertained by the dysfunction.

Juan shook his head. "If you two are done, we need to go now. Or I'm leaving without you."

"They're going to find you," Lenore snapped. Her eyes narrowed into thin slits as she stared at her ex-boyfriend. "They have everything they need to send you to prison till the end of time. Maybe even the gas chamber if I get lucky!"

Juan was on her so quickly that she'd barely had time to blink. He grabbed her by the throat, slamming her hard against the wall. She struggled for air, her legs swinging in the air.

"There you go with that mouth!" he snarled. "Always something to say."

He dropped her back onto her feet. When he loosened his grip, she slapped his hand away and nailed him with a hard punch to his chest.

"Get your damn hands off me!" she yelled.

"I will hurt you, Lenore. Don't think that I won't."

"You better hope my father never gets his hands on you after this," she said.

"Your father! Your father! Do you know how much I hated hearing about your damn father? You talk about him like he's some god, when he's just a common criminal!"

Her expression was haughty as she gave him a smug smile. "My father may be a criminal, but there's not one damn thing about him that's common!"

Juan rolled his eyes toward the ceiling. "I should put you down."

"Then just go ahead and do it!" Charles quipped. "Stop playing games with her. Or did you forget she didn't want you?" His tone was snide.

"Why?" Lenore said, gesturing at Juan with her hands. "Why? Is this the family you wanted to bring me home to?"

His expression was dead, his stare icy. "What? You think we're not like your perfect little family? How are we different? We support each other. Stand by each other's side."

"Torture and murder innocent children. Lie, cheat and live these fake lives. I'd venture to say you don't hold a candle to my family!"

"Like daddy dearest is so innocent!"

"You two are about to get on my last good nerve!" Charles said. He stared at Juan. "You ready?"

"I've been ready!"

"Then take care of your problem so we can get out of here."

Juan shot Lenore a look. "I say we auction her off. Let her make us some money. We may need it."

"She's deadweight, and we can't afford that right now," Charles said.

Lenore shook her head and shifted her gaze toward the coach. "I know you killed Michael-Lynn. I know what you did to her. And you're going to pay for that."

The woman suddenly looked defeated. She leaned back against the table, her breathing static. She shook her head.

"Why'd you do it?" Lenore asked. "And why'd you kill Tralisa?"

"I didn't," the coach replied. "Like you, she was too nosy for her own good. She became a problem. The principal eliminated the problem. Morris killed her."

"Shut up," Charles snapped. "She's not your priest! What the hell are you confessing for?"

"Because I'm tired," the coach suddenly yelled. "I'm tired of it all. And I'm tired of you."

"Beat her!" Richard yelled. "Beat her ass! Don't let her disrespect you. Damn women always being disrespectful."

"You did this!" Lenore snarled. "Why would you do this to your children?"

Richard laughed, waving a dismissive hand in her direction.

"He's a miserable old man," the coach said. "Since we were kids, he made our lives hell!"

"He gave us a home!" Juan snapped. "He took care of us. All we had to do was follow the rules!"

"His rules!" the coach whispered. "Always his rules!"

"Shut up!" Charles interjected. "You're being such an ungrateful whore!"

"Enough!" the coach screamed back, and then she

pulled a small-caliber revolver from her pocket and pulled the trigger.

Everyone in the room stared as the patriarch of their family suddenly grabbed his chest. Shock masked his expression, and then Richard Carmichael fell to the floor dead.

No one spoke, the moment feeling surreal. Lenore's gaze shifted from one face to the other, unable to read any emotion from any of them. It was frightening, and she realized things were not going to end well for her if she didn't do something soon.

Charles stepped over his grandfather's body, reaching for a bag that rested on the counter. "Well, that's one problem eliminated," he said. He gestured toward Lenore. "Get rid of her and we can go."

Juan spewed profanity, rushing back to where Lenore was still standing. "We've got company," he said, grabbing her by the arm and shoving her forward.

Charles rushed to the window to peer out and look for himself. "What do we do now?" he yelled.

The next shot fired sounded like an explosion going off in the room. Lenore ducked, bringing her hands up over her head protectively. Juan dropped down beside her, and they both turned at the same time to see Maxine Carmichael fall to the floor, her pistol still pointed at her own head.

Charles screamed his mother's name, and as he rushed forward, tears streaming down his face, Lenore slammed her heel into Juan's kneecap. Bone shattered, and he screamed out in pain. Before he could think to lift his weapon and shoot, Lenore had run from the room, disappearing toward the other side of the home.

The next moments were sheer chaos as local police and federal agents breached the front and rear doors. The home was suddenly overrun by officers with their guns drawn. Lenore stood perfectly still with her hands raised. A uniformed agent had grabbed her arm, twisting it behind her back to handcuff her, when King called out her name.

Pushing the agent aside, he wrapped his arms around her and pulled her close against him. "What the hell are you doing here?" he asked, pressing damp kisses against her face and mouth. "You could have been killed!"

"I missed you, too!" she said. "Damn, did I miss you!"

After hours of interrogation and questioning, Lenore was past the point of no return. She was exhausted and refused to tell her story one more time when asked. She'd had enough.

King stood in conversation with the woman from the FBI. She had been the first to interview Lenore about everything that had happened. Lenore moved to where the duo stood. King greeted her with a smile.

"Are you okay?"

"I'm exhausted, and I'm going home."

"We appreciate everything you did, Ms. Martin. I'm sure Detective Randolph would agree that we would not have been able to solve this case without your assistance. I hear you really know how to handle yourself out in the field."

Lenore gave her a slight nod. "We do what's necessary when we have to, isn't that right, Agent?"

Vera nodded back. "If we have any more questions,

I'll reach out personally," she said. "You have a good night."

"Thank you."

King excused himself from his conversation. "I'll be back," he said to Vera. "Let me walk Ms. Martin to her car."

Vera grinned. "No worries. I promise we won't keep him too much longer," she said as she gave Lenore a wink of her eye.

"Keep him for however long you need," she said.

"I think I should be offended by that remark," King said as he pressed his palm to her elbow and guided her through the room and out the door.

She smiled. "I'm just exhausted."

When they reached her car, he opened the door, and she turned to face him before he could help her inside. "How much longer before you can leave?" Lenore asked.

"There's a press conference scheduled in the next hour. As soon as I'm finished, I'm going to head home."

She nodded. "I'll leave a key for you at the security desk," she said.

He chuckled, and Lenore realized her faux pas, assuming he was referring to her apartment as his home. She laughed with him.

"We're going to have to make some decisions," she said. "I like waking up to you in the morning. At least, I think I do."

King tossed his head back, his laugh gut-deep. He wrapped his arms tightly around her and held her close as she rested her cheek against his chest.

"I was scared today," she whispered into the shirt

he wore. She took a deep breath and inhaled the faint aroma of his cologne. "I was really worried I wouldn't make it out. They were all unhinged."

King leaned to kiss her forehead. "You are an amazing woman, Lenore Martin. What you did was incredible. They may actually have gotten away if you hadn't stalled them."

"I was lucky you came when you did," she replied.

He smiled. "Yes, you were."

The drive home was quiet. Lenore refused to allow herself to think about anything. Anthony Hamilton crooned on the car stereo, and she was grateful for the time to just sit in the stillness. Before leaving the crime scene, she'd sent a text message to her sisters. She was wanting family and knew they would be there for her no matter what it took.

Her mother answered her front door. The matriarch opened her arms, and Lenore stepped into the embrace without saying a word. As they stood in the doorway, her sisters rose from their seats and moved to greet her. One by one they hugged her tightly and welcomed her home. Cash brought up the rear, doing a little happy dance before giving her a high five.

"We did that!" Cash exclaimed.

"You did that," Lenore said. She hugged her friend and whispered into her ear. "I'm so sorry," she said. "You should never have had to deal with that."

Cash hugged her back. "There are no guarantees every job is going to be easy. We have to take the dirt and grime with the ribbons and lace. That's how life works."

The workstation that had been her dining room table had been packed up and cleared away. Lenore didn't need to ask to know that her mother had taken care of it all.

"The pizza's gotten cold," Alexis said. "We were expecting you hours ago."

"The wine is still good," Sophie said.

Lenore smiled. "I stopped to tell Mama Hattie that we caught Michael-Lynn's killer. I didn't want her or Tralisa's parents to hear it on the news."

Claudia nodded her approval. "I'll run by to see her before I head home. I'll see if she needs anything."

"You look tired," Celeste said.

"I am. I'm ready for a shower and my bed."

"Where's your man?" Sophie questioned, a hint of mirth in her tone.

Lenore gave her sister a look. "My *man* is finishing up his business. He'll be by later."

"I like that young man!" their mother said. "Your father does, too!"

"Damn!" Lenore said, snapping her finger and shaking her head. "Now I'm going to have to break up with him!"

"You would, too," Celeste said with a laugh. "Just to spite your parents!"

Lenore grinned. "Maybe there was a time in my life that I would have, but never again. I have no plans of ever letting King go."

"That sounds slightly stalker-ish," Sophie interjected.

Laughter rang warmly through the room. For the next hour, Lenore caught her sisters up with all that had happened since she'd last seen them. She told them about Juan and how King had been there to support her. She praised Cash's efforts, applauding the accomplishments that had moved their case forward. She acknowledged everyone and everything that had enabled her to endure what she'd gone through.

One of her sisters slipped a wineglass into Lenore's hand.

"A toast," Claudia said as they moved in perfect sync, closing themselves in a circle. Each lifted her glass.

"To Lenore for a job well done," Claudia said.

"To King for being the man Lenore needs a man to be," said Cash.

"To Tralisa and Michael-Lynn, who will both be missed," Alexis chimed in softly.

"To Mama Hattie, who epitomizes every mother's love," Celeste added.

Sophie giggled. "To the daughters of Josiah Martin, who are fine like good wine!"

Then Lenore took a step forward, raising her glass even higher. "To the sisterhood of Sorority Row!"

"The sisterhood!" they all chimed in before tossing back their glasses.

Conclusion

Lenore had no idea what time King had slipped into her bed. She only knew that when she opened her eyes the next morning, he was lying sweetly beside her, sprawled out across the mattress. He snored ever so softly, and that faint little snort made her smile.

Rising, she tiptoed into the bathroom to empty her bladder. When she was done, she returned to bed, curling herself around King's body. He was warm, his skin heated, and his breathing lulled her back into a deep sleep.

The second time she opened her eyes, King wasn't there. He had tucked a blanket around her torso and eased a pillow against her side. A single red rose rested on the pillow beside her. Lifting the flower to her nose, Lenore took a deep inhale, relishing the sweet scent.

Rising from the bed, she moved to the other room. King sat in the family room. He sat on the leather recliner, his legs extended up on the matching ottoman. He sipped a cup of coffee as he read the morning newspaper. The television was on, feeling like background noise. The local station was recapping the previous night's events and replaying the press conference. She smiled as she paused to watch, admiring how distinguished King looked on screen.

He looked up from the article he was reading and smiled. "Good morning."

"Good morning. How'd you sleep?"

"Exceptionally well considering everything that happened."

She moved to where he sat and settled down beside him as he scooted over to make room. King wrapped her in his arms. "How are you feeling?"

Lenore shrugged. "I'm bruised, and I feel like I've been run over by a freight train."

"Well, you need to rest. Your mother called. She wanted to make sure you were staying home today. She says she doesn't want to see you in the office until next week."

"She doesn't mean that. She'll be having a fit if I don't show up tomorrow. Besides, I'm sure there's something I need to do to close out this case."

"I believe the FBI might have questions about how you acquired some of those documents. All I said was that they were given to us by an anonymous source."

"They really need to just say thank you and move on!" Lenore eased her arms around his waist and rested her head against his chest. As she snuggled against him,

Lenore knew she could do it the rest of her life and still not get enough of him. She blew a soft sigh. "So, what's on your agenda today?"

King smiled again. "I plan to stay right here with you. Maybe later we can visit my grandfather so I can introduce you."

"I'd like that," she said.

She reached for the newspaper he'd rested on his lap. The headline touted the capture of a team of sex offenders and serial killers and the dismantling of their trafficking ring and snuff film operation. There was a notation about more information being forthcoming as additional victims were interviewed. They noted the arrest of a high-ranking police official, a school administrator and a college student. Sixty-four other persons were arrested and landed in the local jail for allegedly patronizing their business. An award-winning high school coach was eulogized, the death of her and her father deemed a murder-suicide. There was no mention of any other familial ties, or their connection to the long-lost cult leader convicted of sex trafficking and child molestation. The details were sordid and read like a fiction novel gone awry.

Lenore shook her head. "Do you think they'll be able to connect them to all the victims?"

"It looks promising. Apparently, Charles was very meticulous about documenting everything. The FBI have already connected the father to over sixty murders."

"I still don't understand," Lenore said. "How do you pull your children into your perverse hobby? How sick do you have to be?"

"Apparently very sick. Charles is talking about how they were raised. Brandt has opened up about how Richard pulled them in when they were children. And forensics has begun to fill in some of the gaps as they go through the lieutenant's personal possessions. He was a real piece of work. But they'll pay for their crimes. The prosecutor is already talking the death penalty."

"What about Juan? Is he talking?"

King shook his head. "No. He claims he needs to protect the family and protecting the family means remaining silent."

Lenore paused for split second. "Did we ever find out who Kevin was?"

"Kevin?"

"The boyfriend Michael-Lynn thought was too old for Tralisa?"

King nodded. "He was a client, picking out his next target."

"Did you get him, too?"

"No," King answered. "He's lost in the wind for now. But we'll find him. We did, however, round up ten other men who purchased pornography and other materials from them."

"Other materials?"

"You really don't want to know," he said. He pulled a large hand through the length of her hair, twirling her curls around his fingers. "So, no more conversation about the case today. This case is closed. All I want to do is talk about you and me and where we go from here. We have a future to plan."

"I'd prefer we let our relationship evolve organically.

If we start planning and something goes wrong, I'll be disappointed. And then I'm going to be mad."

King laughed. "Whatever works!"

Lenore stood up. She grabbed the remote and turned off the television. A second later, someone's jazz billowed from the speakers. "I need coffee," she said. "Then I'm going to need you to wreak sexual havoc on my body."

"Why does that sound painful?"

"If you do it right, it won't be," Lenore said, her seductive tone setting the mood.

"I'm officially scared," King said.

Lenore giggled. "And I thought you liked playing with danger," she replied.

She headed out of the room, dropping her bathrobe to the floor. The rest of her garments followed as she tossed them aside one by one. She paused, threw him a glance over her shoulder and beckoned him to her with a curl of her index finger. King nodded as he lifted himself from his seat and followed after her

* * * * *

#2239 COLTON'S DEADLY AFFAIR
The Coltons of New York • by Jennifer D. Bokal

When NYPD detective Wells Blackthorn and FBI special agent Sinead Colton are assigned to lead a task force to stop a serial killer, they both assume they're in charge. But when Wells is almost murdered himself, they're forced to work closer than ever—transforming their quarreling to passion.

#2240 DANGER IN THE DEPTHS
New York Harbor Patrol • by Addison Fox

NYPD diver Wyatt Trumball begins pulling bodies out of the harbor, and he needs Marlowe McCoy to crack the safes they're strapped to. Unfortunately, the evidence points to her own family being involved in the crimes, and the tentative bond between them isn't the only thing in danger.

#2241 PROTECTING HIS CAMERON BABY
Cameron Glen • by Beth Cornelison

Isla Cameron thinks Evan Murray is her soulmate, until he reveals his connection to a the man who's threatening her family. When Evan kidnaps Isla to keep her and their unborn baby safe, he earns forgiveness for his betrayal as he defends her from an unscrupulous and deadly enemy: his father.

#2242 NOT WITHOUT HER CHILD
Sierra's Web • by Tara Taylor Quinn

Jessica Johnson will do anything to find her missing two-year-old daughter, and investigator Brian Powers is worried she's going to lose her life doing so. He isn't willing to risk his heart again, but as they get closer to finding the truth about Jessica's daughter, it becomes clear that they're both in far deeper than they ever realized.

HRSCNM0623

HARLEQUIN
PLUS

Try the best multimedia subscription service for romance readers like you!

Read, Watch and Play.

Experience the easiest way to get the romance content you crave.

Start your **FREE TRIAL** at
www.harlequinplus.com/freetrial.